MENDED
HEARTS

MENDED HEARTS

a novel

Connie Angeline

Covenant Communications, Inc.

Cover image © Scott David Patterson/iStock

Cover design copyrighted 2008 by Covenant Communications, Inc.

Published by Covenant Communications, Inc.
American Fork, Utah

Printed in Canada
First Printing: April 2008

14 13 12 11 10 09 08   10 9 8 7 6 5 4 3 2 1

ISBN 10: 1-59811-331-3
ISBN 13: 978-1-59811-331-0

Prologue

"I don't think we're going to make it!" Sydney shouted as she shot another glance at the darkening sky and tried to see through the blinding rain. The black clouds completely covered the sky that a few minutes before had been clear blue.

She glanced over at Randy who, standing across from her at the helm, was battling to keep the bow of the small sailboat angled toward the swells so that the boat would not capsize. His hair, which had been tousled by the breeze not an hour past, was now plastered to his wet face. Sydney knew Randy was trying not to appear frightened, but his clenched jaw and white-knuckled grip on the wheel betrayed him.

Sydney held on to the side of the boat to keep from sliding off her seat. The wind, which had picked up dramatically, tossed them ruthlessly over the sea. A movement caught her eye, and she turned to see the glass syrup bottle that Randy had tied to the railing earlier. Inside the dangling glass, the tiny ship he'd built for her was already smashed and mangled.

Fat raindrops cut across her skin and eyes, nearly blinding her, but she stayed put. She had refused when Randy had told her to go inside the cabin and get out of the frigid rain, insisting on staying by his side and helping if she could. Now every inch of her was wet and cold, and she no longer knew whether she was shivering because of the drastic drop in temperature or because of the fear that gripped her heart like a vise.

"You're sure your life jacket's on tight?" Randy shouted.

Sydney could barely make out his words over the noise of the storm, but she nodded stiffly.

Neither of them had seen the ominous clouds until the storm was nearly upon them. When they'd finally noticed the impending storm, Randy had immediately pulled up the anchor and Sydney had helped him close all the hatches and ports to avoid any water intake that might swamp their boat. But even though they'd acted quickly, they hadn't been fast enough to outrun the storm. Now every lesson they'd ever learned about boating was being tested.

They were not far from shore and could still see the lights along the coast, but wisdom forced Randy to reduce the boat's speed in order to ensure their safety. He made a quick call to the coast guard just in case, but Sydney hoped their situation wouldn't become that dire. She offered a quick, fervent prayer that they make it safely home.

Please, Heavenly Father, protect us!

Sydney tried to appear calm, but knew that if she managed to lift her hands from where they clutched the boat, their trembling would reveal her fear. *We should have gone to Seattle with his parents. I never should have asked him to take me sailing today.*

Sydney didn't realize that Randy had moved near her until he grasped her by the shoulders, forcing her to look at him. "The storm sail came loose," he shouted. "Take the helm." She had to concentrate on the movements of his mouth to make out his words over the shrieking winds. Slowly, she stood on shaky legs and took the helm between stiff fingers. "Keep her windward," he yelled, and she was relieved that she knew enough about sailing to follow his instructions.

Her heart pounded in her chest as she struggled to keep the boat windward. But when she glanced across the port bow to where Randy was hurrying to secure the sail, her blood froze in her veins. He had not clipped his safety harness to the nylon jackline. One misstep or gust of wind could easily throw him overboard into the rough sea. "Randy!" she screamed, panicking. "You're not secured!" The thunderous wind dissolved her voice. The swells were well over ten feet high—the small boat was surrounded on all sides by darkness, water, and the freezing wind that sprayed in Sydney's eyes.

Cold fear shot through her as Randy lost his balance. He came down hard on one knee, and his body was shoved forcefully against the mast.

"Randy, stop!" she shouted, desperately looking for a way to reach him and secure him to something solid.

The boat's speed increased dangerously over the waves, causing them to slam into the deep troughs.

Randy slid across the slippery deck and fell against the railing as the boat crested another wave. Sydney saw his mouth move as he shouted something to her about the anchor. Praying that she was doing the right thing, she dropped the anchor, trusting that it would slow them down.

"Randy!" she cried in alarm as he slipped again in an attempt to get to his feet. "Don't move!" Sydney secured the helm and reached for the wire that should have been attached to Randy's tether and harness and would have allowed him to move safely on deck. Clutching the wire tightly, she left the cockpit. The boat rocked wildly from side to side, making it more difficult for her to reach him on the slick deck. "Please, Heavenly Father, keep us safe," she prayed, desperately trying to keep her balance.

When she was within a few feet of Randy, something slammed into the boat, tipping it to one side. Sydney felt the pull of her harness around her middle as she was tossed against the railing and her head crashed into its edge.

Numbing pain seared through the side of her head, and bright spots filled her vision. The sailboat rolled, and a gush of freezing water from a crashing wave engulfed her and then quickly subsided as the boat tipped again.

Sydney choked on the salty sea water that filled her mouth and nose. Gasping for breath, she pushed herself away from the railing and tried to disentangle her leg from the heavy rope used to secure the boat.

"Randy," she called weakly. Her vision came back slowly, followed by a dull pounding behind her eyes. She reached up to the side of her head and touched the spot where she'd crashed into the railing. It was wet, like the rest of her, but her chilled fingers came away hot and sticky. She knew it was blood, and she felt it running down her face and into her eyes.

Wavering, she pulled herself to her knees. The wild rocking of the sailboat and splashing of the waves over the deck nearly knocked her down again, but she clung to the rail for support and managed to drag herself to her feet.

"Randy!" she yelled, and the effort caused her head to throb. "Randy, where are you?" she cried out in confusion, her eyes desperately darting around the boat as a new wave of panic engulfed her. A chill that had nothing to do with the water ran down her spine when she failed to find him.

"Randy!" she screamed again with rising terror.

Sydney stumbled a few steps to the bow and saw only the shattered pieces of glass from the ship in a bottle, which had broken loose and crashed onto the deck. And then they too were washed away in the sea.

Her heart tightened in her chest and she choked on a sob of paralyzing agony.

She screamed Randy's name again, her tears mingling with the cold rain. She frantically searched the black water for any sign of him. He would never survive in the freezing sea, even though he had been wearing a life jacket.

"No." The pounding in her head intensified. "Please, Heavenly Father, no!" she cried out, and another wave dropped her to her knees. She felt her heart break like the glass bottle whose shards had lain scattered on the deck. "Not him!" Then everything went black, and she collapsed limply to the deck, as the freezing waters of the Puget Sound continued to crash over the boat, washing away the blood and the tears.

Chapter 1

Five Years Later

"I could strangle you!" Sydney said with a laugh.

"You don't mean that, Sydney, so don't say it."

"You're right," she teased. "How about I just pull out what's left of your hair."

Her grandfather stopped as he turned to move behind his desk. "That's not nice," he said and sat down, placing a pile of mail on the large mahogany desk in front of him.

Sydney hid a smile. If there was one thing retired Lieutenant General Gabriel P. Chase didn't like, it was any reference to his receding hairline. "It's a little funny," she said impishly, as she flopped down on one of the leather armchairs across from him.

Gabriel raised a proud brow and retrieved a letter opener from the desk drawer. "Anyway, Tom is a nice boy," he said, bringing them back to the subject at hand as he proceeded to methodically slide the letter opener through the tops of all the envelopes and then arrange them into three neat piles.

"Exactly!" Sydney said emphatically. "He's a nice *boy*. What were you thinking?" she demanded, appalled once again as she remembered last night's date.

"Come now, Sydney. Don't be dramatic," Gabriel said as he sliced open another envelope.

"Grandpa, he's barely out of his teens." Sydney's arched brows drew together in a frown and her pert nose wrinkled with disgust.

"So?" he asked, puzzled. "Your grandmother is younger than I am."

"But you're a man. It's more awkward if the girl is the older one," she argued. "And I'm almost five years older than he is. It was like babysitting." She grimaced, remembering how uncomfortable Tom had been on their date. "Besides, his age isn't really the problem, and you know it."

Gabriel looked at her curiously over the rim of his rectangular bifocals.

Sydney released an exasperated sigh. "I can find my own dates. I don't need my grandpa to do it for me." Her grandfather had made it his personal mission to round up dates for her since she'd come back to Washington six months before. The first week she'd been back, he'd arranged for one of the local guys to pick her up and show her around town, regardless of the fact that she'd grown up on Whidbey Island and didn't need a tour guide. Luckily for Sydney, the guy had a girlfriend and had only done it as a favor to his mother, who was acquainted with Gabriel.

"Maybe if you *did* find your own dates, I wouldn't have to," Gabriel pointed out as he returned the letter opener to the drawer. Then, with careful attention, he reached for a letter in the first stack of envelopes.

"Grandpa, please promise me you won't do this anymore. The last guy you set me up with showed up at the front door with an ax and a chainsaw." He'd actually been a nice guy—a nice guy who happened to be a professional lumberjack competitor. His idea of a date had been to teach Sydney how to throw an ax at a bull's-eye and then shimmy up a twenty-foot pole. Even though he'd been perturbed at her inability to make a quick, clean slice with his chainsaw, Sydney had to admit that he topped her list of entertaining dates.

"I just don't see what the problem is," Gabriel said, scanning the letter in front of him. After a moment, he folded the letter neatly, slipped it back into its envelope, then set it aside and picked up another. "Tom is the son of an old friend of mine from Seattle. And from what I remember, he's a very nice boy."

Sydney sighed and shook her head. At least he'd known this guy. Some of the guys he'd set her up with—without her permission—had been almost complete strangers: the friend of a son of a friend of an old associate.

"Grandpa, I need your word," Sydney said gravely. She sat forward in her chair to make sure that his eyes met hers. "Please don't do this anymore." Her thick hair, the color of sun-kissed wheat, fell straight to her shoulders and swayed as she moved.

Gabriel paused and worriedly met his granddaughter's stare. "I just want you to be happy," he said with a sigh, and his shoulders fell slightly.

For the first time, Sydney noticed just how old he was. Gray hair that had been thick for as long as she could remember was now so thin it was nearly gone. The map of lines on his face testified of a disciplined life that had begun when he had joined the Marine Corps at the early age of eighteen. But there were also laugh lines around his eyes that revealed profound kindness and a deep love for his family. This was the love that had compelled Sydney to go out with the guys he'd set her up with, even though she had no interest in starting a relationship with anyone.

"I am happy," she said finally.

Gabriel didn't respond, but Sydney saw the doubt behind his eyes.

"I know you mean well," she said softly. She had to admit that she'd enjoyed meeting some of the guys he'd introduced her to, but she simply didn't have any interest in pursuing a relationship with anyone. She had a good life . . . a comfortable life, and she saw no need to change it. "Please, Grandpa. No more."

"You might meet the man of your dreams," he said.

Sydney flinched. "I don't want to meet anyone."

Randy had been her first relationship—a childhood friendship that had evolved into dating. Everyone, including herself, had assumed that it would eventually end in marriage. But Randy had died so young, and she'd lost so much that night on the Sound—much more than her first love. She was tired of feeling obligated to go out with guys simply to spare their feelings and her grandfather's. "Please promise me you won't arrange any more blind dates," she said softly.

Gabriel was silent and glanced down to look at the letter in his hand. He read slowly, and a half smile crept onto his face. He finally looked up at her, and Sydney could see him weigh his options. "I promise that I won't arrange any more dates for you," he conceded carefully.

"Really?" Her smile faltered a bit when she realized how easy it had been to gain a concession from him. The medals decorating his military uniform hadn't been acquired because he was easily swayed.

"Yes. Now, run along. I have a lot of work to do." He tapped the stacks of letters on his desk.

Sydney smiled with relief. "I love you, Grandpa," she said and walked around his desk to plant a kiss on his broad forehead.

* * *

Gabriel sighed, remembering the days when he'd been the one to kiss her forehead and look down at her with tenderness. She was grown now, but his prayers for her happiness had only grown more fervent over the years. She hadn't been the same since Randy died. Gabriel could see the burden she carried and wanted more than anything to shift it onto his own shoulders. But he knew that wasn't possible. He also knew that succumbing to a life of solitude, the direction of her current path, wasn't the answer.

He smiled as he watched her walk out of his office in her riding outfit. She had grown up to be a striking young woman who was less concerned with her appearance than she was with her love of horses. If she didn't clean up so nicely and have the unmistakable stamp of femininity when she moved and spoke, he would have worried that he'd turned her into a tomboy.

Old age is wonderful, he thought as he picked up the phone and dialed the number that had been on the letter. True wisdom only arrived with age, and if he wasn't mistaken, he'd become pretty wise where Sydney was concerned. His gaze wandered to the corner of the office and fell on the elegant glass chess set his wife had bought him years ago. Over the years, he'd refined his ability to play the game of strategy—moving pieces here and there to ensure the most favorable outcome. Thinking of Sydney's relieved smile, he quelled a small twinge of guilt. He wouldn't be breaking the promise he'd just made to her if he simply rearranged the pieces on the chessboard ever so slightly. All he had to do was turn the king and queen until they couldn't help but meet. And looking down at the letter he'd just read, he had just the king in mind.

"How can I help you?" asked the voice on the other end of the line.

"Jackson Kincaid, please." *Check,* Gabriel thought with a sly smile. One move here and another move there and before they knew it . . . *Checkmate!*

* * *

Sydney lifted the saddle from the pony's back and swung it onto the fence next to the others so that it straddled the top rail. She removed the saddle blankets, leaving the animal's coat glistening with sweat, which quickly evaporated in the breeze. When she removed the reins, the pony quickly trotted away toward the others.

Sydney had six pony jumpers that she used for basic seat and riding lessons, and it had taken her entire savings to purchase them. They were docile and good natured, which was important since her students generally had little or no prior experience with horses. She had five students to whom she taught basic horsemanship and riding skills three times a week, and another student who was just learning to mount a horse. Sydney taught her students how to respect and care for animals, and then, if they chose, she helped the beginning riders become distinguished competitors.

Sydney stood watching the horses graze against the breathtaking backdrop of Whidbey Island. She loved Washington and had always appreciated its beauty and freshness, even though growing up here might have made it all seem ordinary.

"Good class today," Adam said as he lifted a saddle in one hand and reached down with the other to lift the rest of the stable gear. The last two children had already climbed into their mothers' minivans and driven off, leaving Sydney and Adam to tidy her grandfather's stables.

"Yes, it was," she said, turning to watch him go. Most of the tack had already been put away by the children themselves.

Adam was the fifty-year-old groom and trainer who, for nearly fifteen years, had been taking care of any horse that occupied her grandfather's stables. Until recently there had been only three horses: two retired sport horses that she rode often and Gabriel's cherished white Arabian gelding that had been a gift from an old Marines colleague back in the day.

With Sydney's ponies and the graduation present her grandparents had given her in the form of a German Hanoverian mare named Duchess, the stables had gone from being nearly empty to being filled to capacity. Even though Sydney knew that Adam enjoyed the added work, she helped him take care of the animals and clean the equipment. In return, Adam helped her with her students during riding lessons.

The only snag in their unspoken arrangement involved Duchess, who had revealed her snobbish personality soon after Gabriel had brought her home with a big red bow tied around her neck. The gorgeous filly thrived on attention and demanded grooming and fawning several times a day.

"She's high and mighty," Adam had complained on the day Duchess had arrived. "She reminds me of my ex-wife." That initial reaction had been a portent of things to come. As if sensing his disdain, Duchess seemed to provoke Adam at every turn, turning her nose up at the food he offered and blatantly ignoring him when he was near.

Feeling like she was intervening between two unruly children, Sydney had taken sole responsibility for Duchess's care to ensure that things continued to run smoothly in her grandfather's stables.

"Hi, Sydney," a cheerful voice called from behind her.

Sydney turned to see her friend Adrianne coming toward her, Adrianne's curly blond hair bouncing with every step. "Adrianne, what are you doing here? I thought that you were going to go pick out your wedding dress today." Her friend had been engaged for seven months, but had put off choosing a wedding dress until the last minute.

"I am, and you're coming with me."

Sydney smiled knowingly. "Where's your mom?"

"Come on, Syd," Adrianne whined, her blue eyes speaking volumes. "You know what she wants. She's planned on me wearing that dress since I was born."

Sydney couldn't hide her smile as she remembered the first time she'd seen the dress back in the tenth grade. It was a shapeless, tunic-style gown made of white satin with no trimming except for the hand-made lace jacket that was to be worn over it. Adrianne's grandmother had sewn it for Adrianne's mother, who now wanted her own daughter to wear it for her wedding.

"She just wants your wedding dress to be special for you." Sydney felt obligated to say it, but she wouldn't be caught dead in the dress herself.

"I know." Adrianne leaned on the fence, guilt-ridden. "She was a little upset at my dad when he told me he would *buy* me a dress instead. It took her forever to agree to let me even go look at some dresses."

"What time do you have to be there?" Sydney asked, looking down at her riding breeches and her T-shirt, which had gotten smudged with dirt. She winced as she noticed the slobber that one of the ponies had left on her shirt when she'd removed the bridle. "I'm not really dressed for the occasion, Ree."

Relieved that Sydney had agreed to go with her, Adrianne relaxed. "Don't worry. We have a couple of hours. You can clean up, and I thought we could go get something to eat first." She turned around to look out at the horses, folding her arms over the fence. "Your grandma didn't come out to watch you today?"

No one had been prouder than Sydney's grandmother that Sydney had started her own business. It had been she who had insisted that Sydney stay with them in their spacious house instead of renting a small apartment. "There's no sense in wasting your money before you get a chance to make it," she'd said staunchly.

Sydney shook her head. "She went into Seattle early this morning with some friends."

"Your mother called to talk to my mom last night."

"She was so happy when they got the news of your wedding."

"I'm glad your parents will be able to make it."

"So am I," Sydney said with a sigh. "My dad's been working so much. It's a miracle he got the time off."

"How were your riding students today?"

"Impatient," Sydney said with an affectionate smile as she, too, folded her arms over the top of the fence. "They can hardly wait to jump fences—when in fact they haven't yet mastered mounting and dismounting."

"Kids are fearless."

"I remember what I was like at their age. Horses were a little piece of that fantasy world that we all hope exists somewhere. The first time my father put me on the back of a horse I was hooked. It's like that with them, too."

"You're an exceptional teacher. I'm sending all of my children to you for lessons."

"That's interesting, because last time I checked, you weren't even married yet," Sydney teased.

Adrianne smiled again. "I can't wait. I want lots of kids," she said dreamily, as only a bride-to-be could.

Sydney didn't let the small sting in her chest ruin her friend's happy mood. She envied Adrianne's peace of mind and fearless view of the future. She remembered the days when she'd been just as hopeful, but it seemed like a lifetime ago. It was as if her chances for happiness had been washed away that day on the Sound. How could she know that something horrible wouldn't happen again?

"I think Josh Nelson is in love with you," Adrianne was saying. "I saw the way he stared at you in church when I went to your ward last week," she added, running her hand through her short mop of hair. Where Sydney was tall and lean, Adrianne was petite and almost fragile; however, if size were measured in energy, Adrianne would've been seven feet tall.

"He's eleven years old, Ree, and way too young to be in love with anyone. Besides, I taught his Primary class for three weeks while the teacher was on vacation. I'm probably one of the only adults he knows."

Adrianne shrugged, but the hint of mischief was not lost on Sydney. "I guess he takes after Rob, huh?" Adrianne asked.

Sydney rolled her eyes at the familiar suggestion. "Rob is not in love with me." Rob Nelson was only a year older than her and Adrianne. He was their close friend as well as a police officer on Whidbey Island. As the only members of the Church at their elementary school, the three of them had been inseparable growing up. When Randy had moved to the island in the seventh grade, he had easily joined the small group of friends.

"Come on, Syd," Adrianne said. "Rob's been looking at you differently since you moved back to Washington."

"We're friends," Sydney insisted. "I just don't feel that way about him." Rob, in spite of his good looks, was like a brother to her. "And I don't think he feels that way about me, either."

Adrianne didn't press the issue, and Sydney was grateful Adrianne realized that whatever happened between Sydney and Rob wasn't up to her. "I'm just surprised your grandpa hasn't tried to push you guys together," Adrianne said.

"Believe me, he has," Sydney said grimly. "But he also knows when to stop pushing. With Rob, it's just different."

"Excuse me," someone said from behind them.

Both Adrianne and Sydney spun around in surprise.

A tall, dark-haired man stood a few feet from them. "Sorry, I didn't mean to startle you," he said.

Sydney's heart seemed to crawl right up into her throat as she and an open-mouthed Adrianne stared at the man in front of them. He had dark hair that curled slightly in the front and deep blue eyes that seemed to bore holes right through her. His jaw was strong and chiseled and offset nicely by a straight nose. He was wearing blue jeans and a white, button-up shirt with the sleeves rolled up to reveal strong, sinewy forearms. Sydney was surprised to find that butterflies had started fluttering in her stomach. She suspected that she might be coming down with the flu.

Adrianne recovered first and quickly elbowed Sydney, who cleared her throat and stepped forward with a smile. "Is there something I can do for you?"

"My name is Jackson Kincaid. I'm a friend of your grandfather's."

When the words finally sank in, Sydney felt a rush of bitter disappointment as she realized he must be another of her grandpa's projects in his Marry-Sydney-Off-to-Whoever-Is-Willing campaign. In the past month, she'd been approached by so many guys who'd introduced themselves as "a friend of your grandfather" that she was almost able to detect them before they even spoke.

Because Gabriel was a man of his word, she knew better than to think that he'd broken his promise and arranged for another guy to ask her on a date. No, he must have made plans with this guy before they had talked that morning.

She had to hand it to him, though. Her grandfather hadn't chosen badly in the attractive department. With his sun-darkened skin and chiseled features, the man now standing in front of her was the most handsome candidate yet. It was too bad that he was one of her grandfather's minions.

"Gabriel's away for the afternoon. Can I take your number so he can call you?"

Sydney didn't introduce herself, hoping to avoid the coming awkwardness. Gabriel had promised he wouldn't arrange any more dates for her, and if that meant he needed to call all the guys he'd already made arrangements with, well . . . he could start with Mr. Jackson Kincaid.

What a pity, she thought as she took another look at him.

"Actually, I'm here to see you," he said without moving.

Sydney hesitated and took a deep breath. Although a superficial part of her wanted her to make an exception for Jackson Kincaid, she wasn't about to go along with another of her grandfather's matchmaking attempts, no matter what the guy looked like. It was best to put an end to this before the guy got his hopes up.

Sydney ignored the way Adrianne's mouth had formed a silent *O* when Jackson had revealed that he was there to see Sydney and not Gabriel. There was no need to embarrass Jackson in front of an audience, so she gave her friend a pointed look that Adrianne was quick to understand.

"Um . . . I really have to run, Syd. I'll stop by for you in about an hour." As Adrianne headed out of the paddock toward her car, she was unable to resist turning once more to get an eyeful of the stranger. "It was nice to meet you," she called back to Jackson, who smiled at her.

Sydney waited for the sound of Adrianne's car engine before turning her attention to Jackson. She reached up to brush a strand of hair out of her eyes and felt her face burn with embarrassment as she realized what she must look like.

Sydney had never really focused on her looks. Just last Saturday, Rob had seen her in a pair of her grandpa's old pajamas. She'd had puffy eyes and messy hair when Rob had come over to see if she wanted to go fishing with him. It had never occurred to her that she had probably looked frightening enough to scare away the very fish they were trying to catch.

After a few seconds Sydney looked up to see Jackson watching her, a slight smile playing at the corners of his mouth. "Like I said, I'm an old friend of your grandfather's. Actually, he and my father were in the Marines together."

"I don't remember ever seeing you around here," she said, searching for the right moment to tell him that she had no intention of dating him.

"From what Gabriel says, by the time I got back from college, you were headed off to get your own education, so we never really had a chance to meet."

"You two sure have gone through the details, haven't you?" she said dryly, knowing she had to put an end to this, and soon. He seemed like a likeable guy, but she had to nip this in the bud rather than build a rapport. Better now than later.

"Anyway, I'm here because Gabriel asked me to—"

"Look, uh . . . Jackson, right?" she said with a small smile of regret. "This . . ." She gestured to the space between them. ". . . just isn't going to work between us." There, she'd said it.

"I beg your pardon?"

"I know that you and Gabriel have probably made all kinds of plans, but I really don't want to date you." *Don't say it like that,* she chastised herself silently. *You don't want to hurt his feelings.* "I mean, not that you aren't a great guy. I'm sure you are. And you're handsome, so I'm sure that girls are probably just dying to date you, but I can find my own dates."

"You can." It was a statement, not a question, and his eyes narrowed thoughtfully.

"Yes," she said, glad he was agreeing with her. "Gabriel probably told you how wonderful I am. And how beautiful and talented I am, right?" She knew her grandfather.

Jackson nodded, and the corner of his mouth curled up slightly.

"I'm really not that great of a catch," she said, wanting to soothe the ego she felt she was surely destroying. "I play with horses all day, so I stink a lot of the time. Plus, I'm really crabby, especially early in the morning. And I rarely wear makeup—as a matter of fact, I only look this done up on a really good day." She motioned to her face, chagrined to think that what she was saying was true. "So you don't want to date me."

"I don't."

"Good. I'm glad we got that all cleared up," she said with relief, and she waited for him to say his good-byes. When he stood there staring at her with a small amused smile, she frowned. "I snore."

"I'm sorry," he said simply and stood watching her as if he were waiting for something.

"You're still here," she said in mild confusion. *Shouldn't he have made his apologies, expressed his relief, and high-tailed it out of here by now?*

"Why don't we try this again?" he said, taking a step toward her.

"Again?" She didn't think she could do it again—it had been hard enough the first time.

He cleared his throat and extended his hand. "Hi. I'm Jackson Kincaid. Gabriel told me a little bit about you and asked me to come talk to you . . . about horses."

She ignored his outstretched hand and stared at him blankly. "Horses?"

"I'm a breeder." He put his hand in his pocket and continued. "I own a warmblood breeding facility on the southern part of the island. He said you were looking for a pedigree so you could breed your filly."

Chapter 2

Sydney stood frozen in place, her ears ringing with the sudden rush of blood that had filled her head. "You're a horse breeder?"

He nodded.

"You're not here to date me?"

He shook his head slowly, and that small half smile played at his mouth again.

Sydney closed her eyes in mortification, wishing she could disappear. But since disappearing acts were out of the question, she slowly opened her eyes and looked at him. "You wouldn't be related to Meredith Kincaid from Eagle Crest Farms, would you?" she asked, hoping he'd say no.

"She's my aunt," he said, and Sydney closed her eyes as another wave of humiliation washed over her. "I take it you've heard of our establishment, then?"

It was her turn to nod. Eagle Crest Farms had become a sort of guarantee for the classic Hanoverian bloodlines that had originated in Germany, and it had produced more champion show and dressage horses than any other breeder on the West Coast. The warmblood Hanoverian was almost exclusively bred to excel in equestrian sports such as eventing, jumping, and dressage. Patriark, the top horse at Eagle Crest Farms, had won more medals than any other breeder could hope to see.

"I thought you were here . . . to date . . . you see, my grandfather keeps . . ." She stopped herself and gave her head a small shake to clear it. Taking a deep breath and forcing a smile, she stuck out her hand and said, "Hi. I'm Sydney Chase."

He shook her hand. "I figured as much."

"I completely mistook you for somebody else."

"I guessed that as well." He grinned. "Long story?"

"You have no idea." She smiled, grateful for his easy manner. "Why don't we go see Duchess, and you can get a better idea of what I'm looking for."

"Sounds good," he said, and they started toward the opening of the paddock.

"I'm sorry about that," she said, motioning as they walked.

"Don't worry about it." He smiled warmly and glanced at her. "I do have one question, though."

"What's that?"

"Do you really snore?"

Sydney choked on a laugh, barely managing to keep from sinking her head into the nearest hole. "Like a freight train," she admitted painfully.

* * *

"Tell me, tell me!" Adrianne pleaded as they browsed through the racks of white gowns zipped in plastic garment bags. The quaint bridal boutique in Oak Harbor belonged to a member of the Church—who was also a friend of Adrianne's mother—and both girls were hoping Adrianne would find something there and avoid having to drive into Seattle. "Who was he, and why did he want to talk to you?"

After clearing up the misunderstanding about Jackson's motives, Sydney had taken him to the north pasture, where Duchess had been left to graze. He had pointed out a few traits to look for when it came time for Sydney to choose a stallion. Later that week she was going to visit Eagle Crest Farms so she could look at stallions that had many of those particular characteristics.

Sydney was spared from having to recount her embarrassing story to Adrianne when the boutique owner, who had just hung up the phone, walked over from the reception desk.

"Good afternoon, girls," Patsy said brightly.

"Hi, Sister Lee," Sydney said.

"Have you girls seen anything you like?" she asked with a warm smile. Her short brown hair complemented the rounded features of her face.

"Lots," Adrianne said with a smile.

"Your mom called and told me you'd be stopping by today."

"She's not very happy," Adrianne said, biting her lip.

"I know, dear," the middle-aged woman said sympathetically.

Years ago, when Sydney and Adrianne were still Laurels in the Young Women program, they'd had an activity about temple marriage. Each girl had worn her mother's wedding dress as part of the show, and Adrianne's mom had confessed to everyone that she wanted her daughter to get married in the same dress. Everyone, including Patsy Lee, had thought it was a lovely gesture until they'd seen Adrianne walk out in the matronly gown.

"I'm afraid I waited too long to get a dress," Adrianne said. Her wedding was now less than two months away.

"You'll have plenty of time," Patsy said with certainty. "As long as you don't choose to have a custom-made dress, you'll be fine."

"I've already seen a few I like." Adrianne motioned toward some satin gowns against the nearest wall.

Patsy Lee beamed. "Wonderful. I've gone through and selected a few myself that I think will look great on you." She walked to the back wall and started hanging dresses on the rack near the dressing room. "Here are this season's newest dresses, and some of the best ones from last season." She hung one gown inside the dressing room and motioned for Adrianne to go inside. "Start trying them on."

Sydney sat down on the plush sofa outside the dressing room and prepared to spend the next hour helping Adrianne narrow down her choices.

"Most of these are temple-ready, Adrianne, but if you choose one that isn't, we can always adjust it," Patsy reassured her. "Just let me know if you girls need any help," she told them both and then went to help two women who had just arrived.

The next two hours ticked by as Adrianne tried on dress after dress. After a while, neither she nor Sydney could distinguish one from another. "I think I'll just wear my mom's dress, after all," Adrianne complained in exhaustion from inside her dressing room as she fidgeted with yet another dress. "Who knew dress shopping was so much work?"

Sydney smiled sympathetically, glad that she wasn't the one trying them all on.

"So, are you going to tell me or not?" Adrianne asked from behind the heavy curtain.

Sydney cringed inwardly as she was forced to remember the incident with Jackson. She sighed in defeat. "Oh, all right. You know how my grandpa has been setting me up on date after date with every guy that crosses his path?"

Her grandfather had started with the most upstanding young men—college-educated, returned missionaries, good reputations—but the pickings had gotten slimmer and slimmer. Right before she had gone out with Grizzly Adams and his collection of axes, Gabriel had arranged to have the guy at the local fish hatchery ask her out on a date. The poor guy, after discovering the hard way that Sydney was a "stuffy, uptight Mormon," hadn't called her back for a second date.

"Anyway, I got Grandpa to promise me he would back off from his goal to get me married," Sydney explained, leaning back on the sofa. "The absolute last date was Tom," she said emphatically. She cringed, remembering how he'd acted as if she'd been old enough to be his mother.

"How did that go, anyway?" Adrianne's question was muffled as she pulled a dress over her head.

"You don't want to know," Sydney said dryly. "But I feel like I'm living in the eighteenth century, where my family is supposed to choose my husband."

"Your grandpa just wants you to be happy."

"You sound like my mother," Sydney accused.

"But it's true. He thinks if you get married then you'll—"

"Forget about Randy," Sydney finished for her, feeling the familiar pang at the mention of his name. She could count on one hand the number of times she'd said his name aloud in the past five years, and it had never gotten easier.

There was silence inside the dressing room, and then a sad-looking Adrianne poked her head through the curtains. "I didn't say that. You know that's not what he wants," Adrianne said mournfully. "He just wants you to fall in love and be happy."

"One doesn't necessarily guarantee the other," Sydney said for the sake of argument.

"If you do it right, it does," Adrianne said pulling the dressing room curtain shut again. "With prayer and faith, love can bring eternal happiness," she said softly.

Sydney didn't disagree—couldn't disagree. She'd been taught this since she was a child, and she believed deeply in temple marriage. She had spent much of her youth dreaming of the day when she'd be able to go to the temple with a worthy man and be sealed for time and all eternity.

But a big factor in a successful eternal marriage—a big factor in a successful life, for that matter—was prayer. Five years ago, when, in spite of her prayers, Randy had died, her faith had faltered. She'd been afraid to ask her Father in Heaven for anything ever since.

"Sydney?" Adrianne prodded, pulling Sydney out of her thoughts.

Sydney looked up. "I can't just fall in love with someone my grandfather picks off the street," she said, wanting to steer the subject away from Randy. "The guys he's chosen have been . . . odd."

"What do you mean? I thought there were a couple of real keepers in the bunch," Adrianne contended.

"Yeah, if you're into picking your teeth with a hunting knife."

"You're being unfair," Adrianne chided. "What about that army guy . . . Todd?"

"Rod," Sydney corrected, remembering Rod's severe haircut and piercing gray eyes. "He was married to the military. I felt like I should say 'yes, sir' anytime he asked me a question."

"And that doctor from Seattle?"

"He was a germ freak." He had carried wet-wipes in his pockets and had disinfected his hands after he touched anything—including her.

"The accountant from Colorado?"

"He was just plain weird," Sydney said distastefully.

"He was not."

"He thought that everything had to be split fifty-fifty—not only, might I add, the price of our dinner, but also the cost of the gas for his car." Sydney frowned, remembering her shock when he had pulled out his calculator and started calculating the mileage and the price of fuel.

"Okay, so your grandpa chose a couple of strange guys. Look at it this way: if he hadn't set you up with them, you wouldn't have dated anybody."

"I don't need my grandfather talking to anyone he knows or meets in an attempt to find me a date. I can pick my own dates, Adrianne."

"But that's just it. If it weren't for your grandfather, you wouldn't date at all. The first date you had in five years was with a guy your grandfather invited over."

"Are you girls doing okay back there?" Patsy called from the front of the store.

"We're doing fine," Adrianne said as she opened the curtain. She padded over to the raised platform in front of the mirrors and grimaced. "I look like I belong on top of a cake," she said, grabbing handfuls of the princess-style dress that consisted of endless layers of taffeta.

"No, you don't," Sydney said, and then smiled slightly. "Well, maybe it *is* just a little bit . . . puffy." She didn't add that she thought it made Adrianne look like a dollop of whipped cream.

Adrianne groaned and stomped back behind the curtain. "I'm done! No more dresses!" she announced and pulled down the zipper, exhaling the breath she'd had to hold to get the dress on. "So, was this Jackson guy just another one of Gabriel's prospects?"

"No," Sydney said, almost with regret—almost.

"Then who was he?"

Sydney braced herself and then divulged the details of her humiliating experience.

There was silence from behind the curtain. Then Adrianne slowly pushed the heavy fabric aside and looked at her friend. "You're kidding, right?"

Sydney shook her head.

"Was he mad?"

Again, Sydney shook her head.

"Well, that's a good sign."

"Of what?" Sydney asked, suspiciously.

"Well, maybe your business relationship can grow into something more personal."

"Why is everyone so obsessed with marriage—particularly my lack of one?"

Adrianne disappeared behind the curtain again. "We want you to be happy."

"I *am* happy," Sydney maintained emphatically. "As a matter of fact, I feel pretty close to being overjoyed. Do I have to get married to convince everybody of that?"

"Sorry to interrupt, girls," Patsy called as she walked up with a pile of white satin in her arms. "I found two more dresses that I think will look wonderful on you, Adrianne." Somehow Patsy missed the groan of agony that came from behind the curtain.

* * *

Sydney had dressed up for dinner, as was the custom in her grandparents' house. Gabriel had grown up in Virginia, the son of a diplomat, and dressing nicely for dinner had been as customary as brushing his teeth. Gabriel's son hadn't enforced the same rules with Sydney, mainly because Sydney's mother had been raised by parents who had run a very relaxed household. But every time Sydney and her parents had had dinner with her grandparents, they'd all had to dress up. As a child, Sydney had thought it was a silly tradition, but now she hardly gave it a second thought.

Her father's job had transferred him to Texas during Sydney's last year of high school. To avoid making her change schools during her senior year, her parents had let her move in with her grandparents for the rest of the school year. And a few years later, when Sydney had finished college in Missouri and was looking to start a business teaching horseback riding, they had eagerly welcomed her back into their home.

Her grandmother, Jane, was a soft-spoken, sweet-natured woman who seemed to get shorter each year. Her grandfather, on the other hand, was a bear of a man who had spent his life commanding everyone and everything around him. There wasn't a person in the world who could make him bend or change his course once his mind was made up—except for his wife. With a soft word or a pointed look, Sydney had seen Jane get him to bawl like a baby.

Since Sydney made her living working with horses and wearing dirty riding pants and boots, dressing up for dinner every evening was a welcome ritual. Tonight she chose a pair of dark trousers and an emerald-colored blouse. Unrestrained by the usual ponytail, her hair flowed around her shoulders.

After dinner, Sydney and her grandparents remained at the table to talk as they usually did in the evening hours, when their daily responsibilities finally left them alone together.

"I'm glad somebody's exercising the poor things," Jane said, talking about the three horses they owned. "Heaven knows we're too old to do it." Until Sydney had arrived, the animals had been exercised primarily on the walking machine behind the stables, which allowed them to walk or trot around the machine in wide circles. Since she'd been back from college, Sydney had taken the horses on long trail rides.

"Just be careful with Aladdin," Gabriel warned. "He's not like your warmbloods. Arabians are spirited, and Aladdin makes the rest of the horses look like teddy bears."

Sydney smiled. This wasn't the first time her grandfather had warned her about his favorite horse. "He's not half as bad as he wants you to believe," she said, having learned at an early age that a horse would try to get and keep the upper hand if allowed.

Gabriel snorted in disagreement.

"Your grandfather tells me that you're going to meet with the Kincaids tomorrow," Jane interjected.

"I have a meeting with Meredith's nephew about breeding Duchess with one of their stallions. Patriark is the clear choice, but I need to see the other stallions and look over their stud books," she said, picking at what remained of her apple pie.

"I'm surprised you haven't been out there before," Jane mused, her translucent skin glowing beneath the soft lights of the chandelier. "We've known the Kincaids for a very long time."

"I planned to when I first got back, but I just kept putting it off for one reason or another." Since coming back from Missouri, where she'd been studying and working for the past five years, Sydney had had little time for anything that didn't relate to her riding lessons. Only recently had she found any time to dedicate to her ambition of becoming a breeder, and now she planned to start by breeding Duchess.

"Well, Jackson has done wonders with Eagle Crest's facilities," Gabriel said fondly. "Until he was in charge it was just a small establishment. In the past couple of years he's turned it into a world-class breeding and training facility."

Over the past couple of years Sydney had often heard people in the field mention Eagle Crest Farms with the utmost respect and admiration. She'd forgotten that Gabriel had once mentioned something about knowing Meredith Kincaid personally until Jackson had shown up.

"I'm sure they have many fine stallions to choose from," Jane said.

Sydney nodded. "I wish it were an easier decision." She knew what she wanted. She knew from experience that a light gait, a temperate disposition, and a willingness to learn were important traits. But she also knew that these traits alone wouldn't guarantee a good result. She had to find a stallion that would match well with her mare's characteristics. If she chose a horse with the right qualities and proven abilities, and then matched those characteristics with the potential that Duchess had shown, she could breed a magnificent animal.

Duchess had shown great promise on the dressage circuit, but, due to a jumping-related injury, she could no longer compete. If Sydney wanted a champion, she would have to breed one.

"Get Jackson's advice," Jane suggested.

"I was hoping that Meredith would be there tomorrow, since she's the big-name trainer, but apparently she's away at a competition until the weekend."

"Jackson knows as much about horses as she does," Gabriel said, taking a drink of his water.

"I know, but from what I understand, he handles more of the business end of things."

"That's just because he owns the place," he countered. "But I've known Jackson since he was a boy, and believe me, there aren't many people who know horses better than he does. If you want any advice on bloodlines and temperament, you won't go wrong by following his suggestions."

Her curiosity suddenly piqued, Sydney looked sideways at her grandfather. "How well do you know Jackson?" she asked.

"Well enough to guarantee his opinion. He doesn't make his breeding choices easily. He studies and then joins the two bloodlines that will most likely result in exceptional horses." Gabriel leaned back and folded his arms. "Patriark is one of those results," he said proudly.

Sydney could barely keep her mouth from hanging open in shock. "You're kidding, right?" she asked. She'd seen the stallion in show and had been enthralled by his smooth, faultless jumps and beautiful lines. Worth a sum well into the six-figure range, Patriark had a pedigree that manifested itself in his many awards and championships.

"Jackson used to ride, too, and wasn't half bad, but he preferred to ride for fun rather than for show. But believe me when I tell you that he has a good eye when it comes to horseflesh. He's the one who introduced me to the man who sold us Romeo—" He stopped himself, and his eyes flickered with regret.

"Romeo?" Sydney asked, not sure that she'd heard right.

Her grandparents exchanged worried glances. Although Sydney's horse Romeo had been the focal point of her adolescence, she no longer mentioned him or anything else that would remind her of that time in her life.

Romeo had been a gift that her grandparents had given her when they had realized her love for horses went beyond weekend trail riding. She had won her fair share of awards up until that point on a mediocre horse, but when she'd ridden Romeo, it had been magic. She had done exceptionally well in the junior ranks and had displayed remarkable success at the amateur jumper ranks. Then she'd gone on to win over fifteen thousand dollars in awards the summer after high school—money that she'd planned to invest in the necessary training at the professional level. But all those plans had ended abruptly.

After Randy died, she had said her good-byes to Romeo and had asked her grandfather to sell him so that the money they'd invested wouldn't be completely lost. "I can't compete anymore," she had said with a disconnected finality. "And if he's not ridden, he'll go to fat." Romeo had been professionally trained and was in his prime. Letting him stand around like a barn horse would have been a waste. He needed to perform, he needed to compete—just not with her.

It had been as if she were punishing herself. She had abandoned equestrian sports and had left everyone she loved to go to school in Missouri, as if distance and time would heal her wounds.

"He knew so much more about show jumpers than I did," Gabriel explained.

Sydney was silent for a while, remembering how much she had loved Romeo and how much they had learned and grown together. Over the last five years there had been many moments like this—moments when she had regretted asking her grandfather to sell him. The decision had been difficult, but it had been borne out of consideration for her horse: keeping him would have meant ending his training and his competitive future.

"Well, Jackson made a good choice," she said finally. "Romeo was an incredible animal." She looked down at her hands. She hadn't kept track of how Romeo had been progressing with his new owner. "I wonder how he's done since we sold him," she said.

She didn't see Jane glance at her husband imploringly or Gabriel shake his head in reply.

"Anyway, Duchess is three years old and ready to be bred," she said, wanting to ease the tension that hovered above them. "With her genes and the right stallion, I might really be able to get a champion from her."

"You'll need a good trainer," Jane said.

"If I can save enough money, I'll have the foal professionally trained at Eagle Crest." Sydney knew that once a horse came under Meredith Kincaid's tutelage, it couldn't help but do well. "Then, maybe, I'll lease it out." Leasing was a common way of ensuring that a horse received continued training and experience when the owner was unable or unwilling to ride it in shows. There were a number of very good riders who couldn't afford their own horses yet, so they leased professionally trained horses that belonged to other people. Both parties came away winners—the owners because they were getting paid to have someone else exercise their horses, and the competitors because they were able to ride in shows without having to spend exorbitant amounts of money to buy quality horses.

"You know, Jackson's sister has already won a few competitions," Jane suggested.

"I didn't even know he had a sister," Sydney replied.

"Meredith has been training her for dressage and hunter/jumper competitions."

"Then she's already at an advantage," Sydney said appreciatively. Meredith Kincaid was the type of big-name trainer that everyone wanted but few could afford.

When the conversation came to its natural end, Sydney excused herself. "There are a few things that I need to do before calling it a night," she said as she stood. "I'll clear the table."

It was after ten before she made it to bed and even later before she managed to fall asleep.

Chapter 3

"I appreciate you doing this," Sydney said as Jackson met her at her car. "I know you're very busy."

"I'm glad to. Besides, my aunt Meredith and your grandparents go way back." He was dressed much as he had been the day before. If it weren't for the dirt on his boots she never would have guessed that he made his living with horses.

Sydney got out of the car, leaving her windows down so that the cool air could circulate. She parked near the training arena as he had suggested when he'd called her that morning.

"This is absolutely beautiful," she said, gazing at the property. "How big is it?"

"We have over a hundred acres," Jackson said, looking around him. "There are twenty-four turnout paddocks and seven large pastures. The rest is forest with some great riding trails. There's a whole network of roads that we just built last year to make everything more accessible," he said, turning back to her.

"Gabriel tells me that you've been in charge of things here since graduating from college."

"I don't know about being in charge," he said sincerely as he leaned against the door of a sleek, silver BMW that was parked next to Sydney's old Jeep. "I've been working the place since I was a kid, but in an official capacity just for the past three years."

"So that makes you, what, about twenty-five?"

"I'm twenty-nine. I served a mission before going to school."

Sydney stared at him. "You're LDS?" she asked, amazed. "I didn't know that Meredith Kincaid was a Mormon."

"She's not," he said with an easy smile. "I was baptized when I was fifteen. My sister joined the Church a couple of years ago."

"I'm stunned that my grandfather failed to mention that you're a Mormon." *And that he hasn't tried to set me up on a date with you,* she thought.

"Why is that shocking?"

She shrugged. "I would have assumed he'd want me to know it." When his eyes questioned her further, she added, "For the same reason that I misunderstood your reasons for visiting me yesterday."

Jackson smiled in comprehension. "For what it's worth, I know a lot about *you.*"

"Given the fact that you're acquainted with Gabriel, that doesn't surprise me." Sydney grimaced awkwardly. "He's done everything short of hiring a plane to fly a banner over Seattle saying 'Please Date My Granddaughter.'"

"That bad, huh?"

"That bad," she assured him. "That's why I assumed that you were there for . . . um, other reasons."

"Easy mistake," he said with a smile. "Well, shall we get started?" He pushed away from the car, motioning toward the path that led to a number of buildings.

"That's the house," he said, pointing to a magnificent gray brick structure in the distance. She had driven past it on the way up and thought it looked like it had grown right out of the rock it rested on. It stood on the crest of a jagged, fifty-foot bluff, proudly overlooking the Puget Sound, and it was framed by exquisitely manicured lawns. It was obvious from the location of the house and training facilities that work and family life, although distinctly separated, were undeniably linked.

It was a beautiful day. The sun had hidden itself behind the clouds, creating a subtle overcast and allowing mist to hover just inches above the Irish-green grass. Rain had sprinkled for a few minutes earlier that morning but remained cushioned in the clouds for the time being.

"It must be incredible to live here," Sydney commented.

Jackson shrugged and led her away from the house, toward a cluster of neatly arranged buildings that made up the training and riding facilities. "When you were raised here, it seems like just another house, but it was pretty nice as a kid," he said, looking over the grounds. "My grandfather had it built when my mother was born. When she got older and started competing, he had the stables put up as a gift to her. My father then expanded the stables and added the two indoor arenas," he explained, pointing out the various structures as he spoke. They went past a jumping course made up of twelve multicolored jumps. Riders and horses were randomly scattered throughout the facilities, training diligently. Beyond the course, Sydney could see tidy pastures framed with white four-board fences, and beyond the pastures lay a lush forest, highlighted by specks of lime and olive green.

Jackson stopped to open the door to the larger of the two indoor arenas. He moved aside and waited for her to pass before closing the door behind them. "A couple of years ago," he continued, "I had this stadium jumping course built, as well as a cross-country course. Last summer we finished the two outdoor arenas and a three-quarter-mile training track, and we expanded the breeding barn to include a heated veterinarian room."

Inside the spacious indoor arena, a young man was taking a tall chestnut mare through the course. Sydney noted that although the mare's lines were smooth, she needed some work with her jumps.

Jackson nodded toward the young man. "That's Andy. He's one of our trainers. Calypso is a mare we've been working with for a couple of weeks. When she came to us, she was rushing her jumps and had ended up throwing a rider in competition." They paused to watch as horse and rider approached a fence. Sydney could tell that the trainer had set the fences lower and farther apart than normal to force the horse to flatten her back while taking the jumps. As Calypso neared the jump, she increased her pace. Jackson shook his head. "She's still a little anxious," he said.

Sydney just smiled. She had no doubt that Calypso's trainers would soon teach her to jump without rushing. Inside, she suddenly felt the slightest hint of longing. It had been so long since she'd felt a horse beneath her. She remembered how it felt to calculate her horse's speed in order to take a jump without throwing a pole. She remembered the days when she had lived and breathed competition. Shaking off the memories, she turned to Jackson. "You have a first-class facility here," she said.

Jackson smiled appreciatively. "It's a lot of work, but it's worth it," he said as they resumed their walk toward the far side of the building. "The stables are connected to this arena, which makes for easy access."

He guided her to the back, where the arena opened up to the main stables. The stable was a long building with yellow-pine stalls on both sides. The entire length of the floor was covered in red cobbled rubber pavers, just like the walkways around the paddocks had been.

There was the expected bustle of activity in a facility as large as this one. Stable hands were busily making sure the horses were fed and watered while grooms saw to their cleaning and brushing. Like well-orchestrated dancers, everyone knew their role and performed it to the best of their abilities. And the director of this dance troupe, the facilities manager at Eagle Crest Farms, was doing a difficult but phenomenal job.

"This main barn has seventy-six stalls," Jackson explained, continuing the tour. "We have some sixty-seven horses currently in residence."

"How many belong to you?" Sydney asked, stopping to run her hand along the nose of a beautiful bay horse that had poked its head through the opening of the Dutch stall door. The stables were built in the shape of a cross so that there were four distinct entrances, each leading to a different part of the property.

"We own twenty-one. Nine mares are here to be bred, seven horses are here for training, and thirty horses are here being boarded. We have a pretty big staff, including a vet and a farrier available around the clock. Meredith oversees the training program, which focuses mainly on current competitors. We leave the training of young riders to facilities like your own."

Sydney grinned and started walking again. "I'm not quite in your league. My students are still miles away from dressage and jumping."

"How many students do you have?" Jackson asked, walking beside her now instead of leading her.

"Only six, which means that right now I still have a little time to focus on breeding my mare. I'm hoping that by next year I'll be swamped."

"Do you like it?"

"Teaching?"

He nodded.

"Yes, I do. There was a time when I thought that I'd never be able to stand being around a horse without wanting to compete. But I've found there is a relaxed enjoyment that comes with teaching and just riding for the joy of it." As they walked, she couldn't help running her hands across the nose of any horse that chose to stick its head out for a greeting.

"Why did you stop competing?" he asked.

Sydney stopped to pet a champagne-colored horse. She avoided looking at Jackson by kissing the animal's cheek. "It lost its appeal."

Jackson paused as if he sensed that there was more to the story than she was letting on, but he didn't press her. "Let me take you back to my office. It's just off of the west tack room," he said, and they took a right down the north wing of the stables. "Then we'll let you take a look at our stallions."

His office was elegant, spacious, and as clean and well-maintained as the rest of the facilities. It was trimmed in oak, and the built-in bookshelves were well stocked with leather-bound books. There was a small sitting room with some cushiony sofas just outside in what appeared to be the lobby.

"You don't spare any expense, do you?" Sydney asked as she ran her hands along the burgundy leather of the armchairs.

"It's Meredith's doing," Jackson defended. With a wry smile, he added, "If it were up to me I'd be working out of one of the stalls."

"I have the paperwork ready on all of the stallions so you can look over it before you see each of them," he said, gesturing to the desk.

"Perfect," Sydney said as she looked around the room. If the location of Jackson's office didn't give away the industry in which he worked, the décor certainly did. A sleek, bronze sculpture of a horse leaping over a fence graced the coffee table. There were also framed photographs of Eagle Crest Farms' prized horses on the walls, and the highlight of the room was an enormous painting of Patriark hanging behind Jackson's desk.

"This is beautiful," Sydney breathed, approaching the large painting. And it *was* beautifully done—the horse stood in an elegant pose, and his coat gleamed in the sunlight.

"Carrie Larsen," Jackson said, coming to stand right next to her.

Sydney noticed the small signature of the artist just as Jackson said the name. "She's very good."

"And she knows it," he added with a grin. "She makes sure everyone else knows it, too, simply by the price of her paintings."

Sydney noted the affection with which Jackson spoke of her and wondered if there wasn't something more to their relationship than just business. It would explain why Sydney's grandfather hadn't attempted to set her up with him.

"It sounds like you know her well," she remarked, watching his reaction with curiosity.

"I do," he said fondly and turned away. "We met a couple of years ago at a show."

Sydney nodded, her mouth lifting at the corners.

"Jackson, the paperwork you were waiting for came in—" A man in his mid-forties with pale hair and a kind face came to an abrupt halt when he saw Sydney. "I'm sorry, I didn't know you were busy. I'll come back."

"David, come in," Jackson said, calling the man back. "I want you to meet Sydney Chase."

David stepped into the room, a wide grin spreading across his face. "Oh yes, Jackson told me about you." He was a couple of inches shorter than Sydney and pleasantly soft in the middle.

"Sydney, this is David Miller. He's our manager and is absolutely invaluable to Eagle Crest Farms."

"He exaggerates," David said, extending his hand to her.

Sydney shook his hand. "From the looks of things, Mr. Miller, I don't think Jackson has exaggerated at all. Everything seems to be extremely well-organized."

David smiled appreciatively, causing his ruddy cheeks to crease with dimples. He was unassuming and sincere, and Sydney liked him immediately.

"Call me David," he invited. Then, remembering why he had sought Jackson out, he tapped the manila envelope in his hand. "I'll set this right here," he said, placing it on Jackson's desk. "If you'll excuse me, we have a stallion out on pasture number four that keeps chewing the fence." He rolled his eyes in exasperation and then looked to Sydney and smiled widely. "It was really nice to meet you. I'm sure I'll see you around," he said with a quick glance at Jackson, and then he turned and left.

"He seems to have it all under control," Sydney commented when they were alone again.

Jackson nodded. "If it weren't for him, it all would have fallen apart long ago."

"He sounds like Adam," Sydney said, almost to herself.

"The Stable Nazi," Jackson mused, and when Sydney looked at him questioningly, he added, "Elizabeth calls Adam the Stable Nazi."

"Elizabeth?"

"Elizabeth is my sister." He gestured toward the armchair. "Please, have a seat." When Sydney had done so, he explained. "Whenever I'd go visit your grandparents, Elizabeth would go visit Adam. I used to think that it was because she loved horses so much, but in retrospect, I think she did it mostly because she liked to pester him. So, she dubbed him the Stable Nazi."

Sydney grinned, imagining how Adam would have reacted to having a recalcitrant child running around and making a mess of his immaculate stables.

"I'm surprised we never met before now," Jackson mused.

"Gabriel always had visitors, but I was too caught up in training to pay much attention to who came around." Nothing had mattered to Sydney but riding in those days. She tried to change the subject. "Has David been with you for very long?"

"David was my father's good friend. He sort of took charge of things when my parents died. I was away at school, and Aunt Meredith lived in Florida at the time. David took care of the place, but more importantly, of Elizabeth, until we could get here."

"I'm sorry, I didn't know about your parents." Sydney couldn't imagine how difficult it had been for him and was immediately sorry for having provoked sad memories.

He nodded and Sydney could see the dulled pain in his eyes. "They died in a car accident three years ago. It was hardest for Elizabeth—she was just a kid." Rather than move behind his desk to sit down, he leaned his hip against it and remained standing a few feet from her. "By the time I flew to Washington, she was inconsolable. When they died, she lost the stability and security that had been wrapped around her as she was growing up. It's the kind of thing you don't miss until it's gone for good."

Sydney knew what it was like to feel that the world had suddenly been turned around. She had stepped outside of herself when she had lost Randy, and by the time she had returned, she had changed and no longer recognized anything that had once been familiar. "How is she now?" Sydney asked.

A smile stole across Jackson's face. "She's a terror," he said warmly. "She graduates from high school this summer, but she's somehow convinced that she's years wiser than I am."

Sydney smirked.

"But enough about me. What about you?" he asked. "Where did you go to school?"

"Well," she began, "I studied equestrian science at William Woods University in Missouri."

"I hear they have a good program," he responded, looking at her intently.

She felt him studying her face and nodded self-consciously, feeling a little like a fish in a glass bowl. She cleared her throat, suddenly unsure of what to say next.

"Are you glad you came back?"

"To Washington?"

He nodded. "It's a great state, but not exactly the horse capital of the world."

Sydney shrugged. "There's something about Whidbey Island that sort of captures you," she said. Then, uncomfortable with the nerves he provoked in her, she stood up. She'd never been particularly jittery around a man before, and she wanted to get out of his line of vision so she could recover her composure. She moved to the bookcases and glanced through the titles.

"It's good you came back," he said.

"Why's that?" she asked, turning toward him.

Now it was Jackson's turn to shrug. "I'm sure your presence will do your grandparents some good. Gabriel is immensely proud of you. He must love having you around."

Sydney grinned wryly. "That must be why he's been trying to marry me off since I arrived."

Jackson smiled in mild amusement, his eyes creasing at the corners as he gazed at her thoughtfully. Then, as if suddenly remembering himself, he blinked and straightened. "Why don't we find you a stallion?"

"Great," she said, glad for the reprieve.

Chapter 4

"Remember the leg cues I taught you, Jesse, and he'll start moving," Sydney instructed and then watched as the little girl did as she was told. The pony immediately started forward again, and the child started to giggle. Jesse was seven years old and had just started group lessons.

"Good girl. Now keep him going with everyone else."

Sydney moved to the middle of the outdoor arena and watched her students until she saw that they were comfortable with the new task of turning their mounts from left to right using leg cues.

"Okay. Now gently bring your mount to a stop. If he doesn't react to your legs, pull back gently on the reins."

She walked over to Jesse and grabbed her pony's lead line while giving her new pupil some extra pointers. "Stiffen your back, and if he still doesn't obey, pull back on the reins," she instructed gently. "Say 'whoa' if he doesn't want to listen," she added, taking the child's hands to show her how to pull back until the pony came to a full stop. Jesse giggled again, as if she had found a new toy that worked without batteries.

Sydney glanced at her watch. "All right. Now everyone dismount." She turned toward a pretty, red-headed girl. "Remember, we dismount from the left side of the horse, Trinity," she called, making sure that the eight-year-old had heard her. Trinity had a tendency to mount and dismount from the right side; this was dangerous, as it put her behind the horse's hind legs.

When all of her students stood on the ground, Sydney instructed them to take the reins and lead their horses to the fence, where Adam would take care of them.

"Good job today, kids," she said and watched as they scattered in the direction of their waiting parents. "Don't forget your helmet, Trinny," she called.

The girl grinned sheepishly and ran back to Sydney to retrieve her helmet.

"Thanks, Miss Chase."

"Sydney," Sydney corrected and playfully pulled on Trinity's braid before the girl ran to her mother's car.

"Josh is doing so much better," said a voice from Sydney's right. Sydney turned to see Sister Nelson, Josh and Rob's mother.

Sydney looked over at Josh, who sat on the grass taking off his riding boots so that he could put on his tennis shoes.

"He's got a knack for it."

"He was afraid of horses, Syd. The only reason he begged me to let him take classes was because you were the one teaching them."

Sydney grinned. "He's sweet."

"He's the youngest, so we indulge him. He's decided that he wants to be a mounted police officer. He's just frustrated that he hasn't yet been able to convince Rob to give up his patrol car for a horse."

Josh finished putting on his shoes and hurried over to where his mother and Sydney were talking. "Thank you for the lesson, Sydney," he said, and a handsome little dimple grew in his cheek. His eyes were blue where Rob's were a deep sable, but the resemblance between the brothers was still strong.

Sydney ruffled his hair. "You keep up the good work and soon you'll be giving *me* riding lessons."

Josh's grin widened, and his mother gently pulled on his sleeve.

"Let's go, Josh," his mother said and started back to her car with Josh in tow. "See you tomorrow, Sydney."

"Bye," Sydney called as she walked over to where Adam was unsaddling the ponies.

"No one fell off," he said, lifting the saddle off a white pony's back.

Sydney laughed, remembering how last week Trinity had fallen off as she was dismounting—from the wrong side. Luckily, Trinity's pony was small, and Trinity had been halfway dismounted. "I swear that girl has the hardest time with horses."

"But she loves them," Adam replied.

"I wish I could say the horses felt the same way about her." The horses always tried to take a bite out of Trinity's carrot-red hair whenever it was within reach, but this didn't discourage her from wanting to ride.

"Rebecca didn't come today," Adam pointed out.

"She's having a hard time trusting horses again," Sydney said, remembering the conversations she'd had with Rebecca's mother. Rebecca had had riding lessons previously, but when she'd fallen off of her horse last summer, she'd lost all confidence in herself and the animals.

When Rebecca's mother had brought her to Sydney, the girl's love for horses had been palpable, but her fear had kept her from even approaching them. Instead, the three times she had come to class, she'd stood against the fence and observed. Sydney decided she would call Rebecca's mother again and suggest that the girl try a couple of private lessons to rebuild her confidence.

"If she can regain her trust in horses, she'll be able to trust herself again," she told Adam.

"I've seen the way she looks at them," Adam said thoughtfully. "She wants to do it. She's just scared." He shot a quick glance at Sydney. "Gabriel told me that you paid a visit to the Kincaid farm today," he said and watched her circumspectly.

Sydney smiled at him affectionately, remembering the nickname that Jackson's sister had given him. "You know the place?" she asked, loosening the cinch on one of the ponies' saddles.

Adam paused before taking another saddle off. "I've been there."

"Oh, yeah? What did you think?" she asked, wondering why he'd never mentioned the farm.

"Of the place or the people?" he responded almost evasively, and before Sydney could call him on it, he continued. "Eagle Crest is top notch when it comes to breeding. A lot of Grand Prix winners have come from their spread."

"Speaking of Grand Prix winners, I think I want Patriark as the stallion for Duchess," Sydney announced, the excitement nearly pouring out of her. "After talking to Jackson last week, I'm pretty sure he'll be my pick. He's expensive, but he'll suit Duchess perfectly."

"He passes his characteristics to his offspring well," Adam agreed. "I've seen a couple of the horses that Patriark has sired. His foals are all stamped with the same traits. It's common knowledge that he's got a marketable pedigree and a great performance record."

"Duchess has some pretty good characteristics herself," Sydney said with a small smirk, knowing that Adam hated to admit this. He didn't react, so she pressed him further. "She has a good temper." She sensed Adam's internal scoff. "You can't deny that her head and neck are stunning and that she has good conformation."

Adam finally nodded reluctantly. "Matched with the right stallion, her foal could be a winner. But she's a maiden mare, so we can't look at any previous foals to see whether she throws her characteristics well. It's a toss up, but if it comes out right, you're set. Let's just hope that her foals aren't as hoity-toity as she is," Adam said flatly.

A car door slammed in the distance, and both of them turned to see who had arrived.

The late-afternoon sun winked off the windows of Rob's black pickup truck.

"Well . . . I've got a few things to take care of before calling it a day," Adam declared, lifting another saddle. "If you need help with anything, you let me know." He waved at Rob as he passed him on the way to the tack room.

"Adam," Rob said with a nod to the older man.

"Hey, Rob," Sydney greeted him with a smile.

"Do you want to go grab a bite to eat?"

"Sure." She glanced down at the dirt on her clothes and hands. "But let me clean up a little."

Rob nodded and followed her as she turned to walk back to the house. "Are you done with classes this week?"

"Until Tuesday," she said.

"I hear Adrianne managed to get the dress she wanted, huh?" he said with a smile.

Sydney chuckled. "And it wasn't easy, either. You should have seen the piles of white satin and taffeta."

"That bad?"

"It was horrible."

Rob winced. "Don't think she didn't try to convince me to go with the two of you. But a man's got to draw the line somewhere."

Sydney laughed, remembering all the times she and Adrianne had forced him to go shopping with them—tricked him into it, actually. Like baking soda and vinegar, Rob and shopping simply didn't get along, but the resulting eruption was so entertaining that Sydney and Adrianne constantly tried to combine them. They had swindled Rob into going shopping with them so often that he'd begun anticipating their intentions and avoiding their traps.

"It's no wonder you're not married," she teased, and her comment earned her a glare.

Even though there were plenty of women on the island praying for him to look their direction, Rob was secretive when it came to dating. If he dated at all, he didn't talk about it, and whenever Sydney or Adrianne grilled him on the subject, he only smiled and evasively changed the subject.

Rob was tall and had dark hair, which he kept short, and he was wearing a dark blue T-shirt that, unbeknownst to him, displayed his well-muscled arms. It was his lack of awareness about his own appeal that made him even more attractive than he already was.

As they walked in the front door, Doris, Jane's part-time house-keeper, spotted them and called, "Sydney, you have a call."

"Talk about timing." Sydney sent Rob a quick glance of apology before going to the living room to pick up the phone.

"This is Sydney," she said. She heard Rob flirt with Doris, who playfully reprimanded him before going back to work.

Rob strolled past Sydney to stand by the fireplace, where pictures of Sydney at all stages of youth lined the mantle. She saw him pick up the photograph of her at seven years old, standing nose to nose with a monster of a horse. She had been fearless then, before her dreams had sunk into the dark waters of the Sound.

"Oh, hi, Jackson," she said, and saw Rob's head turn at the mention of Jackson's name. "I did get them, thank you. Yes, I'm looking forward to it," she responded with a broad smile. "Thanks again." She hung up the receiver.

"Who was that?" Rob asked, setting the picture back on the mantle.

"Jackson Kincaid," she replied, feeling her cheeks grow warm. "He owns Eagle Crest Farms and the stallion that I'm going to breed with Duchess. He was just calling to see if I got the documents he sent for me to look over before our meeting tomorrow."

"Have you known him long?" he asked offhandedly.

"I just met him last week. He came by the house the other day at Gabriel's request."

"Gabriel's request?" Rob repeated with a raised brow.

Sydney saw his expression and laughed. He knew too well the nature of Gabriel's requests in regard to single men and his grand-daughter. "It's not like that. But I have to admit, at first I thought he was here for that reason, too."

"So . . . he's not old, then?"

"No. But old might have been a welcome change from that last guy Grandpa set me up with," she teased as she hurried past him on her way out of the living room. "Sit tight. I'll be ready in no time," she called on her way upstairs.

"That's what you said the last time you dragged me with you to the mall," he called back, dropping down onto the comfortable sofa.

"It was for a good cause," she defended with feigned affront.

"Shopping is never a good cause," he retorted.

"It is when it's for me or Adrianne," she assured him with a teasing wink and disappeared up the stairs.

* * *

Sydney was wearing a pair of olive-green cargo pants with a black, long-sleeved T-shirt. She'd pulled her hair up into a French twist, but short wisps still fell to frame her face.

The Fisherman's Net had been serving the tastiest and freshest seafood for as long as Sydney could remember. She and Rob were seated next to the window overlooking the docks. Lights from the adjoining businesses glared off of the water in different hues, making it look like a sea of multicolored gems. She loved the water when it was like this—calm and tranquil. From a distance it didn't even look like water. She could almost imagine that it hadn't robbed her—almost.

"I love this place," she said, unable to resist. "Good choice."

"I called Adrianne, but she was busy with Colin."

"No surprise there," Sydney said. "So, how's the old pile of rust?" she asked, referring to a Mustang that Rob was rebuilding.

Rob narrowed his eyes as expected. "Make fun of her all you want, but when I finish you won't be able to take your eyes off her."

"Sorry," Sydney said, shaking her head, "but new or old, cars do absolutely nothing for me." When his frown deepened, she raised her hands in surrender. "Fine, I'll change the subject." She reached for a cheddar roll. "How's work?"

"It's good," he answered easily. "I'm working on getting out of uniform."

"Why? You look so good in yours," she said with a teasing smile that only widened when he scowled back at her. "Uniforms are great," she assured him.

Rob shrugged. "Unless you have to wear them."

"If you didn't like the outfit, then why did you become a cop?"

"I didn't join the force so I could wear the uniform, if that's what you mean. I became a cop because I love the work."

"Well then, I think you're pretty much stuck wearing it."

"Maybe not. I put in my application for detective. If I get it, I'll be able to wear plain clothes."

Sydney's eyebrows shot up and she smiled. "You'd make a good detective."

"Yeah?" He gave her a cocky grin as the waiter set their plates on the table.

"Yeah," she insisted. "You're always so serious, so I think a detective job would be perfect for you. Detectives should be strong and somber," she said dramatically, and then she cocked her head to the side. "Do you realize that all of the words that describe you start with an *S*? Solemn. Stern. Steady." She counted them off on her fingers.

"Smart," he added with amusement.

"Conceited," she retorted.

"That starts with a *C*," he scolded.

"Not if I say 'super conceited.'" She wiggled her eyebrows at him. "Being serious, though, I think you'll make a great detective."

"*If* I get the job," he reminded her. "It's highly competitive."

"You will. You're good at what you do, Rob. They'd be stupid to give it to anyone else."

"*Stupid* starts with an *S*," he pointed out and took a large bite of mashed potatoes.

"So does *smart aleck.*"

They spent the rest of the evening in lighthearted conversation. Two hours later, Sydney was just walking out of the restaurant with Rob when she saw Jackson at the front of the restaurant, apparently waiting to be seated. When he looked up and spotted her, he smiled.

"Hi," Sydney said, feeling a sudden flutter in her stomach. He looked good, and his hair was still damp from a recent shower.

"Sydney," he said, smiling widely and glancing from her to Rob and back to her again. "You're just leaving?"

"Yes," she replied, hating that she couldn't think of something more intelligent to say. "Let me introduce you to my friend Rob."

Rob nodded to Jackson but remained silent, watching him intently.

Jackson returned the nod and then, after a slightly awkward pause, turned to the two women waiting with him. "This is Elizabeth, my sister, and my Aunt Meredith," he said.

Sydney smiled and shook their hands. Elizabeth was breathtaking with her long, strawberry-blond curls and her perfect bone structure. She was tall and lithe and had the same mysterious quality in her green eyes that Sydney had noticed in Jackson's—it was as if she knew something that no one else did. Meredith, on the other hand, was tiny and compact, and her rich brown hair barely reached her jawline. Although Meredith was small, Sydney knew that her light frame masked a strength that was essential for training the best horses and riders in the country.

"I've wanted to meet you for a long time," she said to Meredith. "You can't know what an inspiration you've been to me."

"Gabriel has told me so much about you over the years that I feel as though I've known you for ages," Meredith said with a friendly smile.

"I've heard a lot about you, too," Elizabeth said intrepidly.

"Your grandfather likes to brag," Jackson explained.

Meredith chuckled warmly. "He certainly does. But he didn't exaggerate when he said you were beautiful."

Sydney couldn't avoid the blush that instantly colored her cheeks. "You're kind for saying so." Knowing her grandfather, these poor people had probably had to endure hours of boasting.

"You're a very lucky young man," Meredith said to Rob, apparently mistaking him for Sydney's boyfriend.

"Kincaid, party of three? Your table's ready," the hostess announced, drawing their attention.

"That's us," Meredith said, turning back to Sydney and Rob. "It was nice meeting you. You'll both have to come by Eagle Crest sometime soon. We have some great trails."

"Thank you." Sydney slanted a quick look at Jackson. "Enjoy your meal."

"Take care," Jackson said as Sydney and Rob headed out into the darkening night.

* * *

Elizabeth watched her brother carefully as his eyes followed Sydney out of the restaurant. "She's really pretty," she casually remarked, gauging his reaction.

"Yes, she is," he said, refusing to acknowledge her silent inquiry.

"Too bad she's got a boyfriend." She was still watching him carefully.

Apparently Jackson knew better than to respond. With another reflective look at Sydney's retreating form, he turned to follow Meredith to their table.

Elizabeth hadn't missed the look of pleasure that had appeared on Jackson's face when he'd seen Sydney in the restaurant lobby. But what had really shifted her Cupid radar into overdrive was the look of regret that had replaced the smile when Sydney had left with another man.

Chapter 5

"Jack, darling, are you in here?"

Jackson took advantage of the interruption, dropped his pen on the desk, and leaned back in his chair for a much-needed stretch. "Back here," he called.

"There you are," Carrie said, flowing into his office like the scent of her perfume—refreshing and pronounced. She skirted around his desk and placed a kiss on his cheek before turning to admire her most recent painting of Patriark. "Oh, it looks incredible," she crooned. "It really does your horse justice, if I do say so myself." She stood back to properly appreciate it.

Jackson smiled. "You did a wonderful job, as always." If there was one thing that Carrie's artist's temperament required, it was proper acclaim. She lived for praise as much as she lived for painting. "And my pocketbook thanks you too," he added with mild sarcasm, although it had been worth every penny.

Carrie pouted as expected, making Jackson grin. "A girl's got to make a living, doesn't she?"

Jackson chuckled and shook his head. Carrie didn't need to work any more than he needed a root canal. Her father had made millions in the stock market before she'd ever been born, and Carrie Larsen had grown up pampered and spoiled. Her saving graces were that she had true talent when she picked up a paintbrush and that when she made a friend she was loyal to a fault. Due to the nature of her upbringing, she was superficial at times, and the artist in her occasionally exposed a flightiness that could be almost amusing, but the few who were privileged to know the true Carrie saw genuine depth and sensitivity that made everything else just frivolous packaging.

"What are you doing here, Carrie?" he asked, closing the contract he'd just signed. "I thought you weren't going to come down until next weekend." Carrie still lived in her parents' Madison Park mansion in Seattle.

"I got bored." She sighed as if that explained it all, and she smoothed her red-and-white sundress over her knees. "Let's go play," she said excitedly. "We can take Daddy's boat out on the Sound and have lunch on the water."

"I can't, Carrie. I have a lot of work to do," Jackson replied.

Carrie scowled as much as her perfect features would allow. "Work, shmurk." She dismissed his objection with a wave of her hand. "Have I ever told you that you work way too much?"

"Repeatedly," he agreed dryly. His aunt and his sister often accused him of the same thing.

"Who cares about work when you can have fun?"

"People who actually need to make a living," he said, amused at her unashamed lack of responsibility. If he didn't know her better, he would have taken that comment as evidence that she truly didn't comprehend the need for work. Sometimes it was hard to determine if her blatant disregard for responsibility was a result of her incredible wealth or just her free spirit. She seemed to live life on impulse and reserved the right to change her mind whenever she wanted to, and she did want to—often.

"Oh, come on," she said, eyeing her perfectly manicured nails. "You're not exactly . . . *poor.*" She whispered the last word as if it were a profanity and she didn't want to offend anyone.

"That's because I work," he reminded her.

Carrie sighed discontentedly. Her rich, dark-brown hair hung around her shoulders in loose curls that appeared to be as natural as her beauty. But Jackson knew enough about women to know that she'd spent hours in the salon to achieve that look, and he knew enough about Carrie to know that it had been incredibly expensive.

When he had first met Carrie, he'd thought she was spoiled beyond belief, but the more he'd talked to her, the more she had amused and entertained him. It wasn't until they had started spending a lot of time together that he'd learned she was also kind-hearted and generous.

"Can't you make David do the work?" she asked with a glower. "He *is* the manager, so let him . . . manage." She smirked at her own wit.

Jackson smiled but shook his head.

"Just for a couple of hours?" she begged.

"Why don't you ask one of your girlfriends to go with you?" It wasn't as if she was short on friends. She had an entire army of socialites vying for the chance just to be seen with Carrie Larsen.

"They're boring," she replied with a genuine frown. "All they want to do is shop and get their hair done."

Jackson raised his brow meaningfully as he eyed her designer shirt. "Last time I checked, you loved to shop."

Carrie chose to ignore his insinuation. "Not with them, I don't."

"See if Elizabeth wants to go with you."

Carrie exhaled her disappointment. "She hates me."

"She doesn't hate you, Carrie." Feeling tired, he glanced at his watch. Sydney would be arriving soon to see David about the stallions. "She just prefers horses over hairstylists."

"I like horses," she insisted on a near whine.

"Her idea of being around horses means riding them," Jackson pointed out. "Your idea of being around horses means watching a polo match from your box seat with a cool drink in your hand."

"There's nothing wrong with wanting to stay clean."

"Horseback riding isn't exactly a day in the mud."

"That's a matter of perspective." She waved away the subject as if it were a pesky fly. "So are you going to go with me or not?"

"Not," he said simply. "Some other time."

"Fine." She primly clutched the red purse that matched her shoes and stood up. "But this is no way to treat a girlfriend," she complained as she walked to the door. She liked to point out the fact that they had dated, as if it gave her some sort of leverage with him. "Next time I'm doubling my fee," she threatened, stopping to gaze at the painting of Patriark.

Jackson chuckled, because he didn't put it past her. "Then I'll have to make sure to commission a very small painting."

Carrie narrowed her eyes, but humor danced around her lips. "Tyrant," she spat playfully, flashing him the full, brilliant smile that had graced the covers of numerous magazines and newspapers in recent years. Then she turned on her heel.

"Drive careful," he called as she walked away.

* * *

Jackson found Sydney and David talking in the indoor arena. They were sitting on the wooden benches watching as Meredith instructed Elizabeth on different techniques. Apparently Elizabeth didn't like what she was hearing, because she was pursing her lips impudently from her position on Patriark's back. Finally, Elizabeth nodded at what her aunt was telling her and proceeded to take Patriark around the course until she reached the most difficult jump. With effortless elegance they cleared the fence.

"Good choice," Jackson said as he joined them in the viewing gallery and sat down on the bench next to Sydney. He ignored the look that passed between his aunt and sister when they saw him walk into the arena and immediately choose to sit with Sydney.

"I think so," she said, glancing at him only briefly before looking back at the stallion she had chosen for Duchess.

"We'll keep our fingers crossed that Duchess passes her characteristics to her foals." There was no guarantee in breeding horses, and even less guarantee when working with a maiden mare. They just had to wait and see with her first foal whether she threw her traits.

Sydney bit her lip nervously.

"Don't worry," Jackson reassured her. "If David didn't think your mare could turn out a foal with great traits, he wouldn't risk breeding a horse like Patriark with her. It's our reputation, too."

Sydney didn't answer for a moment as she watched the easy way Elizabeth took the horse through its jumps. Meredith called for her to keep her hands from going too high.

"She really knows her stuff," Sydney commented at the way his aunt noticed the small mistake.

"And she won't let you get away with anything less than perfection," he added, having been on the receiving end of her commands when he was young.

Sydney looked at him. "What was it like training with her?"

Jackson met her eyes and smiled. "We both got frustrated before any real training began."

"Did you see that?" Elizabeth called as she finished a jump. She trotted Patriark over to the fence in front of them to get their attention. "My best jump ever, and you didn't even see it!" she accused Jackson.

"I was distracted. Do it again."

"If I could do it again, I wouldn't be this excited in the first place," she snapped.

"It was a good jump, Elizabeth," Meredith agreed. "But you still need to work on keeping your legs still. You should move as little as possible while riding—you know that's what the judges look for."

Elizabeth scowled as she dismounted. "I hardly moved at all," she complained. "It wasn't even noticeable."

"If I saw it, then it was noticeable," Meredith countered, coming to stand near her niece.

"That's because you have bionic vision when it comes to showing horses." Elizabeth unclipped her riding helmet and propped it on the gate pole. "I bet Jackson wouldn't have seen it . . . *if* he'd been watching me." She handed the reins to one of the stable hands, who took Patriark for a cooldown.

"Jackson isn't the best judge when it comes to competition."

"You're right," Elizabeth conceded cheerily and reached around Meredith to smack a loud kiss on her cheek. "But *you* think I'm a great rider, don't you, Aunt Mer?"

Meredith chuckled reluctantly. "Passably good."

"I knew it," Elizabeth said with triumph. "If you knew anything about my aunt," she explained to Sydney, "you'd know that she's just practically admitted that I'm the best rider on the circuit!"

Meredith rolled her eyes.

Elizabeth turned to her brother again. "So, are you still taking me?"

"Taking you where?" he asked.

"To the Skagit Valley Tulip Festival," she whined. "I can't believe you forgot already. I reminded you just this morning."

Jackson groaned. "Can't David take you?"

David stood quickly. "I have to get back to work," he announced, and he started walking away before anyone could think to stop him.

"You'll pay for that, Dave," Elizabeth called to his retreating back. "Now," she said, looking back at Jackson, "go get ready, because you are most definitely driving me."

"And why is it that you can't drive yourself? You are seventeen, after all."

"Eighteen," she corrected.

"Barely," he said pointedly, as if he didn't like the fact that his little sister had reached adulthood.

"Barely, but still eighteen," she replied with a smirk. "But to answer your question, I volunteered to help with the parade, but my friends aren't going till later. We're all going out after the parade, and I don't want to have to leave my car at the festival. So you're taking me. You could actually take advantage of the opportunity and go look at the tulips that you're usually 'too busy' to see." Suddenly, Elizabeth gasped softly and her eyes widened as if she'd just had a brilliant thought. Turning to Sydney, she said, "Do you want to go with him?"

Sydney opened her mouth to decline.

"Sure she would," Meredith answered for her. "You'd like to go, wouldn't you, Sydney? You and Jackson could go look at the tulip fields."

Sydney closed her mouth and smiled in defeat, and Jackson could see that she recognized a dead end when she came to one.

He shrugged his shoulders helplessly. "They do it to me all the time."

* * *

People came from all around the country to see the colorful tulip blooms every spring. And they didn't limit their observations to land. For those who preferred sky views, there were a number of helicopter tours that carried visitors over the thousands of acres of color-coordinated flowers. But most people chose to experience the rainbow of fields on bicycles or on foot, which was how Jackson and Sydney had chosen to see them.

They walked through the endless fields of multicolored tulips in one of the few places that allowed visitors to pick the tulips they wanted to buy. The rows of flowers went as far as the eye could see and were neatly divided into fields of every color of the rainbow. The Cascade Mountains offered a breathtaking backdrop to the brilliant fields. As Sydney and Jackson wandered through the fields of red tulips, the smells of spring permeated the air. Sydney closed her eyes and inhaled deeply. "Isn't it the most wonderful thing you've ever smelled?"

Then, abruptly, Sydney stopped and opened her eyes to find Jackson watching her intently. "Sorry," she said, embarrassed that she'd forgotten who she was with. "I tend to get carried away." Regardless of how easy it was to be around him, and regardless of how he turned her stomach to jelly, he was, more than anything else, a business associate—and a new one at that.

"You've come here a lot, I take it," Jackson remarked, resuming their stroll through the long rows of flowers.

"I used to," she said. "Before I moved away we'd come every spring."

"We?" he asked, stepping aside as a wobbly toddler tried to stumble past him before being caught by his father.

"Adrianne and I."

"The girl from last week?" he surmised, remembering the curly-haired blond.

Sydney nodded. "She's getting married in a couple of months, so tulips are the last thing on her mind right now—unless we're talking about adding them to the bouquet."

"That guy you were with at the restaurant," Jackson began. "Rob, wasn't it? Are you seeing him?"

Sydney looked up at him, her heart suddenly racing in her chest. She shook her head. "No. We're just really good friends."

"Nothing serious?"

"We've known each other a long time," she said candidly. "We're friends."

"Does he know that?" Jackson asked, reaching down to pick a particularly bright tulip.

"What do you mean?"

"He seemed a little . . . proprietary," he stated, handing her the flower.

Sydney took the blossom, feeling a little breathless. "Not Rob," she said, bringing the tulip to her nose. It was sweet and bright beneath the warm rays of the sun. "He's no more interested in a relationship than I am."

"Then you're not dating anyone seriously?" he prodded.

Sydney looked up, wishing she had kept her mouth shut. "I don't really date." Then, worried he would think she was complaining, she hurried to add, "By choice."

"Officially? No exceptions?" He turned to face her so that they were just a few inches apart.

"No exceptions," she said, her eyes darting around uncomfortably, knowing full well that it sounded extreme.

"What about the guys you said Gabriel set you up with?"

Sydney gave a short laugh. "Those weren't dates, they were favors." She sobered instantly. "I know that sounds mean, but it isn't . . . not really. I just went out with them because my grandfather set the dates up, and it was either hurt their feelings or go. Believe me, most of them were happy to never see me again." She grimaced, remembering a particular date who had taken her home early after finding out that her ignorance about baseball had been voluntary. "I'm just not interested in dating anyone."

"Why not?"

No one had ever asked her that, and she didn't know how to respond. Jackson watched her, waiting, but there wasn't a way to answer him without going into the details. "Thanks for the flower," she said, smelling it once more before sidestepping Jackson to continue down the path.

"You're welcome," Jackson said, allowing her to change the subject. He turned to follow her, but a few steps away Sydney had frozen in place and was staring straight ahead. "Are you okay?" he asked when he reached her side.

Sydney felt like she had been transported back in time. She could almost hear the screech of the wind and feel the salty sea spray on her face. For a moment it was as if she was there again, clinging to the sailboat as it crashed over the waves just after Randy had disappeared into the black water. For an instant, she thought she was looking into his eyes.

"Sydney," a voice said so softly it was almost inaudible.

Sydney stared at the thin, older woman standing motionless just a few feet away. She felt the blood drain from her face, and her eyes began to sting with emotion.

"Sydney, are you all right?" Jackson asked again, touching Sydney's arm.

As if being pulled out of a trance, she swung her eyes in his direction and struggled to collect herself. "Yes," she said softly. "Yes, I'm fine," she said more surely and looked back at the woman. With a shaky smile she spoke. "Hello, Mrs. Willett."

"Hello, Sydney," the woman said carefully. "I didn't know you were back."

Sydney nodded, suddenly feeling weak and unsteady. "I came back six months ago," she said. *I would have come to see you, but . . . I couldn't,* she added to herself.

The woman lifted her head in understanding, her smile turning concerned. "How have you been?" She gave Jackson a quick glance.

Sydney felt as if she couldn't breathe, as if at any moment she would lose her grasp on reality and find herself back on the storm-tossed water. "This is Jackson," she said. Then, knowing what it looked like and feeling like she needed to explain, she added, "He's a friend."

Jackson exchanged greetings with the woman, but then he turned back to Sydney with concern in his eyes. "It was nice to meet you," he said to Mrs. Willett. "But we really need to run."

"Of course." Mrs. Willett turned to Sydney again. "Maybe we can talk sometime," she said, and with one last glance at Jackson she walked past them and headed farther into the fields.

"Thank you," Sydney said, hating that tears were pooling in her eyes and hating that Jackson was there to see them. "Would you mind if I left?" she asked quietly, feeling the familiar urge to run.

"I'll take you home." He took her arm and led her back toward his car.

"What about Elizabeth?"

"She's catching a ride with her friends."

Sydney breathed deeply to keep from embarrassing herself by crying in front of someone who was practically a stranger. "Thank you."

They found the car and headed back to Whidbey Island.

After nearly half an hour, Jackson broke the silence. "Who was she?"

Sydney glanced at him briefly before looking back out the window.

"She was the mother of someone I used to know," she said evasively, staring at the emerald waters of Deception Pass.

Jackson didn't miss the fact that she'd used the past tense. "Is this why you don't date anymore?" he asked.

Sydney looked at Jackson Kincaid and realized that there was something about him that made her want to confide in him, to reveal her fears and free her heart. But she couldn't . . . She just couldn't.

"If you ever want to talk about it, I'll listen," he said softly.

Maybe it was habit that made her remain silent; maybe it was that no matter how receptive he appeared, he was still, ultimately . . . a stranger. She smiled appreciatively and turned her head to look at the passing landscape. They rode the rest of the way in silence.

Chapter 6

"If I had known you were coming, I would have arranged to be here earlier," Jackson said as he met Gabriel in the stables several days later.

"I just stopped by for a moment," Gabriel replied. He stood outside the stall that held a finely chiseled, chestnut-colored gelding and ran his hand along the horse's forehead. "Meredith called and told me he was here for the time being."

Jackson opened the stall door and walked inside to stand next to the horse. "His rider had a jumping-related back injury," he explained, firmly patting the animal's sleek withers. "So, for now, this boy is here with us." He patted the horse's shoulder and left the stall.

"That's good."

Jackson noticed Gabriel's worried frown. "You know," Jackson began as he leaned against the door. "When Sydney stopped by last week she didn't even ask about him."

Gabriel rested his arms on the iron grill of the stall and let his head fall forward tiredly.

"She doesn't know, does she?" Jackson prodded.

Gabriel lifted his head, keeping his eyes on the horse, and smiled guiltily. "She asked me to sell him, but I couldn't. She loved this horse more than anything." He shook his head regretfully. "I'd planned on telling her when I thought she was strong enough." He shrugged. "I'm still waiting."

"I asked her why she stopped competing." Jackson watched the old man carefully. "She said that she lost interest."

Gabriel gave him a quick glance. "In a way, I suppose she did," he said remorsefully.

"What happened?"

Gabriel paused, considering how much to say. "Five years ago, Sydney lost someone who was very close to her."

"I remember you mentioning something about it when you brought Romeo." Jackson glanced at the horse. He hadn't asked any questions when Gabriel had brought the horse to him five years ago asking him to take care of the details. He wasn't sure why he wanted to ask now. "A friend, wasn't it?"

Gabriel nodded. "Randy Willet. He was her boyfriend. They were caught in a storm while they were sailing, and he drowned."

Jackson was beginning to understand the reason for Sydney's reaction when she'd bumped into the woman at the tulip festival. It must have brought the whole horrible experience back to her. "Is this why she doesn't date?"

Gabriel's eyes swung to his. "Is that what she told you?"

"Not in so many words."

"She never talks about it." Gabriel straightened. "But I think she's scared to try again. She was so young—barely nineteen—when it happened."

"What will happen if she learns that he's been here all along?" he asked, motioning to the horse.

"I'm afraid to find out."

* * *

"Grandma?" Sydney called, knocking on the door.

"Come in."

Sydney walked in to find her grandmother propped up against the headboard of her bed reading. Smiling, Jane looked up at Sydney and set her book aside.

"Linda did a good job with your hair today," Sydney commented and sat on the edge of Jane's bed. "Is it a new color?" She inspected her grandmother's ice-white hair, which pronounced her regal features. Jane Chase had aged with dignity and grace and had wrapped the years around herself like a fur coat.

"She went a little lighter this time." With a little grimace, Jane patted her short, fluffy curls.

"I like it."

"We'll see what your grandfather says," she said with a wry grin. "If he even notices it." She sighed placidly. "So tell me, what are your plans for the weekend?"

"I have to help Adrianne with the singles' dance tonight." Sydney made a face.

Jane chuckled. "It's a good way to meet young men."

"Not you too." Sydney sighed in defeat. "It's bad enough that Grandpa's trying to marry me off, but you?"

"Come on, now." She patted Sydney's hand. "Your father is forever asking me if you've met anyone yet. I'm running out of excuses."

"Tell him the truth. I've met plenty of guys." The last thing she needed was for her parents to hound her from thousands of miles away.

Her grandmother raised a chastising brow. "Name one."

"Jackson Kincaid," Sydney said, because he was the only one who came to mind.

"I can't argue there," Jane responded. "And he's definitely everything a parent could want."

Sydney picked at the threads of the coverlet. "He seems to be a decent guy."

"And noble," Jane added.

"How do you mean?" Sydney's curiosity was piqued.

"Well," Jane began thoughtfully. "When his parents passed away, Elizabeth was barely fourteen and Jackson was in graduate school. Meredith lived in Florida at the time, and even though she offered to move to Washington to take care of Elizabeth, Jackson refused. He left school, came home, and took full responsibility for his sister. Jackson was selfless and compassionate enough to know what mattered."

"He does seem to have a good relationship with his sister," Sydney mused, remembering the way they teased each other.

"He adores her, and she him," her grandmother stated. "He took a difficult situation and with faith and pure determination, he turned it around. Because of him, Elizabeth is a sound young woman who knows without a doubt that she is loved."

Sydney's smile was thoughtful. There was so much to Jackson that both drew her in and frightened her, and the more time she spent with him and his family, the more of the real Jackson she saw. He was compassionate, kind, and strong. It was alarming to meet a man with so many appealing qualities. But what disturbed her above all was that when she was with Jackson, she felt safe. She hadn't felt that way in a long time. "Well . . . I'd better go get ready." Sydney stood and headed out. At the door she paused and turned back. "Grandma?"

"Yes?"

"Thank you," she said. "You know . . . for everything."

"You're welcome," Jane said just before the door closed. "You're most definitely welcome."

* * *

When Jackson finished his work for the day, the sun was still out. This was rare, since he usually didn't leave the office before sunset.

He relaxed into a teak chair on his deck overlooking the ocean, and his thoughts turned to the person who seemed to hold a monopoly on his attention lately. He hadn't seen Sydney for days, but he had thought of her often—the way she smiled, the way she stirred something within him that made him think of the future . . . of his future. Until he'd met her, he hadn't realized how lonely he was.

"Are you going to get ready soon?" Elizabeth asked, stepping in front of him and adroitly blocking his view of the cove with her mass of strawberry-blond curls.

"For what?" he asked absently and closed his eyes.

"For the multi-stake single adults' dance," she said with sudden panic. "Please don't tell me you forgot."

He opened his eyes slowly. "Dance?"

"You did forget!" she accused, plopping herself on the chair beside him. "You promised that I wouldn't have to go alone." It was her first singles' dance, and she wasn't about to go by herself. Many of her friends were seventeen and still too young to attend.

"I didn't forget," he lied.

Elizabeth glared at him. "It doesn't matter," she said petulantly. "Either way, you're going. So you better get ready . . . and fast," she glanced at her watch as she stood up. "You have exactly thirty minutes," she announced before waltzing off.

Jackson rubbed his hand over his face. The last thing he wanted to do was put himself in the middle of a bunch of people who were out to snare a spouse. Now that Elizabeth had "grown up," she was starting to frequent the places that he had always avoided—chiefly the singles' activities. He couldn't recall how, exactly, his sister had managed to convince him to go with her to a dance of all things. Come to think of it, he didn't remember ever having talked about it.

His eyes narrowed as threads of suspicion crept into his mind. He wouldn't put it past her, and Meredith for that matter, to have conspired to get him involved in anything involving single women. *"You're a workaholic,"* Elizabeth had accused just last month. *"How are you ever going to get married if all you ever do is work?"*

"Twenty-five minutes, now. You'd better hurry!" Elizabeth called from inside the house.

Jackson forced himself to stand up and walk into his bedroom. Already, he felt exhausted.

Chapter 7

The minute Jackson stepped inside the church gym, he had the wild urge to run.

"Don't even think about it," Elizabeth warned him as she scanned the room for familiar faces.

"The minute you find someone you know, I'm out of here," he informed her and glanced at his watch, mentally calculating the amount of time it would take him to make his getaway.

"No . . . you promised."

"Oddly, that promise seems to have slipped my mind. I know what you're up to, Lizzy. I can practically hear Cupid drawing his bow," Jackson said dryly.

Elizabeth rolled her eyes. "At least stay through the meal. It's not like anyone's going to attack you. Look, no one has even noticed you."

"Jackson," a high pitched voice called as if to prove Elizabeth wrong.

"There's Cupid now," Jackson muttered. "You are going to owe me big time for this," he assured Elizabeth through gritted teeth and looked up to smile at a girl he'd met at one activity or another. It didn't surprise him that she still remembered his name; in fact, he wouldn't be surprised to learn that she had started naming their future children soon after they'd met.

"I haven't seen you in forever," she began excitedly as she approached him. "Where have you been hiding?" she asked, nudging him playfully.

"Oh, I've been around." He smiled and prayed for deliverance. "This is my sister, Elizabeth," he said, motioning to her. "My soon to be *dead* sister," he whispered so only Elizabeth could hear.

"Hi, I'm Teresa."

Right . . . Teresa, he thought, recalling her name.

"It's nice to meet you," Elizabeth said with a huge smile. "Well, I just spotted a friend. I'll see you later, Jackson." With an apologetic glance, she left him to the mercy of an expert huntress.

Teresa was a sweet girl, but from what Jackson remembered, she was also a chatterbox with the unique skill of talking about everything while saying nothing important at all.

It was bad enough that he'd been strong-armed into coming. "You look nice," he remarked honestly. She was tiny, barely reaching the middle of his chest, and her hair had been dyed a perfect blond, which was set off by her blue eyes. All in all, Teresa was a beautiful girl, but he couldn't help but wish she was more like Sydney.

"You think so? It took me a month to find this dress, and even then it didn't fit right. I had to search around to find someone who could bring up the hem. I swear it was made for a giant, but the minute I saw it, I just had to have it."

Jackson nodded at the right times and desperately looked for an escape.

* * *

"It's too bad Rob had to work tonight," Adrianne said as she pulled a pan of rolls out of the oven.

"He's not missing much," Sydney grumbled sourly as she arranged the Dixie cups in rows along the counter and poured cherry soda into each one. Had Adrianne not been chair of the activities committee and requested Sydney's help with setting up, Sydney would never have come to the activity. Usually when she got dragged to one of these things she hung out with Rob, who always made it more bearable. But Rob had gotten called in to work at the last minute, and Sydney had been left stranded.

"Come on, Sydney." Adrianne busily filled small bread baskets with hot rolls while two other girls worked to put the finishing touches on the spaghetti, which was the main dish for the buffet dinner. "Give it a chance. You might have fun."

"I'm not saying it's not fun. It's just not *my* idea of fun." Sydney tossed an empty soda bottle into the trash and loosened the cap on a new one.

"Why don't we get the cups on the table before you fill any more?" Adrianne handed her a tray, and Sydney began lining it with cups.

"You girls need any help?" Colin and his brother Toby appeared in the kitchen.

Adrianne's smile nearly lit up the room as she looked at her fiancé. Colin's sandy blond hair was just a little lighter than his brother's, and his good looks had set Adrianne's heart aflutter when they'd first met. "Yes, we do. Could you guys help us take the spaghetti into the gym?" she asked sweetly.

"Sure." Colin kissed her before lifting the heavy tray.

Adrianne sighed and watched him leave as if she hadn't seen him in years. "Isn't he wonderful?" she asked dreamily.

"Come on," Sydney chuckled. "Help me with the drinks."

The gym was crowded with single men and women who were laughing and talking and apparently having a great time doing so. After dinner, there was to be dancing, which Sydney and Rob had planned to skip in favor of a movie. But now that Rob had bailed on her she had no ride home until after the dance.

"Here, let me take that," Toby offered. He took the tray of drinks from Sydney and placed it at the end of the table.

"Thanks." She smiled appreciatively and helped him set the drinks up in neat rows. Adrianne and Colin disappeared back into the kitchen.

"No problem." Toby grinned as he looked at her. "You look scared," he said and raised an amused brow.

"I am." Sydney laughed and glanced behind her to the groups of people. "It's like a meat market. And I feel like I'm on display."

"This is how my brother and Adrianne met, you know." He nodded toward the crowd.

"I know," Sydney replied and leaned toward him to add with a dramatic whisper, "That's what scares me."

Toby laughed. "Maybe you have reason to be afraid." He winked suggestively. "You might find Mr. Right tonight."

"Don't even say it," she threatened, entertained by his audaciousness. The few times that she'd spoken with Toby, he had charmed her. He was better looking than his brother, although Adrianne would never think so. He had a chiseled jaw and was tan from hours of playing baseball under the sun.

"I'll tell you what," Toby began, removing the last cup from the tray, "Dance with me later and I'll show you how to avoid the 'M' word."

"Marriage?"

He shook his head. "Monotony."

Sydney laughed out loud and eyed Colin's handsome younger brother. "You wouldn't be trying to trick me into dancing with you, now would you?"

"Not if you say yes."

"You're just like your brother." Sydney shook her head in amusement. "It's no wonder Colin hooked Adrianne the first night they met. I'm sure if I don't watch out you'll have me saying 'I do' in no time, as well." Sydney could see that if there was anything the Ralston brothers had in common, it was their charisma.

"You're on to me," he said in feigned disappointment.

"I'll just bet."

* * *

Jackson heard her laugh before he saw her. He wasn't sure how he knew it was her, but the sound had him scanning the room until he spotted her.

"And her puppies were as cute as buttons. You should come over and see them." Teresa sighed and gave Jackson a much-needed opening.

"I bet they're adorable," Jackson responded absently, his eyes locked on Sydney across the room. "I'm sorry, Teresa, but if you'll excuse me, I have to go say hi to a friend." And before she could start a discussion on the value of friendship, Jackson was halfway across the gym. By the time he reached Sydney, she was laughing again at something the guy she was with had said.

"I didn't know you'd be here tonight," Jackson said as he came up behind her.

Sydney spun around. "Oh, hi." She greeted him with a wide grin.

"I would have thought you'd avoid things like this." Jackson glanced around him at the room filled with eligible singles.

"I do. I mean, I did." She paused momentarily and smiled. "I just came to help Adrianne."

The man she'd been talking to cleared his throat as if to bring attention to the fact that he was being ignored.

Sydney grinned over at him deprecatingly. "This is Toby. Toby, this is Jackson."

Toby grinned genially when they shook hands. "Hi. I've got to get back to the kitchen. The girls are lost without me." He looked back at Sydney. "Remember what I said about the 'M' word," he reminded with a significant nod of his head in Jackson's direction.

Sydney shot him a silent rebuke before he left, grinning.

"Another friend of yours, I take it," Jackson said as Toby disappeared into the kitchen.

"Adrianne's soon-to-be brother-in-law," Sydney explained, taking a cup of soda and bringing it to her lips. "So, who are you here with?"

"I brought my sister," he replied, searching the room for her. Elizabeth was standing with a group of giggling young girls who were all scoping out the single boys.

"That was nice of you."

"You don't know the half of it," he said dryly, and Sydney smiled.

"Could I please have everyone's attention?" Adrianne's voice carried over the speakers and all eyes turned toward her. "We're ready to get started. We'll start the dance about an hour after dinner, so please clean off your tables when you're through and drag yourselves onto the dance floor. Thank you for coming, and have fun," she finished, and then she moved aside as the evening got underway.

Jackson and Sydney found a table close to the door with Adrianne, Colin, and Toby. Elizabeth and a couple of her girlfriends joined them after the dinner plates had been cleared away. The lights were dimmed slightly and the dance floor was filled with couples moving their arms to the Village People's "YMCA."

"And then Jackson tossed the bucket of water over his head," Elizabeth recounted, giggling. "It wasn't until globs of horse manure dribbled over my dad's face that Jackson realized he'd grabbed the wrong bucket."

Sydney laughed loudly.

Jackson relaxed in his seat and watched, unable to take his eyes off her.

"It sounds like you were a handful as a boy," Sydney said, turning to him.

"With a sister like Elizabeth, I came across as a saint. One important fact that Elizabeth is leaving out of the story is that she was the one to switch the buckets."

"How was I supposed to know that you were going to pour it over Dad's head?" Elizabeth responded. "Besides, Mom and Dad absolutely adored me," she added primly.

"That's because around them you acted like an angel. It wasn't until their backs were turned that you bared your claws," he answered lightheartedly. "I have the scars to prove it."

"The only scars you have are from your own clowning around," Elizabeth corrected, and she turned to Sydney. "One time, he'd decided he was going to be a skydiver when he grew up, so he convinced me to make a parachute out of sheets and jump off the barn with him. Luckily, he hadn't yet figured out how to climb up to the roof of the barn, so we jumped off the fence instead. He landed on a rock, and I landed on top of him," Elizabeth admitted with a laugh. "Even at three years old I was smart enough to wait for him to go first and then arrange my jump based on his landing."

Jackson couldn't help but chuckle at the memory. Elizabeth had been gullible enough as a child to go along with all of his foolish ventures but clever enough to come out on top—literally.

A Richard Marx song about love, distance, and breaking hearts began to play. Adrianne and Colin trailed to the floor to join the other couples under the swirling lights reflected off the disco ball, while others scanned the room for someone with whom to share the romantic moment.

Jackson stood up. "Will you dance with me?" he asked, extending his hand toward her.

* * *

If Sydney thought that breathing had been difficult when she'd been around him before, she had been wrong. Now it was as if her body had forgotten how to do its most fundamental task. She took Jackson's hand, because there didn't seem to be anything else she could do, and he led her onto the dance floor. She saw Toby dancing with a pretty brunette, and when he spotted her hand clasped in Jackson's, he wiggled his eyebrows at her. Sydney sucked in her cheeks to keep from giggling as Jackson stopped and turned around. When he held her right hand to his chest and put his other arm around her waist, all desire to laugh disappeared.

The tender lyrics swirled inside her head as she and Jackson moved to the music and the whole world fell away around them. For a moment, it was as if no one else was in the room—in the world—except the two of them.

"I'm glad you came," Jackson said softly.

Sydney raised her eyes to his, thankful that the dim lights kept her blush hidden. "I am too," she said, and she was surprised to realize that she meant it.

Chapter 8

Sydney lay awake in bed for several reasons, and all of them involved Jackson. He had called her the day after the dance, and she'd agreed to go riding with him through Eagle Crest's trails tomorrow. She was eager to, in fact. And this was the root of her problem. For reasons she didn't want to explore at the moment, she found herself looking forward to seeing him.

Just yesterday, she had been at the grocery store picking up some much-needed ice cream and had felt her pulse race when she'd spotted a man with dark hair in the produce aisle. After discovering that it wasn't Jackson, she'd felt deflated and had been forced to face the fact that she'd wanted to see him again.

Now, lying in bed making shapes of the shadows on her ceiling, Sydney was fully aware that her attraction to Jackson was speeding quickly down a course that led directly to something she'd avoided for a very long time. A part of her said it was about time, but a louder, more insistent voice told her to stop before it was too late.

Sydney rolled over onto her stomach and slammed the pillow over her head to smother her conflicting thoughts. She groaned when she realized that no matter which way she turned and no matter how hard she tried, she couldn't get Jackson out of her mind.

She needed to sleep.

She rolled once more onto her back and stared at the ceiling.

Whatever feelings she thought she was having for him must simply have been born of gratitude. He'd been kind to her when she had bumped into Randy's mother at the tulip festival, and he'd somehow known not to push her for information. She'd been impressed by his strength in the face of his own trials. And she'd been drawn to him by the selfless way he'd shouldered his family responsibilities after his parents' deaths. But as a whole, there really wasn't a chance for whatever it was her heart thought it wanted.

Sydney sighed regretfully. *Perhaps if things had been different.*

But they weren't different. Ever since Randy had died she no longer trusted herself. Her fear had grown almost palpable, overtaking any hope. It was a weed that, unnoticed, had spread until it had infested the whole garden and suffocated the flowers that at one time had bloomed freely. A neglectful gardener, she'd allowed the weeds to dig their roots so deeply into her heart that she no longer saw signs of the life she had once wanted.

Tomorrow she would go riding with Jackson, and she would enjoy herself the way she did when she spent time with Rob, but after that she would avoid him as much as she could until thoughts of him no longer caused her heart to race.

It was settled.

Sydney closed her eyes, commanding herself not to think of him. Slowly, her body obeyed as sleep overcame her.

Her heart didn't obey so easily, however, for just as she succumbed to the world of dreams, where awareness surrenders to welcome oblivion, a pair of deep blue eyes smiled down at her and stole her thoughts.

With an unconscious smile of her own, she surrendered to sleep.

* * *

They had been on the trail for nearly an hour, surrounded by only the sounds of nature and the soft thudding of the horses' hooves on the well-packed dirt. They made their way to a bluff overlooking the ocean, where they secured the horses to the trees along the edge of the clearing and sat on the grass in a small glade.

Their skin was warmed by the sun and cooled by the soft breeze. The whisper of leaves and the chorus of birds contended with the sound of waves breaking against the rocks below.

"This is incredible." Sydney sat with her legs crossed, playing with a blade of warm grass.

"I use to come here as a kid—against my mother's orders—to relax and to just breathe," Jackson said.

"I can see why." To the right and tucked back inside the cove, his house stood proudly on the ridge.

"For the longest time my mother had a telescope out on the deck so that she could make sure I wasn't over here." He grinned affectionately. His legs were crossed at the ankles and he leaned back on his elbows.

Sydney smiled slightly as she imagined how his mother must have known that her unruly son would make his way to the one spot she'd forbidden him to visit. "You talk about them so easily," she reflected, almost to herself.

"Who, my parents?" Jackson looked out over the water. "I didn't at first. I guess I thought not mentioning their names would make it easier. Then a few months after they'd died, I found Elizabeth crying in her bedroom because she couldn't remember what our mother's favorite color was. I realized then that when we talk about them, it's as if we're keeping a part of them with us."

The salty air toyed with Sydney's hair as her eyes met his. She looked away quickly and focused on the distant horizon.

"Were you in love with him?" Jackson asked.

Sydney looked over at him questioningly, unsure of what he meant until she saw his expression.

"Gabriel told me," he explained.

She expected to feel anger or betrayal at knowing that her grandfather had spoken to Jackson about her past, but it was the lack of those emotions that impelled her to speak. "I loved him," she acknowledged.

Sydney looked at the ocean. The sun glared off of the glassy surface of the water, making it shimmer like thousands of diamonds. "Randy loved sailing. His father was a captain for the Washington State Ferries, and so Randy was at home on the ocean." Her eyes fell to her hands, where the blade of grass had started to curl with the heat of her fingers. "But that day he didn't want to go sailing. It was me who convinced him to take the boat out." Unwilling to say more, and unable to sit still beneath the full force of his stare for fear he would see just how culpable she was, she stood up. "We should get back," she suggested with a broad grin that she didn't feel.

Jackson stood slowly.

Sydney took a deep breath and tried to dispel the melancholy mood. "You know, you're the first person I've talked to about that." She continued smiling and moved too quickly toward her horse.

He remained silent.

"The first day we met," Sydney said as she untied the reins from around the tree, "what were you thinking when I went on about why you shouldn't date me?"

Jackson smiled. "I was crushed."

Sydney laughed. "No, really."

They both mounted their horses, settling into the saddles comfortably. "At first I was confused. Then, to tell the truth . . . I was a little alarmed," he confessed, making Sydney chuckle. They started at a leisurely pace down the path that would take them back to the stables. "But it didn't take long for me to find myself intrigued," he admitted.

The look on her face must have been comical, because Jackson chuckled.

"Do you usually find weird and eccentric women intriguing?" she teased.

He shook his head pensively, and although a smile played about his mouth, his gaze was earnest and steady as he watched her. "I find you intriguing."

Sydney didn't know if she should be amused or flattered. She chose to laugh loudly; the blush was involuntary, and the flutter in her belly . . . almost familiar.

* * *

Jackson led her down the length of the stables past nickering horses and busy grooms. Fresh air circulated through open stall windows and combined with the musty smell of hay and grain. Somewhere in the stables a radio was playing a popular song that echoed pleasantly with the whinny of horses and the occasional holler of a stable hand.

"I wanted you to take a look at a gelding that's been with us for some time." Jackson smiled at her as they headed toward the west wing of the stables. "I have a feeling that you'll really like him."

Sydney cleared her throat and looked away, unamused by the butter-flies gathering in her stomach. "Gelding?" she repeated distractedly.

"An eight-year-old gelding, to be precise," he clarified and veered toward a stall where a teenage boy was busy filling the feeder with fresh hay. He turned to the boy, who couldn't have been older than seventeen. "How is he doing today, Ben?"

"Good. We're turning him out to pasture in a little bit," he stated, straightening and wiping his brow with the back of his hand, leaving a few stray pieces of straw pasted to his forehead. He eyed Sydney and flushed slightly when she smiled at him.

"Give us a minute?" Jackson asked. With one last doe-eyed look at Sydney, the boy left. Jackson lifted the latch on the stall door. "He'd been on lease with a rider from California up until a couple of weeks ago, but he'll be training with us for a while."

Sydney cocked her head curiously, distracted by the way Jackson's dark hair curled slightly in the humidity.

There was a soft whinny from inside the stall. A dark nose appeared, nostrils flaring widely, but when the horse stepped forward into Sydney's line of vision and the light fell on him fully, Sydney froze. She was subjected to a few warm puffs of air as the gelding took in her scent.

"Romeo?" she heard herself say, and she instinctively lifted her hand to touch his muzzle. The horse bumped her shoulder with his head until she finally raised her arms and wrapped them around his sleek neck. "Romeo, it's you," she said, mystified.

Romeo nickered softly at her. Her eyes stung as memories flooded her mind. For a moment she was eighteen again, fresh from winning her first big cash award on a horse who knew her as well as she knew him.

We did it, Romeo. We won.

She remembered how happy she'd been in the stalls after the show. Her parents and grandparents hadn't been able to separate her from Romeo for hours.

"He remembers you," Jackson said, watching the old friends reunite. "I thought you might want to see him."

"I didn't know." Sydney swallowed the lump in her throat. She lifted her head from the horse's coat to look at Jackson. "I didn't know that Gabriel sold him to you."

"He didn't." He watched her carefully. "He's been in our care. We've trained him, boarded him occasionally, and leased him, but he still belongs to Gabriel . . . to you."

"I don't understand. Gabriel told me that he'd sold him . . ." Her voice died as she realized that her grandfather had never actually told her what, exactly, he'd done with Romeo, and she had never asked. She'd just assumed that her grandfather had sold him as she had requested. "I don't believe this," she whispered, looking at the beautiful dark bay horse that had been her companion as a teenager. He had been promising then; she knew that under the right training he could have become phenomenal.

"He's very good," Jackson supplied, as if reading her mind. "He has a ground-eating gait and beautiful movement." Romeo nickered as if pleased with the praise and bobbed his head arrogantly. "Doesn't he know it, too?"

Sydney chuckled. "I don't remember you being conceited, Romeo," she reprimanded her old friend, smiling widely when he blew a puff of hot air into her face. She kissed the velvet of his muzzle and rested her head against his cheek. She tilted her head and met Jackson's eyes. "Thank you," she said softly, overwhelmed with a rush of emotion.

"It's not me you need to thank," he answered gently.

* * *

"Where's Grandpa?" Sydney asked her grandmother when she didn't find Gabriel in the study.

Jane, with hands wrist-deep in cookie dough, looked up. "He's out in the stables with the vet," she replied carefully, becoming concerned when she saw Sydney's face. But before she could ask any questions, Sydney was gone.

* * *

"It's just a cold," the veterinarian said to Gabriel as he left Aladdin's stall.

Gabriel's pride and joy. Aladdin was a desert-bred Arabian through and through: sleek lines, a sculpted head, and a spirit to equal that of his ancestors.

"I'll give Adam a rundown of the medications. It should clear up soon enough."

Gabriel caught a movement to his right and turned to see Sydney standing just inside the stable doors. The late afternoon sun behind her darkened her features, so he couldn't read her face, but he sensed her emotions. She was rigid and silent as she watched them. "Thank you, Chuck. Just let Adam know what needs to be done," Gabriel said, then he turned back to Sydney.

The veterinarian greeted Sydney on his way out.

"You just came back from Eagle Crest?" Gabriel asked, watching his granddaughter warily as she took a step forward into better light.

Sydney nodded.

"How did it go?" His words were carefully chosen.

She seemed to debate her response. "You didn't sell him."

Gabriel ducked his head in regret. "I couldn't," he finally confessed sadly, knowing that in a way it had been a betrayal of her trust.

"You never told me," she whispered, and a tear trailed down her cheek.

"I could never find—" He expelled a breath when Sydney threw herself into his arms. His relief was overwhelming. "Come now. You'd lost so much already. I just hoped that one day you'd change your mind."

"Thank you." She hadn't known until today how much she'd missed her horse, how much she'd turned her back on, and how many people had suffered with her. It wasn't until this moment that she realized she had not mourned alone. She hadn't given any thought to easing the pain of those who loved her and had suffered with her.

"This is a happy day, Sydney. You shouldn't be crying."

Sydney pulled back so she could wipe her eyes. "All this time you've been paying to board him, when we've had a perfectly good stable here."

"Do you see what a pain you are?" he rebuked tenderly and laid an arm over her shoulders as they strolled back to the house. "Actually, he's been on lease most of the time, and most of the training and boarding fee came out of that profit. The man who's been riding him has taken good care of him—won some competitions even."

"Jackson says that Romeo is really good. Apparently, he has a whole collection of ribbons to show for it."

"It's too bad he's a gelding or else you'd have a good sire for that foal you're wanting."

"Yeah," she said thoughtfully. "But Patriark and Duchess compliment each other perfectly."

"How is that deal coming along, anyway?"

"Adam's taking Duchess to Eagle Crest sometime next week so we can get started. From then on, it'll just be a matter of waiting. I think it will turn out well."

"I think it already has," he said, and she had a feeling he wasn't talking about the horses.

Chapter 9

"We've come to kidnap you," Rob announced, hooking his arm around Sydney's neck the way he had when they were in high school.

"Don't you think you just spoiled it by telling me?" Sydney questioned and deftly escaped his hold so she could hang the last bridle on the rack. She'd been cleaning up the tack room, which was nearly impossible considering mud and dirt were constantly being tracked in.

"We can still tie you up and stuff you into the trunk," Rob warned as he hoisted himself onto the countertop that lay across a set of rough cabinets along the wall.

"And you were once such a law-abiding policeman, too." Sydney sighed remorsefully and walked over to the small, round table in the middle of the room that she often used to finish up paperwork. She plopped down on a straight-backed, wooden chair.

"I can read you your rights first, if it will make you feel better," he suggested with a shrug.

"Come on, Syd," Adrianne whined, pulling out a chair and sitting across from her. "We hardly see you anymore."

"You can't lay the blame solely at my door," she argued. "Rob is always working, and you're busy planning your wedding with Colin."

"And that's why we're going to go hang out tonight," Adrianne declared cheerily. "But speaking of Colin . . ." she began tentatively and glanced up at Rob before looking back at Sydney. "A friend of Colin's father invited us out for a day on his yacht next week, and . . . we want you and Rob to come with us," she said cautiously. "Rob already said he'd go. Please say yes," she pressed.

"I don't know, Ree." Sydney couldn't help but feel apprehensive whenever she thought about going out onto the open water. She hadn't been on a boat since the accident. She looked at Rob and saw the same look of concern and wondered if, perhaps, all this time she had unconsciously obligated them to carefully choose the words they said and the places they took her. She had never stopped to consider the price they paid to be her friends. Adrianne and Rob were watching her carefully, and Sydney was touched by their love for her. "I think I would like that," Sydney agreed finally and was surprised to find that, regardless of the flicker of fear, she meant it.

Adrianne smiled brightly, but she still appeared hesitant. "Really?"

Sydney nodded. "As long as I don't have to do any of the work, because I don't remember the last thing about sailing." She could feel little nerves jump beneath her skin at the thought of getting on another boat.

"It's a motor yacht," Adrianne clarified. "So we just have to sit back and enjoy the scenery. As a matter of fact, it would be the perfect place to take a bunch of pictures for our wedding scrapbook." Rob groaned from behind her, but she ignored him. "I hope it will be sunny."

"I doubt bad weather would stop you," Rob muttered. Sydney smiled. Adrianne was a woman obsessed when it came to preparing for her wedding. "Enough about weddings and photographs and dresses," Rob grumbled. "Let's go get something to eat."

"I beg your pardon, Robert Nelson." Adrianne sniffed primly and stood as tall as her five feet two inches would allow her. "The day that you get married, I'm going to remind you just how horrible you're being right now."

Rob rolled his eyes. "Are we going to eat, or what?"

"Let's eat." Sydney stood up.

"At least somebody still has her senses." Rob hopped off of the counter and proceeded to look Sydney up and down. He wrinkled his nose. "But you're cleaning up first—you stink."

"You know, Rob," Sydney began as they started for the house, "just when I think Adrianne's being too harsh with you, you say something that proves me wrong."

Rob chuckled. "Yeah. That's what my mother says."

"Have you ever thought that maybe she has a point?"

"Yup," he said unrepentantly.

* * *

They picked up some fried oyster sandwiches and found a spot on the Coupeville Wharf overlooking the glassy, calm waters of Penn Cove. Rob perched on the side of the weathered wood railing and Sydney and Adrianne leaned against it as they ate. The setting sun burned on the water around them, casting shades of orange and pink over everything.

"I still can't believe you went," Adrianne commented and popped the last of her sandwich into her mouth. "I mean, he was what, nineteen?"

"Just turned twenty," Sydney corrected. "He wasn't a bad guy, just a little young is all." She still couldn't, and probably never would, think of him as anything but "little Tommy." If nothing else, her grandfather's matchmaking had furnished her with some great topics for conversation.

"Since boys mature about two years slower than us girls, that made him barely eighteen. Ew!" Adrianne said, making a face.

"Look on the bright side," Rob stated, taking another bite. "The kid will be able to brag to his friends that he went out with an older woman," he suggested with a wiggle of his eyebrows.

"I doubt it. You should have seen his face when he found out how old I was. He kept calling me ma'am," Sydney admitted, mortified. "I swear I never felt so old in my life."

"At least Gabriel isn't trying to set you up anymore," Rob pointed out with a lopsided grin.

"And that's what makes me a little suspicious," Sydney frowned.

"Why?" Adrianne turned to lean back against the railing.

"I've never known him to just back down like that."

"Maybe he realized that it wasn't working."

Sydney shook her head thoughtfully. "I don't think so. If he started it, it was because he honestly thought it would work—he wouldn't just stop because I asked."

"Well, the only reason it was working at all was because you were too nice to say no to the guys who *did* come a-knockin'. It's not like he could force you, you know," Adrianne insisted. She glanced over at Rob for backup, but Rob remained quiet.

"I know, but he knew I'd react that way."

"Do you think he lied, then?" Adrianne asked, turning to the side so that she faced both Sydney and Rob.

"No," Sydney answered earnestly. "He wouldn't lie . . . but he's an expert tactician. He believes in his methods, and if he's decided that this approach isn't working, it's only because he's figured out a different one."

"You make it sound like he's playing chess," Rob interjected, hopping down from the fence. Crunching up the paper that had wrapped his sandwich, he tossed it into the nearest garbage can.

"He was a Marine three-fourths of his life," Sydney exclaimed. "I'd say he's an expert at maneuvering any, and all, of the pieces on the board. You should know," she said, looking at Rob, "since he manipulated you into asking me out." Two months ago, Rob had called to see if she wanted to catch a movie and have dinner with him. It wasn't until later in the evening that he had slipped up and confessed that Gabriel had cornered him in the grocery store, innocently asking why he and Sydney had never dated.

Rob glanced away. "Regardless of how crafty he is, it all boils down to one simple fact: he can't force you to do something you don't want to do. If you don't want to go out on these blind dates, then don't."

"That's the problem right there," Sydney insisted. "When these guys show up, I don't want to hurt their feelings—and my grandfather knows it. He knows how I'll react in any given situation. And that's what makes him dangerous," she said, narrowing her eyes and pursing her lips dramatically.

"Entrapment," Adrianne concluded judiciously.

"And that, my cop friend," Sydney said to Rob, "is a term you should recognize."

Adrianne laughed. "I'm glad he's your grandfather and not your enemy."

"If he were your enemy, we wouldn't be having this discussion," Rob said soberly. "He wants you to be happy."

"And dating is going to make me happy?" Sydney put her hands on her hips, wondering why Rob was taking her grandfather's side all of a sudden.

Rob's face softened. "No, but I know that giving up on life will make you *unhappy*."

Sydney's mouth fell open. "I haven't given up on life."

Adrianne straightened, her eyes bouncing back and forth between her two best friends. She opened her mouth to say something that would lighten the situation, but she was cut off.

"Then why don't you date?" Rob challenged softly.

"Dating isn't life," she pointed out, a frown line forming between her brows.

"It's a big part of it." Rob took a deep breath. "Look, Syd, I'm not saying that your grandpa's tactics are necessarily the right ones, but I understand where he's coming from."

"Enlighten me," Sydney ordered peevishly.

"Ever since that night, you've been running—from things you love, from life . . . from happiness."

"You make it sound like avoiding marriage is the same thing as foregoing any chance at being happy. Have you stopped to consider that maybe I'm happy just the way I am? That maybe I'm not interested in getting married?"

"No," he said seriously, his eyes focused on hers. "Because I know you."

Rob took a step forward until they were toe to toe. "He doesn't want you to make the wrong decision—none of us do," he added tenderly, his hands coming up to her arms. "You've been living in a prison, and we're worried that you'll stay there."

Sydney was speechless as she stared at the two friends she'd grown up with. They had been there when she'd fallen on stage and chipped her tooth during the fifth grade rendition of *The Wizard of Oz*. They had been there when, in the photograph of her first horse show, the flash glared off of her braces, creating a big white light where her face should have been. They knew her—loved her—and it was this fact that made her shoulders fall in defeat. She was silent, unable to argue with what she knew was right, no matter how hard it was to admit.

"We don't want you to do something that will sentence you to a life you'll regret," Rob said softly.

"But I haven't done anything," she insisted in a last effort to redeem herself.

"Sometimes doing nothing can do more damage than doing something we fear."

Chapter 10

"I'm starting to believe it's true."

Sydney jumped and spun around, dropping the brush she'd been using to stroke Duchess's back. "Jackson!" she said with a flustered laugh and retrieved the brush. "You're starting to believe what's true?" She tried to calm her suddenly electrified senses.

"What you said when we first met," he said, coming farther into the stables to stop just a few feet from her. He ran his hands over the silky coat of the filly.

"What did I say when we first met?" she asked, unable to think of anything but the way he was looking at her.

"That you play with horses all day."

Sydney managed a smile. "I think I also said that I stink most of the time . . . and snore."

"You must have been lying."

It took all of her strength to break eye contact with him. "Maybe a little," she admitted with a grin. "Except for the snoring part." Sydney cleared her throat, which suddenly felt dry. "So, what are you doing here?" She made the mistake of looking at him again and felt her insides turn over. He looked good in a pair of jeans and a white polo shirt that bore the small insignia of Eagle Crest Farms on the pocket.

"I stopped by to see if you wanted to get a bite to eat and then maybe go for a drive," he said, smiling at her.

"A drive?" she repeated distractedly, noticing the way his eyes were almost amethyst in the overcast afternoon.

"To the pass," he clarified, and he grinned.

"The pass?" Jackson had awakened a part of her that had lain dormant for so long, and she was suddenly aware of his every detail.

"Deception Pass," he prompted, but when she stared at him blankly, he continued. "You know, the bridge?" Still nothing. "The really tall bridge?"

"Bridge," she said vacantly, until she noticed his growing amusement. "Oh! Of course, Deception Pass," she said quickly and turned around so he wouldn't see her mortification. She began grooming Duchess's coat with more zeal than was necessary, and the mare snorted impatiently and flicked her heavy tail so that it slapped Sydney in the face. Sydney sputtered and spit out a few thick strands of hair. "Yes, I know Deception Pass. What about it?"

"Do you want to go for a drive with me to the pass?" he repeated patiently.

"Sure," she said, shifting position so that the mare stood between them. "Sure. I'd love to go. Just let me finish up, okay?"

"Good." He smiled and watched her hands attentively. "Uh . . . need any help?" he asked wryly.

"No, I'm almost done," she said and gave him a sweet smile.

He nodded slowly but appeared to be fighting back a laugh. "You know, it might work a little better if you turned the brush over."

"Huh?" Sydney asked, looking up at him. He was staring at her hand, so she glanced down. Her cheeks instantly turned bright pink as she gaped at the palm of her hand, where the bristles had left thousands of tiny indentations on her skin. Wincing in embarrassment, she met his eyes. "Would you believe me if I told you it was a new European grooming technique?"

Jackson laughed loudly.

Duchess turned her head sanctimoniously to look back at Sydney and with a haughty snort turned away again. Sydney suspected that if her mare could have rolled her eyes in that moment, she would have.

* * *

They parked at the Deception Pass Bridge and took a short trail down the mountain toward the beach. Fragmented rays of light splintered through the cover of trees and onto their skin as the sun played peek-a-boo with the thick clouds.

Sydney could see glimpses of the emerald waters through the dense foliage. The earth was kept damp by sudden and regular rainfall, and the aroma of flowers danced around them, luring them farther into the forest's depths. Thick ferns surrounded moss-covered tree trunks, and ropes of woody vines draped across the branches.

"You're not working today?" Sydney asked when they finally descended and came out into the clearing where the trail leveled off. The pebbled beach was covered with piles of faded driftwood that lay scattered on the short coastline like confetti.

"I managed to get away for a few hours . . . I wasn't getting a lot done." The look on his face was thoughtful. "Long hours at the office don't hold the appeal that they had before. I found myself wanting to be somewhere else," he added as he gazed at her.

Sydney swallowed hard and cleared her throat, unsure how to respond. "Are Saturdays usually busy for you?"

He nodded as if he knew that she had purposely circumvented the significance of his comment. With a smile he answered her question. "Breeders from out of town usually fly in over the weekend, or I fly out to them. What about you? I would have thought that Saturdays would be the most hectic, especially during the school year."

"I usually save Saturdays for private lessons, but since most of the kids started together I've had some much-needed free time. It'll change during the summer when some of my students get ready to compete." Sydney stopped next to a cluster of sun-bleached driftwood. Moving to the end of the largest trunk, where the blunted root spanned out like webbed fingers, she sat down on the smooth wood. She was tempted to take off her shoes and let the cool pebbles massage her bare feet, but she resisted the impulse.

"Do you miss Missouri?" he asked, sitting next to her.

"No," she said, and she grinned at how easily she'd answered. "My parents would be happy to hear me say that." She turned a little to face him. "They didn't like it that I was so far away from home."

"From them?" Jackson asked wisely.

"As a matter of fact, they'd love nothing better than for me to move to Texas."

"Do you plan to?"

"I don't know. Washington feels more like home than any other place I've been."

Jackson smiled warmly. "I'm glad." His gaze was intense and steady as he looked at her.

Sydney looked away. "But they'll be coming for Adrianne's wedding next month. Maybe I'll introduce you," she added in an attempt to fill the silence that magnified the feelings his nearness stirred in her.

The corner of his mouth lifted. "I'd like that."

Me too, she thought, but she couldn't say it.

"How is Adrianne, anyway?" he asked.

Grateful for the change of subject, Sydney sighed. "Adrianne's getting crazier and crazier the closer she gets to her wedding day."

"I hear that's common."

She glanced at him sideways, amused by his response. "You sound like Colin."

"How so?"

She shrugged. "You sound like you're watching from the sidelines . . . sort of detached. Colin's the-wedding-is-your-domain attitude has been the main reason for Adrianne's sudden loss of sanity."

"I can see how that might be a problem."

"You see what I mean," she said with a small laugh. "You'd make a good psychiatrist. You make people feel like they're lying on that black couch." When he raised a questioning brow she explained. "You could make people bare their deepest, darkest secrets before they even realized they'd done it."

"So what deep dark secret do you have to share?"

That I can't stop thinking about you. "I don't have any secrets," she smiled and turned her gaze to a black-and-white tugboat that was pulling a train of logs through Deception Pass.

"I do."

She turned to look at him, unable to hide her curiosity. "You do?" she asked with a mischievous smile. "Want to share?"

He nodded slowly, and she found herself hypnotized by eyes that had suddenly became dark and soft. "Since I met you, I've wanted to kiss you."

If aliens had landed on the beach right in front of them saying, "take me to your leader," she could not have been more stunned. Had they offered her a gallon of black cherry ice cream sprinkled with slivered almonds, she could not have been more tempted.

If her life had depended on it, she could not have moved when he leaned toward her, ran his hand through her hair until his fingers cradled her head, and pressed his lips to hers.

Chapter 11

The waves crashed against the rocks below, creating a relaxing hum. A light breeze, freshly swept from the cold waters of the Puget Sound, gently drifted across the patio and over Jackson's feet, which he'd propped on the glass top of the coffee table.

He heard footsteps pad gently across the cool, red tiles of the balcony floor.

"Mind if I join you?" Elizabeth didn't wait for an answer; she simply plopped down on the luxuriously cushioned patio bench next to her brother. "You've been out here more in the past couple of weeks than you have been in the past three years," she commented, making herself comfortable. They both sat staring out across the water, their legs stretched out before them, their arms folded across their chests, and their heads resting against the back of the bench as they watched the sun fall behind the water.

Jackson knew his sister. She was curious. And if she'd come out here, it was because she wanted to know something. He silently started counting down from five.

"Where did you go yesterday?" Elizabeth finally asked.

"I was with Sydney," he answered. He should have started at three.

"That's what I thought. Aunt Meredith owes me dinner," she revealed smugly.

"What's that supposed to mean?" He glanced in her direction.

"She didn't believe that you felt that way about Sydney, and she bet me that she'd make me dinner if she was wrong. She doesn't have my keen sense of observation."

"What do you mean 'felt that way' about Sydney?" He was suddenly interested.

"You know."

"No. I don't know."

"That you're in love with her." She said it so matter-of-factly that, had he not been suspecting it himself, her response might have swayed him.

"In love with her," he repeated solemnly and looked back over the water. He hadn't even realized until yesterday that he was more than just attracted to her. And now, his kid sister—who wasn't so much of a kid anymore—declared it herself.

"You didn't deny it," she pointed out with an impish smile.

He gave her an insipid look.

"So, what are you going to do about it?"

"About what?" He avoided the question.

"About Sydney, of course."

"Of course," he said without any inflection in his voice.

Elizabeth rolled her eyes. "I swear I'd get more dialogue from a wall."

Jackson smiled then because Sydney had said something along those same lines to him yesterday. "When did you get so lippy?"

Elizabeth smiled and twirled a strand of strawberry-blond hair around her finger. "So, did you tell her?"

"Tell who, what?" he asked evenly.

"Oh, stop it!" she protested, knowing that he was being purposely obtuse. "Did you tell Sydney that you're in love with her?"

"You know, for a child, you're awfully curious about the whole love and marriage deal."

"I am not a child," she defended sulkily. "Legally, I'm just as much of an adult as you are."

Jackson snorted.

"As a matter of fact," she began with a noticeable twinkle in her eye, "I could get married tomorrow and wouldn't even need your permission."

The look he gave her was glacial.

Elizabeth grinned. "So, are you going to tell me, or are you going to make me drive over there and ask her?"

"She doesn't know," he admitted, because he knew very well that if he didn't answer, Elizabeth would not hesitate to ask Sydney.

"When are you going to tell her?"

"It's more complicated than that." He was glad when Elizabeth didn't ask for further explanation.

"I like her," Elizabeth uttered finally and rested her head on her brother's shoulder.

"So do I," Jackson said with a slow smile.

"She's really beautiful."

"Among other things." Sydney was also intelligent and sweet and funny . . .

"She seemed sad, though," Elizabeth added pensively.

"Why do you say that?"

"When we were at the dance, I saw her smile a lot, but it didn't seem to quite reach her eyes." She paused momentarily as if lost in her thoughts. "Granted, I didn't spend that much time with her, but I definitely saw grief there."

Jackson was silent. He suspected that Elizabeth had seen in Sydney the grief Elizabeth herself had seen for so long when she'd looked in the mirror. The death of their parents had been difficult to overcome. Initially, Jackson had seen the same thing when he had looked at Sydney, but recently he had begun to see that smile expand until he could feel its warmth.

"I forgot to tell you that Carrie called today."

Elizabeth's sudden change of subject nearly gave him whiplash. "What did she say?"

She shrugged. "She wants you to call her back."

He was quiet for a moment. "Do you like Carrie?" he asked finally, remembering the conversation he'd had with Carrie a couple of weeks earlier. "Because she seems to think you don't."

"I like her," Elizabeth responded noncommittally. "I just don't like her for you."

"Who ever said she was for me?"

"Why else does she come around?" Elizabeth countered neatly.

"Because we're good friends."

"But for a while you were more than friends." Before Jackson could speak she continued. "How do you know she doesn't want to start a relationship again?"

"Because I know Carrie," Jackson answered easily. He would have never continued their friendship if he thought Carrie harbored any feelings for him.

Elizabeth shrugged and abruptly lifted her head. Her eyes sparkled mischievously as she looked at him. "I think Sydney likes you, too."

Jackson didn't think Sydney quite knew what she wanted yet, but he wanted to help her figure it out.

"Kind of makes you wonder," Elizabeth said wryly. "Should Cupid make her presence known in this little affair?" she taunted.

"Lizzy," Jackson warned, knowing that tone of voice.

"Sydney doesn't look like she's going to make the first move, and from what I've gleaned of our little conversation, neither are you. Sometimes a sister has to do what a sister has to do."

"Don't even think about it, Lizzy."

She smiled sweetly and shrugged her shoulders. "Someone needs to do the matchmaking around here. How else am I going to become the best aunt in the world?"

"I'll make you wish you were born in a different century."

"Why? I might just help you," she offered innocently.

"Elizabeth." He drew out her name in warning, feeling like he was losing control of the situation.

"You might thank me when it's all said and done," she insisted.

"If you do anything or say anything to compromise my relationship with Sydney, you'll live to regret it the rest of your life, and I promise you, it will be an extremely long life."

"Oh, relax," she advised with a smile and stood up to stretch.

"Stay out of it, Elizabeth."

"I won't do anything to compromise your relationship with Sydney," she promised, and before he could say anything else, she pranced off into the house.

Somehow he wasn't comforted by her smile. And her assurance had sounded suspiciously like a trap.

* * *

"Miss Chase."

Sydney had been lost in the memory of Jackson's kiss. Her face turned bright red, and she looked up at Trinity, who had stayed after class for help with her balance. Trinity's red curls were covered by her black riding helmet, which made her small dimple all the more noticeable.

"Do you think unicorns are real?" Trinity asked as she teetered in her saddle, completely dismissing the instructions that Sydney had given her.

"Concentrate, Trinity," Sydney admonished gently. "Until you're comfortable being on a horse's back I need you to concentrate on what I'm saying, all right?"

Trinity nodded ruefully, but Sydney could see that her thoughts were still on unicorns.

"Now remember, you shouldn't be able to see your toes from where you're sitting. If you can see them, then you're not properly seated. So, you'll need to push them back like this." She aligned Trinity's heels with her hips. "And make sure to keep your toes pointing forward."

The little girl nodded again.

"Good." Sydney smiled warmly. "You're a natural-born rider, Trinity."

Trinity beamed. "I love horses."

"I know you do," Sydney said with an understanding smile.

"I'm not very good at riding, though." Trinity frowned.

"You know what?" Sydney leaned forward until they were nearly eye to eye. "The very first time that I got on a horse, I started crying."

"You did?" Trinity looked doubtful.

Sydney nodded. "I sure did. And I swore that I would never ride another horse again for as long as I lived. But my mom took me back the next day, and I cried just a tiny bit less. But I still couldn't get the horse to move in any direction," she added with an exaggerated sigh. "I think my horse found it funny that all the other kids laughed when I couldn't get him to move."

Trinity giggled. "How mean."

"I thought so, too," Sydney agreed. "Anyway, after many months of practicing, I finally started to get it right. Two years later I won my first competition. So, no matter how hard it is for you now, just remember that it took me a really long time, too."

"And now you're a teacher," Trinity exclaimed as though it were the most prestigious position in the world of horses.

"And now I'm a teacher." Sydney smiled sweetly. "And I promise that with a little more practice, you will be a great rider," she said and was touched when Trinity's eyes became wide with excitement. "But now—" Sydney glanced at the black suburban that waited in the drive—"it's time for you to go home. Your daddy looks hungry."

Trinity turned to glance at her father, who was tapping his fingers on the car door where his hand rested. She beamed at Sydney. "We're having pizza!"

"Well, then you'd better dismount and get going." Sydney stepped back to give her room. "Ah," she reminded pointedly, and Trinity changed legs and dismounted on the left. "Go on, I'll take care of Chocolate," Sydney offered, running her hands along the horse's neck. "Oh, and Trinity," she called, just as the girl was leaving the arena.

Trinity turned around to look at her. "Yes?"

"I think unicorns *do* exist—pink ones with silver horns," Sydney said and watched the child's eyes light up before she turned and ran to her car.

* * *

Sydney finished cleaning up and put the saddle and reins back in the tack room. The phone rang and she picked it up. "Hello?"

"Hi, honey."

"Mom," Sydney said with a pleased smile and sat down at the table. "How are you?"

"Not good, since you rarely call. It's been almost two weeks since I last heard from you."

"I know. I'm sorry," she said repentantly. "I've been so busy with classes and with Duchess that it slipped my mind."

"Your grandma tells me that you've found Duchess a stallion."

"Yes, and I'm taking her over there tomorrow."

"Are you excited?" her mother asked.

"You have no idea. Once you see Patriark you can't help but imagine what a beautiful foal he'll sire." Jackson had been right to suggest the prized stallion. A shiver of happiness went through her when she thought of Jackson, and her mind slipped back to the beach at Deception Pass. When he'd looked at her after their kiss, his smile had been devastating.

"We'll have to meet him when we come out for the wedding."

"Who?" Sydney asked, wondering if her grandmother had told her parents about Jackson.

"Patriark," her mother clarified, and there was a smart pause. "Who'd you think I meant?"

"Nobody," Sydney replied quickly.

Another pause. "Are you doing okay, Sydney?"

Sydney switched the phone to her other ear. "Yeah, why?"

"Jane was telling me that your grandpa's been playing matchmaker."

"He *was.* Not anymore."

"And how did that go?"

"I met a couple of really interesting guys," Sydney explained with a small laugh.

"I can imagine."

"How's Dad?" Sydney asked, wanting to avoid the subject of her social life because their conversation would eventually lead to Jackson.

"He's good. He's at a meeting right now, so you'll have to call him later. Anyway, I just wanted to check and see that you were okay. I'll let you finish up there."

"I'm glad you called, Mom."

"So am I. When you came to visit us after you finished school, it wasn't nearly long enough."

"Maybe you guys should move back to Washington," Sydney suggested.

She laughed. "Maybe you should move to Texas."

"We can always meet in the middle," Sydney said with a smile. "What do you think of Lake Tahoe?"

"I think we can make it to Washington every once in a while. You know how your father feels about the coast."

"I love you, Mom. I'll talk to you later." Sydney said and waited for the line to go dead.

When she hung up the phone she was smiling. She began leafing through the latest issue of *Breeder's Guide* that had just come in the mail.

The phone rang again, and she picked it up distractedly. "Hello?"

"Could I please speak with Sydney Chase?" the woman asked.

"This is Sydney," she answered offhandedly and tossed some junk mail into the trash can next to the table.

"Oh," said the woman. "Sydney, this is Laura Willett."

Sydney froze.

"I was told that you're staying with your grandparents."

Silence.

"I've been thinking about you a lot lately, and . . . and I was wondering if maybe we could meet."

Sydney couldn't hear past the sudden ringing in her ears.

"Sydney?"

"Yes. I'm sorry, I'm still here." Her knuckles turned white as she gripped the phone.

"Would you like to come over sometime?" Laura asked.

Sydney shook her head and squeezed her eyes shut. "I don't . . ."

Rob's words echoed in her head. *You're running from your past.*

"Um, I uh . . ." *You've given up on life.*

"Well . . . sure," she said finally, surprised the word didn't stick in her throat. "That would be great."

There was audible relief in the other woman's voice. "Wonderful."

After Sydney hung up the phone, she sat for several moments staring at the back of the envelope where she'd jotted down the details of the meeting. She didn't remember at what point she'd picked up the pencil and scribbled the notes. She didn't even remember most of what had been said, but her beating heart and the dampness on her palms testified that she had agreed to face the moment she'd avoided for almost six years.

And six years had not been nearly long enough.

Chapter 12

"How long do you think it will take?" Sydney asked David as they watched Adam take Duchess by the reins and lead her out of the trailer into the breeding facilities. The structure was kept separate from the main stables, but it was close enough to the stallion barns to make it easily accessible.

"There's no saying," David explained as they followed the filly to her stall. "I would give it a couple of months. If all goes well, she might be in foal by next month, but most likely it won't be until July."

A couple of the stable hands helped get Duchess into her stall. To her credit, and to the credit of any offspring she might have, Duchess was not a jittery horse. She calmly took in her new environment and neighed softly when a broodmare whinnied a greeting to her.

Duchess nickered when Sydney approached. Sydney began talking softly to her as she ran her hands over her forehead.

"She's in good hands," David stated with a paternal smile. "You made a good choice by boarding her here until after the foal is born. We'll make sure she's well taken care of."

"I know," she smiled softly. "I'm more excited than worried."

"If all goes well, in about eleven months you'll have a healthy and fine-looking foal, if his dam is any indication," David remarked in admiration of the mare. "She's what, sixteen hands?"

"Sixteen point three." Patriark was just over seventeen hands tall, which almost guaranteed a tall and elegant foal.

"She looks comfortable enough," Adam grumbled, coming out of the stall. "She'll be even more spoiled here than she was at our place."

"It suits her," Sydney said indulgently.

Adam shook his head. "You shouldn't say that in front of her," he warned with a glance at the mare. "We'll never get her to cooperate when wash time comes around."

Sydney smiled and turned to David to explain. "She's a little playful when it's time to wash her. She enjoys getting everyone else wet along with herself."

"Me in particular," Adam muttered acerbically, and Duchess huffed loudly in response.

"She just knows how upset it makes you." Sydney gave a small laugh.

"We'll let the wash boys know to watch out." David closed the stall and the two stable hands left to gather feed and water for their new resident.

"How is she?" Sydney turned to see Elizabeth approaching them.

"This one can't stay out of anyone's business." David gestured toward Elizabeth. "A new horse comes to Eagle Crest and she needs to know when, why, and in what trailer."

"I heard that, you grouchy old man," Elizabeth teased as she joined them. "I heard you were bringing your filly today." She smiled widely as she drew near the narcissistic Duchess, who was devouring her attention. "Oh, she's gorgeous," Elizabeth crooned admiringly through the grill.

Adam harrumphed loudly. "She'll be impossible by the time she gets back to us," he complained with a shake of his head, and Sydney laughed.

"If there's nothing else, I have some more work to do," David interjected, and he excused himself. "If you need anything, please call me," he called on his way out.

"Hi there, pretty girl." Elizabeth fussed over the mare, kissing her on the muzzle.

"Are we ready?" Adam asked impatiently, tapping the bridle that he'd taken from Duchess against his leg.

Elizabeth turned her head suddenly. "You're not going yet, are you?" she whined. "Can't you stay just a little longer?"

"I'm afraid we can't, young lady," Adam objected. "And don't you be spoiling that one while we're gone," he said, pointing to Duchess.

"Adam," Elizabeth began with an impertinent raise of her brow, "for a man who knows so much about horses, you know absolutely nothing about females."

"And I'm supposed to think you do?" he asked, apparently accustomed to her antics.

"I am a woman, after all," she said pertly and pointedly ignored his snort. "If you give Duchess what she wants, she'll do what *you* want. Won't you Duchess?" She turned once again to the filly but addressed Adam. "One of these days you'll take my advice and find that your stables run much smoother."

"You keep your nose out of my stables," he warned. "If I give her everything she wants, she'll turn out just as spoiled as you are."

Elizabeth narrowed her eyes at him, and Adam almost smiled.

"Why don't we get going?" Sydney interrupted.

"I'll wait in the truck." Adam started toward the truck, but not before giving the glaring Elizabeth another look. He shook his head, and Sydney heard something that sounded suspiciously like a chuckle.

"It was nice to see you, Elizabeth," Sydney said, turning to Jackson's sister.

"Are you sure you can't stay for a while?"

Sydney shook her head. "I have a lot of work to do before my students arrive for class today."

"Maybe some other time, then?" Elizabeth asked hopefully.

"Some other time." Sydney smiled and turned to leave.

"Did Jackson know you would be here today?" Elizabeth asked.

Sydney stopped and looked back at her. "I don't know. Why?" she asked curiously. David had mentioned that Jackson had flown out of town on a quick business trip.

"Knowing Jackson, I just think he would have wanted to be here if he had known you were here." She watched Sydney carefully.

Sydney gave a short nod, unsure of what to make of Elizabeth's comment. "See you around," she said finally, and turned and walked away.

* * *

Elizabeth watched as the dark blue truck pulled away from the stables, hauling the black horse trailer behind it. With a satisfied grin, she turned back to Duchess. "Score one point for Cupid," she announced, placing a kiss on the filly's cheek. "Only a couple more arrows and I'll have done my job."

* * *

Rebecca stood watching the horse as if she were trapped inside a cage with a wild animal. She worried her lip and raised her frightened eyes to Sydney. "I can't."

"Do you like horses, Rebecca?" Sydney asked softly.

The ten-year-old nodded.

"Did you like to ride?" When she nodded again, Sydney smiled. "I know it can be scary when you take a fall, but you can't let it keep you from doing what you love." The hardest—yet the most crucial—part about falling off of a horse was getting back on.

"Have you ever fallen off?"

Sydney smiled. "When I was taking riding lessons, my teacher used to tell me that I wouldn't be a good rider until I had fallen off at least a hundred times. Please believe me when I tell you that all riders fall off of their horses at least once. The first time that I fell off, my coach patted me on the back and said 'good job.' The fifth time I fell, he told me I was well on my way to being a great rider. After the tenth time, I stopped counting."

Rebecca eyed Applejax warily. The pony's caramel-colored coat glimmered like silk beneath the late-afternoon sun. "He *is* a little smaller than the horse that I fell off of," she reasoned.

"Why don't you try talking to him?" Sydney suggested and ran an appreciative hand down Applejax's neck. "Treat him as if he were a person, Rebecca. Get to know him and let him get to know you, because once you start riding again, you'll become great friends," she assured her confidently. "Riding horses is a partnership. You need to know and respect each other."

"Where are you from, Applejax?" the girl asked the animal hesitantly, and Sydney smiled when Rebecca appeared to wait for an answer.

"Try telling him about your feelings."

Rebecca looked up at Sydney and then back at the horse. "I'm scared to ride you," she admitted finally, as if saying it had cost her dearly. "The last time I rode, I got bucked off and hurt my shoulder," she said. "But you don't look so big." She eyed Applejax's short legs. "I don't think it would hurt so bad to fall off your back," she concluded, and the pony glanced at her sideways. Rebecca smiled and reached out to run the tips of her fingers over the pony's cheek. It was the first time she had touched a horse since her fall.

Sydney decided to take it a step further. "Why don't we take this one step at a time? You don't have to ride just yet, but how about sitting on top of him?" she asked, and the girl immediately brought her hand back down to her side.

"I don't think I can," Rebecca said, but she didn't appear to be near tears like she'd been the first time her mother brought her to class. Sydney could see that beneath her fear of riding again, Rebecca yearned to be back in the saddle. "What if he spooks and bucks me off?"

"Applejax is a very gentle pony, Rebecca," Sydney assured her. "He doesn't spook easily."

"But what if he feels that I'm nervous and then gets jumpy?"

"He *will* feel that you're nervous, but we'll give you both some time to get used to each other," Sydney advised. "Applejax here is used to having people who are very scared on his back. That's why I use him to train students who have never been on a horse before. He'll stay calm, I promise. And besides, I only want you to sit on top of him so that your body remembers what it feels like. I'll stand right here next to you."

"Can't I just do it next time?" she asked, looking for an escape. Her brows were drawn together in a worried frown.

Had Sydney not sensed the girl's longing to ride, she would not have pushed her. Pushing a student to do something he or she wasn't ready to do could be as harmful as pushing a horse to take a jump it hadn't been trained for. Sometimes, however, either a student or a horse just needed to be guided through the last few steps.

"Do you think it will be any easier next time? When you fall off of a horse, you must get right back on and ride, Rebecca. The longer you wait, the more afraid you will become." After her fall, Rebecca should have been encouraged to get back on immediately. Instead, she had shied away until her fear of riding grew more powerful than her love for horses. "If you don't try, you'll regret it for the rest of your life." Sydney saw Rebecca's self-doubt cloud her eyes, and Sydney felt as if she were looking in a mirror. For the past six years, Sydney had been paralyzed by her own fear, and she had allowed that fear to keep her from living her life.

"You can't let one bad experience ruin your chances for happiness," she said, feeling as if the words had been ripped from her chest. How could she tell her students not to give up when she failed to apply her own words of advice? When she'd first come back to Oak Harbor, Adam had taught her a proverb that she hadn't quite grasped at the time. "There is nothing better for the inside of a man than the outside of a horse," he had said as she got on Duchess's back for the first time. Only now did she truly understand the meaning. The lessons she'd learned while riding horses applied to every aspect of life. Why hadn't she been wise enough to implement them?

Standing next to Rebecca with her hand on the pony's back, Sydney no longer felt like the teacher. A greater teacher was guiding her—and had always been guiding her. Slowly, patiently, He had led her to this spot so that her eyes would be opened and she would see the path laid out before her.

"You'll stand right here the whole time?" Rebecca asked cautiously, drawing Sydney's attention back to her.

"I will be standing right here," she promised as a lump caught in her throat.

"Okay," Rebecca agreed, but the lines between her brows were deep with self-doubt.

"Do you remember how to mount?" Sydney asked, positioning herself next to Applejax's head and holding the lead line.

Rebecca nodded awkwardly. Taking the reins in her hands, she proceeded to slip her foot into the stirrup. She grabbed onto the front of the saddle, and on shaky legs, she hoisted herself up into it as rigidly as a pole. Applejax shifted his weight in an attempt to adjust to the stiff burden that had been placed on his back.

"Good," Sydney said calmly.

The girl's eyes were huge, and her knuckles were white where she held onto the saddle as if afraid that a slight wind would blow her off.

"Now I want you to try to relax so that Applejax can feel that you're comfortable up there." Sydney glanced at the girl's feet. "Relax your legs a bit and keep your toes pointed forward. Now, for the most important part of all." She smiled broadly. "Try to remember how much fun it was to ride."

Rebecca blinked and slowly eased her grip on the saddle. Her legs relaxed slightly against Applejax's belly, and her shoulders lost some of their tension.

"You see?" Sydney smiled proudly. "That's not so bad, is it?" Rebecca managed to crack a wobbly smile.

"Can I just stay this way for a little while?" Rebecca asked.

"Sure you can." Sydney gave her an assuring smile. "The hard part is over," she said, petting Applejax's forehead. "From here on out, it only gets better."

Chapter 13

"Are you sure you want to do this?" Adrianne asked cautiously.

"I'm sure." Although she felt her legs shaking as she took the stairs up to the main deck of *Never Never Land,* Sydney was determined to take this step.

The enormous three-deck yacht belonged to a friend and client of Colin's father. The yacht was sleek and elegant with smooth lines that were designed to glide over the water with flair. Sydney was sure she could work her entire life and never be able to afford a ship like this. She and Adrianne made themselves comfortable at the large teak table that was situated in the center of the deck.

"We're going whale watching," Toby said from the doorway. "Why wouldn't she want to do this?" Behind him Sydney could see a spacious salon replete with cream-colored sofas arranged around a huge flat-screen television. "Left your sea legs on the dock, did you?" he teased lightheartedly, mistaking Sydney's unease for seasickness.

Sydney couldn't help but smile. "Right next to your humility," she quipped.

He grabbed his chest dramatically. "You wound me."

Adrianne scoffed. "You are such a flirt, Toby Ralston."

"Are you jealous, Ree?" he asked, turning his attention to her. "Because it's not too late to give my brother the boot and marry me instead."

"I heard that," Colin called from somewhere inside the salon, where he was talking on his cell phone.

"You're incorrigible, Toby," Adrianne admonished with a laugh. "Someday that mouth of yours is going to get you in trouble."

"Come now, little sister, you know that I have three times the charm as Colin."

Adrianne snorted loudly.

Toby grinned in response and then turned to Sydney. "When you get your legs under you, come on inside. They have all sorts of treats in there," he added with a mischievous wink before going back inside the luxuriously furnished salon.

The marina was alive with boaters anxious for a clear, sunny day on the water, and dock workers rushed about to help them get there. The crying seagulls swooped along the docks, diligently searching the water and boats for abandoned goodies.

"I was wondering if you were going to make it," Rob said as he came out on deck and took a seat next to her. "I was getting ready to leave if you didn't."

"That's rude," Adrianne protested. "I would still have been here to keep you company."

"But I give you five minutes after we head out into the open water before you forget that anyone but Colin is here, which brings me back to my point." He turned to Sydney once more. "I'm glad you're here."

Two young boys rushed down the stairs and stopped in front of Rob. They pulled out imaginary guns and shot at him. "Bang, bang!" they called and hurried off the yacht.

"They found out that I'm a cop," Rob explained wryly as he watched the two boys run down the dock. "Want me to give you the grand tour?" he asked Sydney, having already experienced the yacht's jaw-dropping extravagance with Adrianne when they had first arrived.

"I'm okay here. I think I need to get my bearings first." The closest she'd ever come to being on the water since the accident was standing on the beach looking out over the sea.

"It's just as well." Rob made a face. "You won't believe your eyes. It's terrible." He shook his head. "The guy who owns this is richer than Hades. Would you believe that he actually keeps a full-time crew on the yacht to take care of everything so that the guests can stay busy enjoying themselves?" He blew out a breath in amazement. "There's a chef in the galley—and yes, I did say 'chef'—preparing some kind of fancy lobster snack to tide us over until we get to the island."

Sydney managed to chuckle. Rob had never been particularly fond of the well-to-do, and when he had become a police officer, his distaste for big money had only grown. After being exposed to people in the poorest circumstances while in the line of duty, he'd become a little jaded where affluence was concerned.

"I guess we can count ourselves lucky that we're guests." She motioned to the deck, where the hosts were chatting with Colin's mother and father. "Or else you might feel tempted to give them a lecture on capital excess."

Rob grinned. "I still might—after that lobster lunch, of course."

"Shame on you, Robert," Adrianne chided. "Colin's dad has been their lawyer for years. Colin and Toby practically grew up with their daughter. They're really nice people."

"She's right," Rob said to Sydney. "They're surprisingly normal." Sydney looked over at the couple who owned the floating mansion. The man was bald except for some dark hair on the sides of his head. His wife boasted a bushel of blond hair that fell to prim shoulders. They appeared welcoming and cordial and impossible to dislike.

"They even made sure there was no alcohol on board, because they know we're all Mormons," Adrianne added. "Why don't we go inside? You'll forget you're on a boat once you're in there."

"I'm fine, you guys . . . really," Sydney insisted when she saw the doubtful looks on their faces. "If I'm going to be on a boat, then I at least want to enjoy the water."

"Okay," Adrianne said. "But remember, there are a couple of guest rooms you can use if you start to feel sick." From the look on her face, however, Sydney could tell she knew that feeling seasick wasn't going to be Sydney's problem.

"I can't believe there are people that live like this," Sydney said in wonder as she looked around her.

There were hundreds of boats in the marina, but most of them were small, modest vessels that belonged to average Joes who had saved their whole lives to buy them. This yacht was an entirely different breed of boat, and it reflected a lifestyle that Sydney had only seen in the movies. Even though Gabriel had been raised with money, it hadn't been used for the opulence that this standard of living presented.

"Does he have a boat here?" Rob asked, looking down the length of the dock toward the marina.

"Who?" Sydney and Adrianne said simultaneously and turned their heads in the direction Rob was looking.

Jackson and Elizabeth were strolling down the dock. With them was a gorgeous brunette who looked like she was modeling for a yachting magazine. She was wearing a pair of blue, cropped sailor pants and a white-and-blue striped shirt. Sydney ignored the uncomfortable feeling that was growing somewhere in the region of her heart.

She sank down in her chair and hoped Jackson would continue on without looking in her direction, but instead he headed straight down the dock that led solely to *Never Never Land.*

* * *

"Is that Sydney?" Elizabeth asked, suddenly animated. She hadn't particularly been looking forward to spending the afternoon with Jackson and Carrie, but her brother had all but forced her to come along.

Jackson's gaze shot toward the ship and his eyes made immediate contact with Sydney's.

"They must be with Todd and Elaine," Carrie mused casually as she glanced at the three people she didn't recognize on the deck. "I told you my father's lawyer and his family were joining us," she said as they approached the yacht.

"You didn't tell me she was going to be here, Jackson," Elizabeth accused as she waved at Sydney, but she was rapidly feeling better about the entire trip.

"Do you know her?" Carrie asked of the pretty blond who waved back demurely.

"Yes," Jackson answered as if mesmerized.

"You do?" Carrie inquired with a quick look in his direction. "Who is she?"

"It's his girlfriend," Elizabeth supplied, and she hurried up ahead. Maybe it wasn't exactly true yet, but she was determined to make sure it would be soon.

Carrie's head whipped around abruptly at Elizabeth's revelation. "Your what?" she asked, suddenly interested. "You never told me you were seeing anyone, Jackson."

Carrie's two little brothers rushed past them with a pair of new water guns in their hands and deftly sidestepped Elizabeth as they boarded the yacht.

* * *

"We can always leave," Rob suggested, studying Sydney's face.

"Did you know he was going to be here?" Sydney asked Adrianne without taking her eyes off Jackson.

"No, I promise. I didn't even know Carrie knew him."

As the pair got closer, Sydney dragged her eyes away and looked at Adrianne. "Carrie? You know her?"

"Her parents own the yacht. She's a good friend of Colin and Toby."

Elizabeth came bounding up the steps toward them. "It's so good to see you, Syd," she pronounced, and she threw herself down on one of the empty chairs.

"Hi, Elizabeth." Sydney smiled, genuinely happy to see her.

"I'm so glad you're here," Elizabeth said to Sydney with exaggerated relief. "I would have been so bored if I had to be here all by myself." She exhaled loudly and glanced at Rob. Her smile widened. "Hello again," she greeted him.

Rob smiled at her. "Hello yourself."

"We met at the restaurant," Elizabeth explained, in case he'd forgotten.

"I remember," Rob replied with an amused grin.

"You're late," Toby said to Carrie. At some point he had come out on deck, and now he leaned against the rail. Carrie flashed him a dazzling smile as she and Jackson came up the steps to the main deck followed by Colin's parents.

"Where have you been hiding yourself lately?" Carrie's father was asking Jackson.

"I've been busy," he explained.

"Why don't you join us for the polo match next Sunday?" Carrie's father wrapped an arm around Jackson's shoulders, as was his habit.

Jackson lifted a sardonic brow. "Why don't you come to church with me instead?" he asked with a wry grin.

Carrie's father laughed loudly and slapped him heartily on the back.

"Oh, Daddy, leave him alone," Carrie complained.

"Small world," Toby said, and he turned to Jackson with a friendly handshake as he stepped on deck.

"Oh . . . you two know each other?" Carrie asked.

"We met at a dance. At the time I was offering my dancing skills to a beautiful young lady," he said with a quick wink at Sydney. "Why? Jealous?" Toby replied with a quick raise of his eyebrows, ignoring Adrianne's loud snicker.

Carrie rolled her eyes. "Toby, you need a wife."

"That's what I told your father," he quipped good-naturedly. "But he wouldn't go for it."

Jackson laughed. "I can imagine."

"The day I give you my daughter . . ." Carrie's father said jovially, leaving his warning unfinished.

". . . will be the best day of your life," Toby finished, obviously accustomed to his bantering.

Carrie's father huffed but let the subject drop. "You kids enjoy yourselves," he said. "We'll be up in the wheelhouse." He and his wife then disappeared up the stairs behind Toby's parents.

Jackson made his way over to the small group sitting around the table. "This is a surprise." He stopped behind Elizabeth's chair and smiled at Sydney.

Sydney's grin was too bright. "I know," she said. "You remember Rob and Adrianne."

Jackson greeted them both, but his eyes came back to rest on Sydney.

"So, how long have you two known each other?" Toby asked Carrie.

"Years and years," Carrie answered. "Jackson commissions me to paint portraits of his horses," she explained.

Carrie Larsen. Of course, Sydney thought. This was the artist who had done the magnificent painting of Patriark that hung in Jackson's office. Jackson had told her that he and Carrie were friends; she didn't want to believe that he had been deceitful. She couldn't believe that he would have kissed her if he'd been involved with someone else.

Colin came out of the salon and stuffed his cell phone into his pocket. "Sorry it took so long. Work," he explained to Adrianne, who smiled at him devotedly as he came to stand by her. "Carrie, this is my fiancée, Adrianne."

"It's nice to finally meet the lucky girl," Carrie said sweetly. "Now we just have to get Toby married off, and all womankind will be safe."

"There are three available candidates right here," Toby said blithely, rubbing his hands together in delight.

"Oh please," Carrie scoffed, voicing everyone's thoughts.

"This is Sydney and her friend Rob," Jackson interjected to finish the introductions. "Sydney is a riding instructor."

"Right up your alley," Carrie said to Jackson with an approving smile. "If I had known you were Jackson's girlfriend, I would have invited you personally," she told Sydney. "But Jackson hadn't told me about you." She turned back to Jackson with her hands on her hips. "Which I won't forgive anytime soon," she teased.

Sydney's and Adrianne's mouths fell open, Rob's brow arched up, and Elizabeth bit her lip guiltily. Jackson smiled in amusement but didn't correct Carrie.

"We're ready to pull out of the slip," the deckhand called, and he and another crew member began releasing the lines.

"Why don't we go inside and make ourselves more comfortable," Carrie suggested. She headed into the salon, unaware of the uncomfortable silence she had left at the table. Her brothers dashed past her and bumped her into the wall. "Slow down, you little monsters!" she called after them.

"Let's go get something to eat," Colin offered to Adrianne, who, with a questioning look at both Sydney and Jackson, stood and followed him inside. Elizabeth didn't miss the you'll-pay-for-that look Jackson shot her before she and Toby went into the salon.

"Are you coming?" Rob asked, rising to his feet.

"Not yet," Sydney replied. With a short nod and a quick look at Jackson, Rob joined the others.

"Sorry about that," Jackson apologized with a small smile. "She misunderstood something Lizzy said."

Sydney's face was bright red, and she smiled dismissively. "Taking the day off for a little R and R, huh?"

"Until I saw you, I didn't think this was a good idea."

Sydney swallowed and looked away. As the yacht started to pull out of the slip, her pulse accelerated for reasons that had nothing to do with Jackson. She glanced around, instinctively searching for an escape. They were just far enough from the dock that she couldn't jump onto it from the boat, so unless she was willing to swim, her only option was to find a quiet spot somewhere away from prying eyes, until she managed to get her bearings.

"Are you all right?" Jackson asked, concerned. His eyes searched hers with care.

"I need air," she whispered, feeling claustrophobic. She glanced nervously at the roomful of people.

Jackson's eyes narrowed, apparently considering the fact that they were out on the deck and that she was already getting air. "Is this the first time you've been on the water since the boating accident?" he asked bluntly.

Sydney nodded and tried to laugh it off, until the yacht gave another small lurch. Her hands instinctively gripped the table for stability and she looked again at the small crowd inside the salon, hoping that they wouldn't see her make a fool of herself. She could see Rob and Adrianne watching her, ready to come to her rescue.

Jackson stood up. "Come on." He reached for Sydney's arm. "Let's go up to the next deck."

Jackson led her up the spiral stairs that led to the more private aft bridge deck. She found a spot on the built-in seats that faced the water and closed her eyes. "You can go," she offered, her expression becoming more and more strained as they headed farther away from the marina into the open waters of the Sound.

"I don't want to go," he said, and he sat next to her.

Too late to turn back now, she thought as the dock grew smaller in the distance.

They sat in silence. Sydney watched the land as if it were a lifeline too far to reach. "Why did you come?" Jackson asked finally, worried that she wasn't ready for this step.

"I thought I'd be able to do it. I needed to do it." She struggled to smile as she felt the brisk air on her skin and was assaulted by the heady smell of the ocean.

The yacht cut through the water, creating foamy wakes that trailed behind them only to dissipate into the constant rise and fall of the ocean waves.

Sydney glanced up at the sky. It was blue, not dark. There was no lightning.

"Hurry, Randy—It's getting stronger!"

Raindrops cut across her skin.

Sydney lifted her hand to wipe the rain from her face, only to find that there was none. It wasn't raining. There was no storm.

It was Jackson who was sitting beside her, not Randy.

As the speed of the yacht increased, the soft purr of the motor vibrated up from Sydney's feet into her legs.

"Randy! You're not secured!"

Sydney watched as he slid across the slippery deck and fell against the railing.

"Randy!" she shouted again. "Don't move!"

Something slammed into the boat, violently tipping it to one side. Sydney was tossed against the railing, her head crashing into the edge. Numbing pain seared through the side of her head.

She reached for her temples, trying to rid herself of the powerful headache.

"Sydney, are you all right?" She heard the familiar voice from a great distance.

"Randy, Where are you?"

"Randy!" she shouted wildly.

"No! Please . . . no!"

"Look at me, Sydney." Jackson reached up to turn her face toward his. "Okay," he said calmly. "Now breathe." He'd seen the same wild look in his sister's eyes after their parents had died, when her suffocating screams had jerked him out of his sleep.

"Look at me," he ordered gently when she tried to look at the water again. "Try to take a deep breath." She was breathing quickly with shallow gasps of air. "You're not there, Sydney." He made sure she kept her eyes on his. "You're here. You're all right."

Sydney nodded, trying to focus on his eyes . . . eyes as blue as the sea . . . as blue as the sky above them. The day was sunny and calm. She nodded more firmly and took a deep breath, but her heart continued to race.

"Are you okay?" he asked, studying her.

She closed her eyes and then nodded. Her fingers clutched the cushioned seat beneath her.

"Do you want to go back inside?"

She shook her head. *Please help me, Heavenly Father.*

Jackson sat next to her in silence, unwilling to leave her side. After what seemed like hours, Sydney's breathing evened out. He watched her intently but said nothing.

"How much did my grandfather tell you?"

"Not much. Just that you lost your boyfriend during a storm."

Sydney nodded and swallowed.

"You don't have to tell me anything more," he responded. "I'm not here because I'm curious about your past."

Sydney looked out over the water that trailed behind them. Whidbey Island was now just a deep green blur against the dark blue water. *Sunny skies and an altogether great day for sailing.* She remembered the encouraging words of the weather forecast almost six years ago. "It was a day just like this one," she began softly. "Not a cloud in the skies."

Sydney watched the small, mountainous island start to fade into the horizon. To the right and the left of them they passed verdant land masses that were made up of dozens of little islands that occupied the waters of the Puget Sound. "Randy was getting ready to go on his mission, and I had the bright idea to spend the day sailing as a sort of good-bye. He wanted to catch a movie instead, but I insisted." She glanced down at her hands, clasping them together to keep them from trembling.

Jackson remained silent as she spoke, but she could see the compassion in his eyes.

"We found a spot not too far from shore and dropped anchor. He gave me a present," she smiled as she remembered. "It was a ship he had built inside of a syrup bottle." She had been captivated by the lifelike miniature.

Randy hung the little ship from the railing. "If you stare at it long enough, it will start to look like a real ship sailing in the distance."

"After lunch, Randy went to the cabin, where he was working on another little ship, and I fell asleep on deck. By the time I opened my eyes, it was too late. It happened so fast. Before we knew it, the sky had gone completely black." She looked at Jackson. "You have no idea how noisy the sea can be in a storm, how dark . . . how scary."

"Hey, it's getting dark, Randy," Sydney called, still a little sleepy as she sat up to look at the sky. She wondered how long she had slept.

Randy stuck his head out the cabin window and his eyes widened in alarm. The wind had picked up and the black clouds were closing in rapidly. "It's a storm," he shouted, hurrying to retrieve the anchor. He powered forward slowly. "Help me, Syd. We don't want to get caught in this." He motioned for her to secure the line.

"It seemed like we were going to make it," Sydney recalled hollowly, looking back up at the sky to make sure it was still blue. "Until I saw the height of the swells and the waves started spilling over the deck. That's when I knew that we were caught right in the middle of it. Randy kept the shore in view and kept trying to reach it." She motioned toward land as if she could see it.

"We put our life vests on, and he helped me secure my harness. I didn't notice until it was too late that he had forgotten to secure his. I should have paid more attention."

Jackson said nothing, and she continued.

"A large piece of debris hit the side of the boat, and I fell and hit my head." She lifted her hand to a place just above her right temple. "By the time I managed to get up . . . Randy was gone." Sydney squeezed her eyes shut, reliving the moment.

"When they found me, I had a concussion, a laceration on my head, and some scrapes and bruises. But it was hypothermia that did the most damage." She rubbed her hands over her bare arms. "No one told me about Randy at first." Her voice was vacant. "When I woke up in the hospital, I was disoriented. I didn't know why I was there or what had happened." It had been a nurse who had finally slipped and told her Randy was dead. And when the memories had come flooding back, no one had been able stop the screams that tore from her throat.

"He can't be gone," she cried, choking on her tears.

"It's my fault," she told her mother and grandfather as she lay in the hospital. Heat packs, heating lamps, and warm blankets covered her as doctors and nurses worked to fight off the hypothermia and shock that had taken hold of her body.

"I would have gone into the water after him if I hadn't blacked out." She revealed her despair, remembering the anguish she had felt when she'd realized that Randy had been swept overboard.

"I remember bits and pieces from when the coast guard pulled me off the boat," she continued. "I'd been laying facedown in a puddle of freezing water. From what they tell me, if the boat hadn't been rocking so furiously and moving the water from one side to the other, and if not for my life jacket, which kept my mouth lifted off the deck, I would have drowned."

"In the hospital, each time I'd wake up, it was like I was learning all over again that he'd been killed. I'd cry myself to sleep only to wake up and go through it all over again." She shook her head slowly. "It was unreal. I couldn't differentiate between my dreams and my memories. I felt a desperation I can't begin to explain." Her eyes met his and she realized that she didn't have to explain. He had gone through a similar experience—perhaps much worse. "You know how it feels," she stated, comforted somehow that his loss brought him closer to her.

Jackson shook his head. "I can't imagine the pain of losing someone you loved when you were close enough to feel like you could have prevented it."

His frank understanding was more soothing than any words could have been. "At first I thought that talking about it would dull the pain, but that only seemed to worsen it. So," she paused, looking out at the sea, "I stopped talking about it . . . tried not to think about it."

She pressed her hands together and looked down at them. "I never told anyone that it was my idea to go out on the water that day." She had been so afraid to hear the blame she already felt. "Randy didn't want to go. He even said no, initially, but he took me out anyway." The anguish that filled her chest was overwhelming. "If I had never asked him to take me, he would still be alive." She hurried to wipe away at the tears in her eyes.

Jackson pulled her into his arms as if he'd been resisting the urge to do so for some time. She rested her head on his shoulder. "You had no control over what happened that day," he assured her softly. "It was in hands more powerful than yours."

"Why am I alive?" she asked her parents as they sat with her in the dark hospital room. "I shouldn't be alive. It's all my fault," she sobbed. "It's my fault. I'm so sorry."

Chapter 14

"So, you're a painter, are you?" Rob asked, taking a seat at the dining room table across from Carrie, who was sketching on a piece of paper.

Everyone else was gathered around the cream-colored sofa, watching a movie on the large screen that occupied most of the far wall—except for Toby and Colin, who were busy raiding the food that was spread out on the buffet.

"I am," Carrie answered, lifting her chin almost defensively. "Why?"

He looked at their surroundings and shrugged. "It's fitting, I guess."

Her eyes narrowed. "How so?"

He shrugged. "It's not like you're forced to find a real job. Not with all of this."

"What's that supposed to mean?" she asked, lifting her chin another notch.

"It just means that people like you have the freedom to do whatever they want without having to worry about whether they can make a living or not."

"I'll have you know that I happen to make a good living with my paintings."

"Congratulations," he said dryly.

Carrie's mouth dropped open. "You're a snob," she muttered as if amazed at her discovery.

"I'm not the one with a luxury yacht," he responded, and he took a sip of his soda.

"Neither am I," she retorted. "It belongs to my parents."

"My father has a canoe."

"Is that supposed to make me feel bad?" Carrie countered.

"I was just showing you the difference between us." Rob realized that he was being unaccountably rude to her. She had been perfectly nice to everyone since she'd come on board. Perhaps that was the problem. Everything about her was perfect: her hair, her eyes, her manners. A traitorous voice inside of him said that his uneasiness had more to do with how she made him feel. He wasn't supposed to find spoiled rich girls attractive or intriguing or anything else that he'd felt when she'd first turned her green eyes his way.

"I can very well see the differences between us," she said haughtily.

Rob couldn't help but admire her spunk and wondered if perhaps he hadn't misjudged her. He hadn't been a cop long enough to be too jaded.

As if sensing his thoughts, Carrie narrowed her eyes. "And what is it that you do, exactly?"

"I'm a police officer," he said proudly.

"Oh . . . that's too bad," she said with a pert smile.

Rob's smile was wiped clean off his face.

Before he could say anything else, Carrie stood up. "I'm going to go find Jackson," she announced to no one in particular.

Rob got to his feet as well. "I'll come with you."

She clenched her teeth. "Suit yourself."

"Where are you guys going?" Toby asked as he munched on a handful of pistachio nuts.

"I was just going outside." Carrie blatantly ignored the way Rob was studying her. "I'm sure we're almost there."

"Let's all go," Adrianne said and followed them outside. The sun was shining brightly and nearly blinded them as they stepped out of the cabin.

"Where's Sydney?" Adrianne asked Rob.

"I don't know." He resisted the urge to go looking for Sydney because he'd seen the way she had looked at Jackson. It didn't take a rocket scientist to know that Jackson reciprocated those feelings. If Sydney was falling for Jackson, there was nothing Rob could do about it.

"There they are," Carrie announced as Sydney and Jackson descended the stairs.

"Are you guys enjoying the view?" Jackson spoke before anyone could ask questions.

Adrianne turned toward Sydney. "You okay?"

"Yeah."

"Thanks a lot for leaving me alone with Her Majesty," Rob said near Sydney's ear.

"Who?" She frowned in confusion.

"The Princess." He glanced at Carrie, who was shaking her head at something Toby was saying. As if sensing that Rob was looking at her, Carrie looked in his direction only to pointedly look away.

"Rob," Sydney chided, "she doesn't seem snobbish at all."

Rob just shook his head.

* * *

The San Juan Islands consisted of 170 heavily forested islands scattered to the north of the Puget Sound. From a distance, it looked like someone had crumbled a large handful of earth and dropped the pieces into the water. Orcas Island was the largest of the three main islands, which also included San Juan and Lopez. Many smaller islands dotted the beautiful view with rocky cliffs and verdant mountains.

As they approached San Juan's rocky coastline, they could see dozens of whale watchers perched on rocks at Lime Kiln Point State Park, cameras in hand, waiting for their first, breathtaking sight of the majestic sea mammals.

The west side of San Juan Island was a favorite fishing spot for the orca whale. This was because the waters known as the Haro Strait were abundant in salmon. People from all over the world flew to Washington during spring and summer for a chance to see over ninety of the graceful giants in their daily water ballet.

The yacht slowed and turned slightly so that everyone on deck was facing the coast. Then it stopped completely some three-hundred yards from the shore.

Both Colin's and Carrie's parents joined them on deck. "Do you guys see anything?" Carrie's mother asked as she stood at the rail.

"Maybe it's still too early in the season." Carrie looked over the surface of the water. "Last year I don't think they showed until May."

Carrie's brothers sat at the top of the stairs that led down to the swimming platform near the water. Everyone scanned the sea except Jackson, who leaned against the doorway of the salon, apparently consumed by his thoughts as he watched Sydney.

"Wait," Toby said, pointing straight ahead. "I think I see something."

"Let's go to the top decks, where we'll have a better view," someone called, and everyone but Sydney hurried up the stairs to the bridge and the sun decks in order to have an unobstructed, bird's-eye view of the water around them.

Unaware that Jackson had remained behind with her, Sydney moved to the railing and lowered herself onto the cushioned seat along the side of the yacht. Closing her eyes, she let the strong smell of the ocean and the noisy cry of the seagulls wash over her.

She opened her eyes when she heard people clapping and cheering from the top deck. The wind carried the excited voices of her friends, indicating that they had spotted the tall dorsal fin of a killer whale jutting out of the water. Someone hushed the others, and the noise above deck died down. Everyone whispered in amazement, awed by the majesty of the whales.

Sydney watched as other fins popped up out of the water next to the first. They glided in and out, providing short glimpses of slick, black-and-white bodies as they wove through the water like silk waving in the wind. The pod of about eight whales bobbed up and down, staying near the surface.

As Sydney watched the grace and harmony of their movements, she felt herself slowly relax and she began to reflect on her past. Although so much of her life was up to her and so many choices were hers to make, there was a large portion that was entirely out of her control—events that depended wholly on the Lord. She had survived the storm because He had wanted her to. And Randy had died because he'd been called home.

Slowly, she began to accept that the Lord was over all; there was no reason to fear if she opened her heart enough to trust in Him. A warm wave of calm washed over her, and for the first time in what felt like a lifetime, she was at peace. Drawing her knees up to her chest, she rested her head against her arms and closed her eyes in silent prayer.

Sydney heard it before she saw it—the sound of someone running a hand through the water. She opened her eyes and saw that in the water to her right, not five feet away, a glossy black orca had surfaced alongside the yacht. Her heart jumped into her throat and her mouth dropped open. She slowly set her feet on the deck and stood.

With a loud puff, the orca blew a spray of water skyward before rolling back into the depths of the ocean, leaving Sydney doused in the fine coat of mist that had been carried by the wind.

She stood still for several seconds afterward, her mouth opening and closing like that of a fish out of water and an amazed smile growing on her face. She heard amused laughter, and she spun around to see Jackson watching her.

"Did you see that?" she cried, spinning back around to lean over the railing. "It was practically in the boat with me," she said in an almost giddy voice. "Did you see it?" She scanned the water for the whale.

"I saw it." Jackson came forward until he was standing right next to her. He reached out a hand to push away a strand of hair that had stuck to her damp face.

"Can you believe it?" She laughed. "I've never been that close before." Her eyes sparkled with exhilaration. "Have you?"

Jackson shook his head but kept smiling at her, enjoying the childlike animation on her face.

"Gabriel will never believe me," she mused as she looked out over the ocean. She spotted the slight rise of the whale's body as it joined the pod.

"I'm a witness."

She looked at him, her head tilted to the side with curiosity. "How long were you standing there?"

"Long enough."

Her eyes focused more fully on him. "How long is long enough?"

"I didn't want to leave you alone."

"You mean you've been down here all along?"

"Like I said, I didn't want to leave you alone."

Sydney felt her heartbeat accelerate. "Oh," she managed to say, and she tried to look away.

Jackson took her chin with his fingers and brought her gaze back to his. "You're beautiful, Sydney," he said softly as he explored the contours of her face. Then he closed the distance between them.

The joy that she had experienced when the whale had slid out of the water next to her was nothing compared to what she felt when Jackson pressed his lips to hers.

The sound of grumbling and complaining from above brought them back to the present, and Jackson stepped back. He tucked a lock of hair behind her ear and looked at her tenderly. "We should go up with the others." Sydney felt dazed, but she nodded, and he led her up to join everyone on the bridge deck.

Sydney exhaled deeply. The whales were gone, leaving the disappointment of their admirers in their wake. She had been granted a small bit of inner peace today, something which had eluded her for a long time.

But along with her joy, she had made a discovery. Here on the ocean, a place that had brought such pain and such happiness to her life, she had just made her most startling discovery yet: She was falling in love. And those unfamiliar waters were perhaps the scariest of all.

* * *

"So is she the one?"

Carrie and Jackson were sitting on the rocks below the balcony of her parents' vacation home, overlooking the private beach. Sydney, Colin, and Adrianne had been sitting on a blanket on the sand for the past hour as Toby and Rob played a hand of smashball. Carrie's two little brothers and Elizabeth were exploring the water's edge for seashells, which they benevolently threw back into the water.

Their late lunch would be ready soon, and then they would head back to Whidbey Island before the sun sunk into the ocean.

Jackson glanced at Carrie and smiled in amusement. "The one? I never thought you were the romantic type."

Carrie laughed. "Yeah, well, we all change, don't we?"

Jackson's eyes drifted in Sydney's direction. "What do you mean?"

Carrie lifted a shoulder. "I just mean that I see a difference in you that I didn't think I would ever see. It's especially noticeable when you look at her."

Sydney ran a hand through her hair and laughed out loud at something Adrianne had said. The corner of Jackson's mouth lifted slightly.

"My father will be immensely relieved." Carrie made a face. She had tried to assure her father many times that she and Jackson were just friends; if Jackson got married, he'd finally believe it.

Carrie's father didn't have a problem with Mormons; he even enjoyed their company on a regular basis, since his close friend and attorney was an active Latter-day Saint. He didn't mind that his daughter associated with Colin, Toby, and Jackson, because they were upright and trustworthy. To his way of thinking, this was a sort of guarantee that his only daughter's reputation would remain spotless. But when it came to allowing her to marry someone of "that religion," Grant Alexander Larson III put his foot down with a bang.

When he'd found out that Carrie was dating Jackson, a returned Mormon missionary, there had been dramatic arguments between him and his daughter that had only died down when her relationship with Jackson had. It wasn't until he knew that she and Jackson were just friends that he had relaxed.

Carrie grinned when Toby tripped and fell flat on his face and Sydney burst out laughing. "I think I like her," Carrie said. She watched as Toby ran over to Sydney and dropped a handful of sand on her head.

Carrie's smile withered when her gaze came to rest on Rob. "I'm not so sure about her friend."

"Who, Adrianne?"

"The cop."

"Rob?" Jackson studied Carrie closely. "Why not?"

She shrugged in an attempt to appear nonchalant. "He's patronizing."

"Have you talked to him?"

"Yes, and having talked to him, I don't want to talk *about* him," she retorted emphatically.

Jackson lifted his hands in defense. "You're the one who brought it up."

"So . . . are you going to tell me, or not?" Carrie asked. When Jackson just looked at her, she expounded, impatiently reeling the air in front of her with her hands. "Do you think she's the one?"

Jackson seemed to consider the question as he watched the scene play out on the beach. Sydney was in the midst of her retaliation effort. She stalked to the water's edge, where the small waves pulsed onto the beach, and bent down to grab a fistful of wet sand. It was already too late when Toby realized that she was standing behind him; the glob of wet sand dripped off his head like a blob of melted cheddar. A roar of laughter resonated from the others as Toby yelped in surprise.

Jackson broke into a smile and chuckled audibly as he watched Sydney take off at a dead run.

"Oh yeah," Carrie pronounced theatrically, "She's definitely the one."

Chapter 15

"Today we're going to focus specifically on tacking up, or saddling your horses," Sydney instructed the children as they stood next to their ponies. "You have all had a little experience with this by now, but today I want each of you to try saddling your horse on your own from start to finish." Her news garnered a wide range of reactions. The older children seemed excited to be handed greater responsibility, while the younger ones looked at their small ponies dubiously.

"You've already groomed your horse in preparation for the saddle, so we're ready to go." Sydney moved to stand close to Trinity and Jesse, who were her youngest students. "You always saddle your horse from the near side. And what side is that, Trinity?" she asked the redhead who was distractedly petting her pony's speckled coat.

"The left side?" she replied hesitantly.

"Very good." Sydney smiled. "The left side," she repeated. "Place the saddle pad on your pony's back so that it's just on top of its withers. And what are the withers, Josh?" she asked as she watched her young students do as they were told and slightly adjusted Trinny's work.

"The front shoulders of the horse," Josh answered proudly.

"Good job, Josh," she commended, and she moved to inspect Jesse's and Will's work while Adam helped Josh and Mary. "Now, slide the pad back so it's just in front of the withers. We do this to straighten the horse's hair that's under the saddle."

"Next, we're going to gently place the saddle on the pony's back. Never drop the saddle on the horse, because you can injure it or you could injure yourself if the horse were to bolt." She helped her students until they had all done as instructed.

"Who can tell me the difference between an English saddle and a western saddle?" she quizzed.

"Western saddles have horns, and their stirrups aren't built to come off," Mary answered.

"That's right." Sydney gave the girl an appreciative smile. "The stirrups on our English saddles detach in case of an emergency, right?"

Sydney spent the next half hour going over the steps of tacking up, and then she allowed the students a few minutes to ride and work on their position and balance.

"Now we're going to do everything backward, guys," Sydney called when they all had their ponies safely tied to the fence again. "We're going to untack the horse. Start by removing the bridle, and then work on the saddle."

She heard the sound of a car door closing and glanced in the direction of the gravel parking area in the back. She smiled broadly. Jackson was headed her way.

"You guys have done a really good job. I'm very impressed with how fast you've all picked up on your lessons. Before you know it, you'll be moving up to the next level," she said with pride. "Now, everyone put your tack away like I showed you. Adam will help you."

Sydney turned around just as Jackson joined her inside the arena. "Are you here to take some riding lessons?"

"Are you willing to teach me?"

"That depends."

"On what?"

"On whether you'll fit on one of my ponies."

Jackson glanced at the five mounts that stood just about waist level and chuckled. "That might be a problem for your ponies."

The children came out of the tack room and gathered around her, knowing that the class was not over until Sydney had dismissed them.

Mary eyed Jackson inquisitively and flushed when he looked down at her and winked. "Are you her boyfriend?"

Sydney and Jackson answered simultaneously.

"No."

"Yes."

Sydney's eyes flew up to meet Jackson's, all humor vanishing from her face at his reply.

Josh glared at his new rival. "Sydney said no," he pointed out gruffly.

Jackson grinned down at the boy. "She meant yes," he assured him as he turned back to Sydney. "Will you go on a date with me?"

Jesse started giggling. "He's asking her out."

"Gross," Will said with a grimace.

Mary frowned down at her little brother. "It's not gross, it's romantic!" She sighed with starry-eyed exaggeration.

"You're not going to say yes, are you?" Josh asked Sydney worriedly.

Sydney's eyes swung from Josh to Jackson, and she felt caught. Dating sounded so official—not that kissing him had been casual— but if she went out with him, she wouldn't be able to hide behind the pretext that theirs was simply a business relationship. There would no longer be a safety net.

Sydney took a deep breath as five pairs of eyes watched her expectantly. "Your parents are waiting, guys," Sydney said finally and motioned to the waiting cars. "Remember that next week a veterinarian will be visiting us to teach us a little more about our horses."

While the rest of the children ran toward their waiting parents, Josh lingered, eyeing Jackson warily. Josh looked at Sydney with a worried frown. "*Is* he your boyfriend?" he asked gravely.

Sydney bent down so that she was looking him in the eye and smiled softly. She could say no—and crush his heart if he saw them together again—or she could say yes, which wasn't completely accurate, either. She wasn't anywhere near ready to say yes.

"I don't know," she whispered, and she saw a myriad of emotions reflected in his young eyes.

Josh finally looked up at Jackson and, showing signs of the man he would someday be, pressed his lips together and stuck out his hand. Jackson didn't crack a smile as he shook the little boy's hand.

"Be nice to her," Josh said solemnly. And with the short nod of a man three times his age, he turned and walked away.

Sydney straightened, touched. In Josh's conduct, she glimpsed what Rob must have been like at this age. She watched Josh's little legs carry him to his mother's car, and she waved when the car pulled out of the driveway.

"Had I known you had a secret admirer, I would have waited to ask you out."

"I think he'll be fine," Sydney said with a quick glance at Jackson, then she started leading the ponies into the paddock so they could graze freely.

"Here, let me help you." Jackson took a couple of the leads.

"Thanks."

"You know," Jackson said, setting the ponies loose, "you never answered my question."

Sydney wasn't quite sure why she was afraid to go out on a date with him. It wasn't as if she'd never been out with him before. He had taken her to lunch before they'd driven to Deception Pass. She'd gone for a ride with him at Eagle Crest and had enjoyed every minute of the time she'd spent with him.

Reason told her that it was only a matter of semantics—just because he hadn't called their outings dates hadn't made them any less personal. So why did it feel like she was standing at the edge of a tall cliff looking down? She could easily say no and go back to living her life the way she had been—no involvement, no complication.

She felt as though she stood on the verge of making a monumental decision. She had made a bad decision that day when she'd asked Randy to take her sailing. How could she trust herself after her choice had cost Randy his life? Wasn't it better to avoid making any more mistakes? Wasn't it safer?

Sometimes doing nothing can do more damage than doing something we fear.

Rob's words echoed in her mind.

Jackson kept his eyes fixed on Sydney while she struggled with the conflicting emotions.

Sydney looked up at him, her expression a mixture of hope and trepidation. "What do you have in mind?"

* * *

"When you said you were taking me to watch the sunrise, I didn't think you meant from five thousand feet," Sydney said breathlessly, watching the sunrise glimmer through the fluffy cluster of clouds. From their vantage point in the basket of the colorful hot air balloon, the sky was cloaked in deep purples, pinks, and blues, and the warm morning sunshine illuminated everything in sight with the most amazing palette of colors she had ever seen.

The sapphire blanket of the Puget Sound was sprinkled with the clutter of emerald gems that were the San Juan Islands. As if waiting for the sun to meet them, the Olympic Mountains stood proudly in the distance.

"I've never seen anything so beautiful."

"It's amazing, isn't it?" Jackson had reached down to lace his fingers with hers. Sydney glanced up at him and smiled before turning once more to look at the beautiful colors around them.

A peaceful silence enveloped them as they drifted in the calm wind. The only sound was the occasional, comforting purr of the propane burners as the pilot gently kept the balloon aloft. When the sun had first shown its face in the west and they had been bathed in the warm, amber light, the pilot had descended twice so that they could witness the sunrise again. Three times in a row they had relived those first seconds of morning glory. Their hour-long ride neared its end as they started their descent back to earth, and it was as if they'd been allowed a glimpse of paradise.

They landed safely in a green field. Moments later they were joined by the chase crew that followed the balloon during landing in order to help pack up the equipment and transport the passengers back to their cars.

"That was the most incredible experience I've ever had," Sydney said, looking up at the sky longingly as they made their way back to Jackson's car. "Thank you."

Jackson smiled at her as he opened the car door and waited for her to climb in. "It's not over yet."

"What do you mean?"

"It's early still." He glanced at his watch. "As a matter of fact, it's time for breakfast. What do you say we drive to my house so I can make you breakfast."

Sydney smiled as she nodded. "Wow. Is there anything you can't do?"

Jackson gave her a dubious look. "You might want to hold your praise until after you've tasted the pancakes."

"Uh-oh," she said with feigned concern.

Chapter 16

As it turned out, Sydney had nothing to worry about; Jackson was as comfortable in the kitchen as he was in the stables. With efficiency and skill, Jackson had breakfast well underway by the time there was any movement upstairs.

"She's awake," Jackson announced with amusement as he flipped the pancake on the griddle that was built into the kitchen island. He gave the clock on the microwave a quick glance before turning back to grin at Sydney. "It's the smell of food that woke the beast," he joked. "Otherwise, she'd sleep until noon."

"Mmm. I can't remember the last time I was able to sleep in, but it sounds good." Sydney was sitting at the large, granite-top island that occupied the center of Jackson's spacious kitchen. She had offered to help cook when they'd arrived, and Jackson had assigned her to make the scrambled eggs as he busied himself with the pancakes and bacon. Sydney had finished long before him, so she'd popped the eggs into the oven to keep them warm.

"It sounds great unless you live with Meredith." Jackson removed another pancake and added the last of the batter to the griddle. "My aunt doesn't believe in wasting time sleeping. She thinks that if you work with horses, then sleeping is only a disruption." Jackson set the spatula on the counter and gave Sydney his full attention. Since their trip on the yacht she'd seemed much more relaxed and at ease.

"I hate to say that I agree, but I do understand what she means," Sydney said with a small smile. "I remember how hard it was when I started training as a kid. While all my friends were having slumber parties and sleeping in on Saturday mornings, I was getting up at five to feed, exercise, and groom Romeo. Then I had to help clean out the stalls and get ready for my trainer to arrive by seven. And that was before I started my serious training. After that, it seemed like every hour I spent sleeping was another hour I could have spent training. There were times when I sleepwalked through half of my chores. But that was the arrangement I'd made with my parents and my grandfather. They bought me a horse and paid for a trainer, and I took care of the horse and the stables."

Jackson smiled. He would have liked to know the younger, more carefree Sydney before she had been struck with so much pain.

When he'd first met her, he had instantly been intrigued by the beautiful woman with the guarded look and smart sense of humor. Now he found himself wanting to know everything about her, and that fact surprised him.

Over the years he had managed to get by with minimal involvement in any relationship other than those involving his family or work. Except for Carrie, he hadn't really dated anyone at all. She'd been the only one who had managed to penetrate the barrier that he had unknowingly erected.

It had been a self-imposed isolation. He had turned inward to get through the loss of his parents and focus on his sister and the ranch. Not even the time he'd spent with Carrie had made him realize how alone he was. But now his loneliness reared up like an angry stallion.

What was it about Sydney that made the things he'd found so important for the last few years seem meaningless? She was beautiful, yes. But he had known a lot of beautiful women, and they had never made him want to be more than he was. Her honesty was refreshing, her humor was invigorating, and the somber serenity she often wore was reassuring.

What would Sydney think, and how would she react, if she knew how much he really cared for her? He knew her well enough by now to know that she had wanted to run at first. He knew that she was afraid to feel again, but he was afraid to waste precious time now that he'd found her.

Sydney was picking at a bowl of fresh berries that Jackson had set out for the pancakes. She hadn't noticed the way he had been watching her as she talked. "Unfortunately there is a severe trade-off when you want to compete in this industry," she was saying. "Love of sleep or love of horses . . . take your pick," she said with an easy smirk and a longing sigh.

Jackson smiled. "That's more or less what Meredith told Elizabeth. My sister, however, wasn't as receptive to her reasoning as you are, so they compromised."

Sydney raised a curious brow, and Jackson explained. "Elizabeth is allowed to sleep in on Saturdays as long as she puts in extra hours during the week to clean out the stalls."

"And she agrees?"

"You don't know how much Lizzy loves her sleep."

"You got that right." Elizabeth sauntered into the kitchen. Her hair was wet from a recent shower, and wiry curls poked out in every direction like metal coils. "Which is why I'm so upset that the smell of food woke me up early. You're lucky I'm starving enough to forgive you." She eyed Jackson and sat down in the stool next to Sydney. Stretching like a cat, she yawned loudly before turning her attention to Sydney. "Hi."

Sydney smiled. "Good morning."

"You should have told me you were bringing Sydney over for breakfast, Jackson." She spoke without looking at her brother. "I would have made you *my* pancakes. They're famous, right, Jackson?" She didn't wait for a response as she proceeded to grab a handful of berries and pop them into her mouth one by one.

"Famous," Jackson repeated with an amused wink at Sydney, who tried to hide her grin.

"So, how was your date?" Elizabeth asked. Jackson didn't miss the uncertainty that flashed in Sydney's eyes at his sister's words.

"It was amazing. Have you ever been in a hot air balloon?" Sydney asked.

"Are you kidding?" Elizabeth asked. She glanced at her brother, who had just pulled the bacon and eggs out of the oven and was busy taking the last of the pancakes off the griddle. If her brother was going to take his sweet time in letting Sydney know that his feelings were serious, then Elizabeth would just have to help him along a bit. "Jackson always says that you only take a hot air balloon ride when you're in love."

Jackson's eyes shot to Elizabeth, pinning his meddling sister with his gaze. He glanced at Sydney, who sat rigidly on the bar stool, staring intently at her hands. Her face was turning bright red, and he wasn't sure if she was embarrassed or terrified. Unable to deny his sister's assertion because he was sure he had indeed said that at one time or another to get out of having to take Elizabeth on a hot air balloon, Jackson found himself at a loss for words. With another warning look at Elizabeth, he carried the pancakes to the table.

"I figure I'll wait until I'm engaged," Elizabeth continued innocently, "but I'm glad you two had fun."

"Elizabeth," Jackson warned, and before he could say anything else, the telephone rang.

"I'll get it." Elizabeth jumped off her stool and hurried over to the telephone that hung on the wall near the refrigerator.

* * *

Sydney wanted to disappear. She wasn't surprised that Elizabeth's words had made her heart start pounding in her chest. What surprised her was that her heart wasn't pounding in panic but in elation. She hadn't realized that the thought of getting more serious with Jackson appealed to her until Elizabeth had suggested it. She didn't dare look up at Jackson for fear that she wouldn't see the same feelings reflected on his face. For all she knew, he might only see her as a good friend. *Then why did he kiss me?* she reasoned.

"It's for you, Jackson,"

"Who is it?"

Elizabeth made a face. "Carrie."

Sydney looked up just as Jackson quickly glanced in her direction. She was surprised to see the look of guilt on his face.

"Tell her I'll call her back."

"I did, but she said you told her to call."

Jackson hesitated. "I'll be just a moment." He apologized to Sydney and took the phone from his sister.

Sydney wanted to believe that she'd imagined Jackson's sudden discomfort. There was nothing between him and Carrie, was there? He had told her himself that they were just friends. But if so, why did he look like he was trying to hide something?

"She's obsessed," Elizabeth said offhandedly.

Sydney swallowed but said nothing as she glanced at Jackson, whose back was to her as he spoke to Carrie.

"She's been after Jackson for a long time," Elizabeth explained. "But it's obvious that you're the one he wants. He doesn't even know she exists now that you're here."

Sydney swallowed past the dry lump in her throat. If he wasn't interested in Carrie, then why had he looked so guilty when he'd taken her phone call?

Chapter 17

"Well, I've got to hand it to you," Sydney called reluctantly. "I didn't think it was possible to make this look more like a car and less like the pile of rust that it used to be."

Rob grinned when he lifted his head from beneath the hood of his '67 Mustang and saw Sydney walking up his drive. Of course, the old beauty didn't start and needed some major body work and an entirely new interior, but no one had been able to convince him that it wasn't a project worth undertaking. It had started as a simple hobby, a way to spend some of his free time, but after a while it had turned into something close to an obsession.

"That's because you've been spending too much time around horses." He straightened and reached for the stained rag that dangled from his back pocket. "You need to have vision in order to see her potential."

"I think it takes a whole lot more than just vision to see it for anything but junk," she argued, and then she laughed loudly at the expression on Rob's face. "Sorry," she amended. Rob glanced at his car as if to make sure it hadn't overheard Sydney's insulting words, which only made Sydney laugh again. "At least you're not the kind of guy who would make me apologize for hurting your car's feelings."

"I would if I thought you'd do it," he admitted.

Sydney shook her head hopelessly. "Rob, you need a girlfriend," she said, and she instantly covered her mouth with her hand as if to physically take back the words. "I'm sorry, Rob." Sydney was horrified. "We're friends, and my saying that is as bad as my grandfather trying to set me up. I promise I'll never say anything like that again.

Just because Adrianne is getting married doesn't mean that we have to, does it?" she joked.

Rob looked back at her, his eyes crinkling at the edges as he smiled. "Yes, I get the feeling that you and I are never going to get married," he said, sure that she didn't understand his meaning by the curious look on her face.

Sydney smiled. "Probably not."

Rob continued to look at her as he stuffed the rag back into his pocket. Then he turned back to look under the hood of his car. "So, what's up?" he asked, picking up the wrench to work at loosening the bolts on the old battery.

"I just stopped by to see what you were up to," she said, casually picking at the oily pieces of metal that he'd set along the rim of the car.

Rob gave Sydney a quick look, knowing that she didn't do anything casually. If she had stopped by, there was a reason, and if she didn't own up to it, it was because she was embarrassed. There wasn't much that embarrassed Sydney, at least not around Adrianne and him, so this made her behavior all the more curious.

"You know that I work on my car on my days off," he answered just as casually.

Sydney nodded distractedly. "Have you eaten lunch yet?"

Rob straightened and motioned to the open box of pizza that sat on top of his red tool chest. There were three cold pieces left of a large supreme. "Help yourself." Sydney made a face and Rob chuckled. "There's a microwave inside."

She glared at him. "Only a man would think that cold pizza constitutes lunch."

"You forgot breakfast and dinner, too."

Sydney shook her head in amusement. "You should not look the way you do, considering how you eat," she said with a pointed look at his muscular arms and lean build.

"I chase the bad guys all night. It's a workout," he explained with a small grunt as he worked to twist a rusted bolt off. Finally loosening it, he placed it on the side with the rest.

"You drive a patrol car," she pointed out, poking at the grimy bolt he'd just released and getting grease on her finger. Without taking his eyes off the next bolt he was working on, Rob reached his free hand behind him and handed his rag to her. Sydney continued. "I'm pretty sure it's not your job that keeps you thin. It's your genes."

Rob frowned thoughtfully. "Old Navy. Thirty bucks."

Sydney scowled dramatically as she took the rag and wiped her hand clean. "Thanks." She thought it was a wonder the cloth didn't make her hand dirtier considering its condition. "Do you work today?"

Rob glanced at his watch. "In a couple of hours. Why?" he asked, finally realizing that she was not going to volunteer the reason for her visit.

She shrugged. "Just wanted to talk." She set the cloth next to the bolts.

"What about?" Rob could see that she was slightly embarrassed to broach whatever was on her mind, but he and Sydney were best friends, and he knew she would work up the nerve soon enough. He could wait.

She shrugged again, and when she didn't say anything else, he raised a questioning brow. "If this is twenty questions, you have to answer yes or no, at least."

Sydney smiled and exhaled. "Sorry. I'm a little nervous."

Rob set down his wrench. "What's going on, Syd?"

She glanced up the street and Rob followed the direction of her gaze. There were a couple of kids riding bikes up and down their driveway while their mother sat on the lawn with a toddler. "I needed to talk to someone, and Adrianne's busy with the wedding."

"So I'm second choice."

Sydney looked at him as if to say he knew better, and he shrugged his shoulders casually. She smiled. "I thought that you could help me figure things out."

"What things?" He was suddenly alert.

"Well, you're a guy, right?"

"Last time I checked."

Sydney ignored the comment. "And since you're a guy, maybe you could explain the way guys think and feel."

Rob's eyes narrowed. "We're pretty much the same as other humans," he said sarcastically, having a premonition of where the conversation was headed and not sure if he wanted to go there with her. "You know, hearts and brains are pretty much the same regardless of gender."

"Rob," she complained. "You're being deliberately obtuse."

"You're being deliberately ambiguous."

She thinned her lips and took a deep breath. "Okay. I'm confused about something . . . someone . . . and I need you to help me figure it—him—out."

Rob was silent a moment as he watched her.

"Will you help me?"

"Is this about Jackson?" he asked, feeling an ache growing in the region of his chest. She didn't realize what this conversation was going to cost him.

She nodded.

Rob was silent, and he mindlessly reached for the rag she'd set down. "Are you in love with him?" he asked, mechanically wiping his hands with the cloth and avoiding eye contact. He knew the answer to his question. He had been suspecting it all along, but he still didn't want to look into her eyes and actually see his suspicions confirmed. It was bad enough knowing that she was in love with someone else; he didn't want to see it written all over her face. Not yet.

Sydney was silent for a moment and then exhaled loudly. "Wow. You get right to the point, don't you."

"If you're here, it's because you want to hear what I think, right?"

She nodded.

"So?" he prodded.

"I'm not sure," she said softly.

Rob's hands tightened on the rag before he stuffed it into his back pocket and took a deep breath. "I think you are," he assured her gently. Even as he said it, he couldn't help wishing it were him she was talking about. He hadn't planned on having these feelings for Sydney. They'd been friends since they were kids, so he had always liked her. But it hadn't been until she'd come back to Washington that he'd discovered the woman she had become. She had a generous nature and a mischievous sense of humor that lightened any situation. She had lived through a traumatic event, and it had made her a better person. He cared deeply about Sydney, and for that reason he was going to let her rip his heart from his chest no matter how badly it hurt.

Rob had always made sure to keep his feelings toward Sydney carefully concealed. He had never confessed that he was in love with her, because he had wanted her to heal first. He just hadn't realized that her heart had already mended. Sydney was stronger than she believed herself to be, and she deserved happiness more than anyone he knew. So if she was in love with Jackson and had the chance to find happiness with him, then he would keep his feelings to himself, step aside, and wish her well.

"That's just it," Sydney said with a worried brow. "I don't know if I am. I mean, I think I might be, but it's so different from what I felt for Randy that I can't be sure." She took a couple of steps over to a pile of tires and sat on them. Leaning forward, she rested her elbows on her knees.

"It was different with Randy. I loved him, but I didn't feel for him what I feel for Jackson. With Randy, it was easy and relaxed and steady. There was a surety there that sort of guaranteed we'd be happy." She looked back up at Rob, who was watching her silently. "But with Jackson, I'm not so sure. How do I know what he feels for me? How do I know whether he has the same feelings for me or whether this is just a passing fancy for him? How do I know anything? How do I know if I'm ready for this?"

Rob swallowed and smiled gently. "If you're asking these questions, then you're ready."

Sydney's smile was fleeting. "I wish I could do that."

"What?"

"You don't hold back. You're not afraid to say what you think."

She was wrong, but he wouldn't correct her. "Have you told Jackson how you feel?"

She shook her head. "I'm afraid he might not feel the same way."

"Why would you think that?"

"Well, you remember Carrie Larsen, right?"

"The artist," he admitted. Carrie wasn't the type of woman one easily forgot, and she knew it. He got the feeling that someday he was going to have to make amends for his rude behavior on her family's yacht. But the thought of seeing her again didn't sit well with him, and that in and of itself made him uneasy.

"She and Jackson are really close."

"I got the impression they were friends," Rob said.

Sydney nodded. "Close friends. But I think for a while they were more than friends."

"So?"

"Well . . ." She started to run her fingers through her hair but remembered it was up in a ponytail and dropped her hand. "What if he still has feelings for her? I mean, you saw her—she's gorgeous."

"So are you," Rob stated easily.

Sydney smiled appreciatively. "You know what I mean."

"Ask him," he said, leaning a hip against his car.

"I can't." Sydney shook her head in horror. "I can't just ask him if he has feelings for his friend any more than I can come out and tell him that I think I'm falling in love with him."

And there it was. Rob could almost feel the cracking within his chest.

After a short silence, Rob spoke. "They seemed to be just friends." He omitted mentioning the fact that although he and Sydney had been "just friends," it hadn't stopped him from falling in love with her. "And Jackson doesn't seem like the kind of man who would play with someone's feelings." As much as he had wanted to find fault with him, Rob hadn't been able to feel anything but respect for Jackson. "I can't say the same for Carrie, because I don't know her."

Rob wasn't such a fool that he didn't recognize this opportunity to influence Sydney's choice. With the right word or carefully crafted phrase, he could plant enough doubt in her to destroy any possibility of a relationship between her and Jackson.

But he couldn't do it. He respected Sydney enough to be honest with her, and he loved her enough to want her happiness. "If I were to venture a guess, I'd say Jackson is not in love with Carrie," Rob assured her finally.

Sydney looked miserable as she looked at him. "Have you ever been in love?" She unwittingly threw him a curveball.

He slowly nodded, because he didn't trust himself to speak.

Sydney looked surprised by Rob's revelation. He had never told her and Adrianne that he'd been in love with anyone, and they hadn't seen him spend time with anyone in particular. "Do I know her?"

Rob smiled. "Why do you want to know, Sydney?"

"You're my best friend. I think I have a right to know."

Rob watched her thoughtfully, and then he pushed away from the car and turned around to mess with the parts he'd removed from the Mustang's engine. "It's in the past."

Sydney stood up and went to stand by him. "Well, did she love you back?"

"In her way, she did," he answered and turned to look at her. "As much as she could, I guess."

Sydney felt a deep sadness in his response and saw sorrow in his eyes. It disturbed her that she'd known him for so long and hadn't ever suspected that he had unresolved pain lurking beneath his handsome smile. "I'm sorry, Rob."

"I know you are, Syd," he said, looking into her heartbreaking eyes. That was what had captured him in the first place—that genuine concern she showed for those she loved. How could she know that she was apologizing for pain she'd inadvertently caused? He changed the subject. "So what's keeping you from telling Jackson how you feel?"

Sydney hesitated, as if reluctant to change the subject. "I don't know."

"What are you afraid of?" He had asked himself that same question a few weeks earlier. His own fears seemed so easily surmountable in retrospect. He hadn't wanted to pressure her. He'd known that Sydney still carried a great deal of pain from Randy's accident, and he hadn't wanted to add more to her load. He had chosen to wait and to give her more time, and in so doing, he had lost her.

"What if I'm wrong?" she nearly whispered, and she moved back over to the tires and sat down. She dropped her head to look at the oil-stained driveway. "What if he doesn't love me? What if this doesn't work out?" she asked, and she swallowed. "What if I lose him?"

Rob didn't hesitate. He walked over to where she sat on the stack of tires and crouched down in front of her so that their eyes met. "What if you don't do anything and lose the chance for the happiness you might have?" Rob wished he had taken his own advice, but he knew that it probably wouldn't have made a difference. Sometimes things turned out exactly the way they were supposed to, and no amount of wishing or praying could change them. Sydney wasn't meant for him.

"So you think I should tell him how I feel?"

"I think you shouldn't be afraid to accept and admit that you've fallen in love with Jackson. And unless my gut is suddenly failing me, I'd say that he feels the same way about you."

"Really?"

Rob grinned softly. "For someone as beautiful as you are, Syd, it's a wonder you're so insecure."

A slow smile grew on her face, and he saw the old Sydney in her eyes—the Sydney from before the accident who had laughed often, loved fearlessly, and teased incessantly. She stood up. "For someone as wonderful as you are, Rob, it's a wonder you're still single." Still smiling, she turned and walked away.

"Sydney," Rob called to her as she walked down his driveway.

She stopped and turned to look at him. "Yeah?"

He paused thoughtfully as he watched her. "He'd be a fool if he didn't love you."

Sydney smiled widely as she turned to leave.

Rob watched her get into her car and drive off. Reaching for his wrench, he swallowed, took a deep breath, and got back to work.

Chapter 18

Sydney pulled into the drive of the beige, ranch-style home that she had once known so well. She forced herself to turn off the engine of her car and open the door.

The lawn was still as neatly mown as ever and not a single leaf from the trees that surrounded the property could be seen on the grass. She remembered how Laura Willett had constantly been disposing of any stray branches or unlucky weeds that had mistakenly chosen to grow in her yard.

She got out of the car and quietly closed the door, not wanting to draw Laura's attention—not that she planned on turning around and making her escape before anyone could see her. Her car keys were clutched tightly in her hand as if she were holding on to a much-needed lifeline.

This was it. This was the moment she'd been avoiding since waking up in the hospital bed five years ago. The time had come to confess to Randy's mother that she was to blame for Randy's death.

Sydney straightened, lifted her chin resolutely, and took her first step.

She didn't have to knock, for just as she reached the end of the small walkway, the door opened.

Laura emerged wearing a small smile and held open the screen door. "I was afraid you wouldn't come."

I almost didn't. "You're still an immaculate gardener," Sydney observed, wanting to talk about anything but why she was there.

"Obsessive is more like it," Laura corrected with a mischievous grin. "It drives Lewis crazy," she said, referring to her husband. "But that's only because he has to mow the lawn twice a week."

Sydney smiled. "How is he? Lewis, I mean," she asked, recalling Randy's kind father, whose portly frame had made him the perfect candidate for Santa at Church Christmas parties.

"Come inside," Laura started, as if remembering her manners, and she stepped aside so Sydney could pass. "He's still working for the Washington State Ferries." She closed the door behind them. "Have a seat," she invited once they had made their way to the small but pristine living room. "Anyway, Lewis could have retired by now, but he's convinced that if he were to stay home I'd have him cutting grass daily."

Sydney smiled.

"I told him you were coming today. He sends his love."

Sydney's smile faltered a little. "I should have come before," she apologized with a dry throat, still clutching her keys in both hands as they rested in her lap.

"We heard that you'd moved away."

Sydney nodded, unable to hold eye contact. "I've been back for a while now." She took a slow breath. "I, um . . . I didn't come sooner because . . ."

"Would you like something to drink?" Laura asked, and she stood suddenly as if she was unprepared to hear what Sydney had to say. She didn't wait for Sydney to answer but walked into the open kitchen that was to their left. A few minutes later, she returned with two glasses filled with pink lemonade. Laura handed Sydney a glass and took a seat across from her again.

"Thank you." Sydney took the glass and sipped from it to wet her throat. Staring down at the glass in her hands, she spoke. "The truth is that I've avoided seeing you."

When Laura said nothing, Sydney glanced up. She was surprised to find the woman watching her compassionately.

"I know, Sydney," she said softly.

"I'm sorry," Sydney whispered, staring at her directly.

"I understand."

"No. I mean . . . about . . . I'm sorry about Randy." She felt her heart constrict as the words left her lips.

"Sydney—" Laura began.

"He didn't want to go." Sydney shook her head as she remembered. "It was my idea to go sailing. He didn't want to go. Please forgive me." She finished and waited for the shock—waited for the tears and the blame. "If it weren't for me, he'd still be alive. He died because of me." She dipped her head, wanting more than anything to disappear. She desperately wanted to escape the blunt pain that came with the revelation of her guilt.

After a long silence, Laura finally spoke. "You haven't been blaming yourself all this time, have you?"

Sydney's head snapped up, and she wiped away the tears that were clouding her vision. She opened her mouth to speak, but nothing came out.

Laura was watching her with a troubled frown. "You have," she whispered finally, in sympathetic disbelief.

"If we had just done what he wanted, if we had done anything else, we never would have gotten caught in the storm," Sydney explained regretfully, in case Laura didn't quite understand what she was confessing. "He'd still be alive."

Laura's face fell as if she wanted nothing more than to have Randy back. The sorrow had never completely disappeared. It was still visible beneath the layers of life that she had lived in his absence. "It was his time," Laura said, shaking her head slowly. "No matter what you could have done differently, it was still his time to go, Sydney. Life and death are ultimately out of our hands," she stated with a sad smile. "It took me so long to accept that, but when I did, I was finally able to put my baby to rest."

Sydney swallowed and watched her carefully. "You're not angry?"

"For a while I was furious," she said as if remembering days as dark as—or darker than—the ones that Sydney had lived. "I blamed everyone: Lewis, myself. If only Lewis hadn't bought that boat; if only he had never taught Randy how to sail. If only I had never let him go; if only I had insisted that you two go with us to Seattle that day. If only . . . if only." She finished with a sad laugh.

"I nearly drove myself crazy thinking about what I could have . . . should have . . . done differently. And then I realized that there was absolutely nothing that I could have done—that anyone could have done—to change the fact that it was his time to go. It was only when I finally accepted that, when I finally understood that everything is in Heavenly Father's hands, that I felt peace for the first time since

Randy was taken from us. Only at that point did I fully understand the Savior's Atonement—His sacrifice for us."

Laura paused as she studied Sydney. "You see, Sydney. If you trust Him, and if you leave in His hands those things you're not able to change or comprehend, everything will be all right. I find such hope in knowing that we'll see Randy again someday—that Heavenly Father has given us a way to reunite with our loved ones after this life and live with them forever."

Sydney was unable to speak as the words that she had expected to be harsh and accusing had instead been kind and forgiving.

"You see, Sydney, the reason I wanted to see you so badly was to ask you to forgive *me*. I was so caught up in my own grief that I never thought about you. I never thought to go see you in the hospital or to call and see how you were doing. I should have thought about what you had been through and how desolate you must have felt. I'm afraid that your devastating experience was made worse by my selfishness."

Sydney stood and moved to sit next to Laura and hesitated only momentarily before wrapping her arms around her. "I thought you would be destroyed when I told you." Sydney paused, wiping at her eyes. "I didn't think I'd ever tell you or anyone. If you hadn't asked me to come . . ." Sydney swallowed. "Do you . . . do you want me to tell you about that day?" The coast guard and the police had gathered the necessary facts, but only she knew the details of Randy's last moments.

Laura shook her head. "I know all that I need to know," she answered quietly, and then the corner of her mouth lifted slightly. "The boy you were with at the tulip festival," she said, and Sydney knew she meant Jackson. "Is he someone special to you?"

Sydney glanced away. "I think so."

"He seemed to think you were," she said intuitively, remembering how he had excused them both when he'd noticed Sydney's stricken look. "He was very handsome."

Sydney smiled in silent agreement. She glanced at her watch and was surprised at the amount of time that had passed. "I need to go."

"You won't stay and wait for Lewis?"

"I'm afraid I won't be able to. My parents are flying in today, and I need to pick them up at the airport."

"Another time, then." She stood to walk Sydney out.

"Another time," Sydney agreed, and she stopped just outside the door. "Thank you, Mrs. Willet." Sydney hugged the woman who had, with her kind words, mended a part of her she thought had been torn forever.

* * *

Before Sydney left for the airport she made a stop that was long overdue. She walked down the quiet path until she found it. His name was engraved in black granite that shimmered beneath the sun.

She read the words that were carved beneath his name and knew the truth of them.

Always loved, never forgotten.

Sydney reached down and laid a yellow tulip next to the fresh flowers that had been neatly placed in vases on either side of the headstone.

"I love you, Randy," she whispered with a sad smile. "And I miss you."

She stood, lost in thought, embraced by the rocking arms of sweet emotion. She closed her eyes and gave silent thanks for the healing gift of forgiveness and for the Savior's loving sacrifice that allowed families to be together after this life.

Kissing her fingertips, she touched the cool stone and then turned and slowly walked away.

Chapter 19

"I don't think we're going to make it!" Sydney shouted as she shot another glance up at the darkening sky. The black water was closing in on them. With a crushing blow, it beckoned Randy into its harrowing depths.

"Sydney, save me! Please!"

Sydney spun around, frantically looking for him.

"Sydney, don't let me die!"

Sobbing, Sydney came fully awake. Her dreams no longer jerked her out of her sleep as they had for so many years after that night. The nightmares now crept upon her, a slow transition that steadily brought her into painful awareness.

She didn't cry loudly, but the tears flowed freely. "Please," she pleaded, not sure what she was begging for anymore. She had loved Randy dearly, and losing him had been a blow she hadn't thought she would be able to overcome. But in time, she had become accustomed to his absence—it was always painful, but it had gotten easier.

Sydney forced herself to slide to the floor and onto her knees, her sobs strong enough to keep her breath from steadying. She had never stopped praying, but she had stopped believing that she would get an answer.

Closing her eyes, Sydney did the only thing she could: she begged for forgiveness. Over the past few years her faith in her prayers had faltered. And now, when she hurt the most, she realized just how badly she needed her Father in Heaven. She had thought the Lord had stopped answering her prayers, had thought that she had done something so terrible that He had stopped listening. But she now knew that it had been her own feeling of guilt that had kept her from trusting Him. In this way she had kept herself from healing.

As she poured out her soul to Him, a spark of warmth began to expand inside her chest, and she cried as she recognized the comforting touch of the Spirit. With conviction, she recognized that the Lord had not left her alone and had never stopped answering her prayers.

In small ways that she had been too blind to recognize, He had helped her grow stronger and taught her to walk on her own again. She remembered the face of the baby that had reminded her that she was glad that she was still alive; she could still hear the words of her bishop reaffirming her beliefs and comforting her with promise. She knew without a doubt that the loving presence of the Lord had sustained her when she had been too weak to stand alone and too lost to realize it. With this new clarity, her prayer turned from one of meek supplication to one of humble gratitude.

When her tears subsided and her breathing returned to normal, she quietly crawled back into bed and turned on her bedside lamp, careful not to make any noise. The second night she'd been back in Washington, the distress of being back on Whidbey Island had brought back nightmares that she had thought she'd already over-come, and she'd called out in her sleep. Her grandparents had rushed into her room, and when they had found her crying on her bed, their worries had intensified. Soon thereafter, young men had started showing up on her doorstep.

The alarm clock read 5:23 A.M. She still had an hour before she would need to busy herself in the stables. Reaching for the scriptures she kept on her nightstand, she turned to where she had left off the day before. There would be comfort here, she knew, and its source was without equal.

* * *

"I won't be back until after the wedding," Jackson explained, wishing that his plans could be changed. But Meredith had been preparing Elizabeth and Patriark for this event for months, and he couldn't miss his sister's performance. "I already sent Adrianne an apology."

Sydney bit her lip and looked around at the abandoned battlements of Fort Casey State Park. They had had lunch on the grass and had spent part of the afternoon exploring the deserted fort. Because the park was large enough and the visitors few enough, they'd been able to spend the afternoon undisturbed.

Sydney hadn't realized that she had been anticipating Jackson's presence at Adrianne's wedding until he told her he wouldn't be there. "I'll miss you," she said. The minute the words left her mouth, she froze, horrified that she had voiced such personal thoughts. Wanting to disappear, Sydney turned her head slightly and looked at anything but him.

"I'll miss you, too," he said, his voice drawing Sydney's gaze. "You know, if it weren't for the wedding and the fact that she's your best friend, I'd ask you to come with us."

She ran her hands along the cold cement walls of the parapet they'd been walking along for the past half hour. "I haven't been to a horse show in years," she reflected.

"Well then, we'll have to remedy that."

It wasn't lost on Sydney that he had said "we," as if he had suddenly assumed the task of granting her wishes. Not knowing how to respond, she chose to remain quiet as they strolled up the cement steps.

Built in 1908, Fort Casey had been constructed on Admiralty Inlet of the Puget Sound. One of three fortifications, intended to defend against a waterborne attack, was eventually decommissioned and turned into a state park. The most popular attraction in the park was a charming lighthouse that had been built, torn down, and rebuilt over the years. What remained of the structure was a white, chapel-like building with a red roof and a single tower. The main draw of a visit to the lighthouse was the chance to travel up the spiral staircase to the top of the tower where, cloaked in fog during the mornings and bathed in sunlight during the afternoons, one could appreciate the prettiest view in the park.

Sydney looked out at the stunning scene from their vantage in the tower. In all the years she'd lived in Washington, she had never been to Fort Casey. She had thought it was merely a boring military camp that would be enjoyed only by war enthusiasts. However, surrounded by empty cement bunkers and a network of iron walkways and stairs, she couldn't help but find the entire scene somewhat fascinating. With the view of the water in front of them and the green, grassy fields behind them, she couldn't imagine that at one time this place had been designated for war.

Jackson came to a stop near the platform of something that looked like a giant, technologically improved cannon. The information placard explained that the "10-inch disappearing gun" was one of two relics on display at the park. Left over from the early twentieth century, the thirty-foot guns were built on immense carriages that were designed to sink down behind concrete parapets after being fired so as to remain hidden from enemy attack. As if frozen in time, the WWI guns remained stationed over an inlet that had never seen battle.

"In October there's an event horse championship in Virginia. It would be a great reintroduction to horse shows. Why don't you come with us?" Jackson asked, folding his arms and leaning against the platform.

Sydney gave him a quick look and placed her foot on the first rung of the iron steps that led up to the massive gun barrel, her hands wrapping around the cold metal handrails. Her steps resounded loudly on the steel staircase as she climbed.

October is so far away, Sydney thought. She was hesitant to make plans that could so easily fall apart. She and Randy had made a great many plans, and she had never imagined that he wouldn't be around to fulfill them. After Randy had died, the moments they'd intended to experience together—birthdays, graduation, weddings—she had lived through by herself. And each one had cut ruthlessly at the wound inside of her.

She had loved Randy. With him, she had felt an easy companionship, a security that had eliminated the need for grand declarations of affection. They had understood each other, had known each other's feelings without having to put them into words. She had believed that this was the only way to love—and that she would never find love again. But she had been wrong on both counts. What she felt for Jackson was different from what she had felt for Randy—and so much more powerful. She was discovering that with Jackson she needed the words; she needed to hear his feelings as much as she felt compelled to express her own. It was almost as if giving them voice in some way fortified them.

She felt safe with Jackson, and when he wasn't with her, she felt his absence in the depths of her heart. She hadn't expected to fall in love with him, yet she wasn't sure if she could live through losing him. She knew from experience that the measure of suffering was directly proportionate to the measure of love. The more one cared for someone, the more pain that person's absence inflicted.

"So much could happen between now and October," Sydney said softly. The day on the yacht had banked many of her fears, but there remained shadows of uncertainty—embers that, like doubt, could be fanned into a fiery panic.

Jackson fell silent at her response and looked at her thoughtfully. He pushed away from the wall and followed her up the steps until he was standing just a few inches from her where she had stopped on a narrow bridge that ended just a few feet behind her. Jackson was blocking the only exit. "Anything could happen between now and tomorrow as well," he said quietly.

Sydney forced a little smile. "I'm just saying that sometimes things are out of our hands."

"And sometimes things are up to us. If you want something, you don't wait for it to happen. You make it happen. If you want to go with me in October, it's up to you."

Sydney looked into the dark blue depths of his eyes and saw only sincerity looking back at her. In that moment, she knew that he would not have asked her if he still had lingering feelings for Carrie. She decided that she must have misunderstood his behavior the day before at breakfast.

Jackson raised a brow at her silence and tilted his head thoughtfully to the side. He watched as the wind played liberally with her hair, which she had left down today. "You know, Sydney," he said, tucking a strand of hair behind her ear, "you'd be surprised how much time can be wasted and how many opportunities can be lost if you stand on the sidelines watching."

Sydney felt, more than saw, the flash of loneliness in his eyes. She wondered if he was talking from personal experience. "Was it really hard for you raising Elizabeth when you were so young yourself?" Sydney asked.

Jackson smiled but didn't hesitate to nod his head. "It was a tremendous adjustment. I did what I thought was right at the time. In retrospect, I can see my mistakes. But when you're living through something, it's hard to see what becomes so clear in hindsight."

"My grandmother tells me that you sacrificed everything to take care of Elizabeth and of Eagle Crest, even when you didn't have to. She said your aunt and David could have easily handled things while you were finishing your schooling."

Jackson shook his head. "She's my sister," he stated as if that explained it all. "It's not a sacrifice when it's for someone you love. Raising Elizabeth was a privilege. When it's something important, something you care about, it all comes down to a simple decision. It was only a matter of shifting my attention to what mattered most. Elizabeth and the ranch became the focus of my life."

Sydney's chest swelled with renewed admiration for the man standing in front of her. He didn't even recognize his sacrifice for what it was. He had given what most people found the hardest to share: he had given of himself. Elizabeth was one lucky young lady to have a brother who loved her so much that he thought it an honor to take care of her. "She was right about you, my grandmother. You are incredibly noble."

Jackson chuckled. "Your grandparents are flattering but often inaccurate. What your grandmother calls noble, Meredith calls reclusive."

Sydney frowned in confusion. "She thinks you're reclusive?"

"She and Elizabeth both."

"Why?"

"When my parents died, and I was left to pick up all the pieces, I didn't have the wisdom to balance everything that was required of me with all the things I might want for myself. I sort of put certain aspects of my life on the back burner."

"You mean, you forfeited your social life in order to focus on your personal life?" she surmised with a small grin.

His mouth lifted up at the corners. "Some would say that they're one and the same," he suggested, leaning a hip against the railing. "I couldn't afford any distractions, and I thought that dating would be the biggest distraction of all. I didn't realize that it didn't have to be that way. Not until much later."

Sydney wondered what had prompted that realization. "Did you and Carrie ever date?" she asked. She could have kicked herself. Instead of sounding casual, the question had come out sounding charged with interest. "I'm sorry. You don't have to answer that. It's none of my business," she stammered, and her face turned bright red. "I don't know why I asked that," she said, and she stepped forward so he would move aside and let her pass. Jackson stood his ground.

"Sydney—"

"It's private, and I shouldn't have asked—"

"Sydney," he said calmly as he took her by the shoulders. "It's okay. I don't mind. It's no big deal."

She quickly ran her hand through her hair in mortification, and when at last she met his stare, her face was hot with embarrassment. "It's a highly personal subject and none of my business," she repeated.

"It's your business if I make it your business."

"Jackson, you really don't have to talk about this. It's not important."

Jackson smiled. "Then don't worry so much about it," he said easily, taking hold of her chin so she would meet his eyes. "Carrie and I dated for a while, yes."

"Okay," Sydney said quickly, pulling her chin free. Her gaze bounced around at anything but him. Her overenthusiastic reply sounded exactly what it was—phony. She was trying to end their conversation, and she was trying for the life of her to squeeze past him.

Jackson chuckled but didn't let her pass. "You trying to drop the subject of my personal life is a little ironic, don't you think?" he said with some amusement, once again pushing away a strand of hair that had blown across her eyes.

Sydney paused. She realized she wouldn't be able to get past him unless she physically pushed him out of the way. Given the fact that he had a good sixty pounds on her—and the fact that they were suspended ten feet in the air—she didn't think that pushing him aside was a good option.

She braced herself and finally looked at him. His eyes were amazing, revealing strengths in his nature that both attracted her and made her apprehensive. When he smiled, his eyes crinkled at the corners, exposing a nature that was easily amused and had a tendency toward kindness. They also revealed a man who was relentless when in pursuit of something he thought was important. When he looked at her the way he was now, his eyes revealed an intensity that she found enthralling. "Why is it ironic?" she asked, finally realizing that he had spoken last and that she was staring.

"It's ironic, Sydney," he began, "because to me, you are *part* of my personal life. An increasingly important part." As he spoke, he cupped the side of her face with his hand, his thumb gently caressing the skin on her cheek as he watched the way a flutter of emotions flashed in her eyes.

Sydney's heart started to thud in her chest. She thought surely he would hear it. She wanted to laugh or say something witty in response to his incredibly intimate revelation, but no sound would come out past her suddenly dry throat.

"That makes you nervous, doesn't it?" he observed frankly.

She managed a small laugh. "You have no problem calling a spade a spade, do you?" she said, and then she grew solemn. "But yes, it does," she admitted, sure that her nerves were quite apparent.

"Do you doubt it?"

Sydney exhaled. "You have to admit, we haven't known each other that long."

"And does that matter?"

"It should." But she knew that it didn't. She felt that she had known Jackson for years, and the feelings she had toward him, though new to her, felt like they had been a part of her for years, growing stronger and more enduring with each passing day.

"But it doesn't matter, does it?" he asked, unwittingly echoing her thoughts as he watched her eyes for the slightest reaction to the conversation.

Sydney shook her head slowly, unable to pull her gaze from his. "It doesn't."

When he lowered his face to meet her lips this time, Sydney was ready. She anticipated the warmth of his kiss, the flash of delight she knew she would feel all the way to her toes. What she wasn't prepared for, however, was the melting away of all her misgivings when she felt the reverence with which he held her.

Though their kiss was brief, it conveyed more than either of their words could have expressed, and Sydney kept her eyes closed when

Jackson pulled away. It wasn't until he took the slightest amused breath that she blinked and managed to focus on his face.

Jackson smiled softly. "I'll be forever grateful to Gabriel."

It took Sydney a moment to follow the change of subject. "Why?"

"If he hadn't called and asked me to pay you a visit about your mare, who knows if we ever would have met."

Sydney cleared her throat, grateful that she didn't feel awkward after their kiss. "Don't tell him that, or you might put ideas into his head." If her grandfather got wind that she and Jackson were anything more than business associates, he would be planning her wedding and buying baby clothes before the week was out.

"Why don't we start heading back?"

Sydney nodded and squeezed past him when he stepped aside for her to go down the steps. "I was thinking that I'd spend a little time with Romeo while you're gone, if you don't mind. I've missed him."

Jackson stepped down onto the concrete next to her and to her surprise took her hand in his, interlocking their fingers as they made their way out of the battlements. "I've kept him busy this past week," he said, but he didn't go into the details. "And yes, you are always welcome to stop in and see him. As a matter of fact, he's there now if you want to see him today."

Sydney nodded and Jackson released her hand so she could go down a set of narrow stairs that led onto the spacious field. "I think I will. Oh, and Jackson," she began.

"Yes?" he answered intently.

"I'll think about October."

Chapter 20

"Just let me get the article I was telling you about," Jackson said as he and Sydney stepped into his office. David kept clippings of all the articles that had been written about any of the horses they had kept at Eagle Crest, and Jackson had told Sydney about the book they had on Romeo. He had a few business calls he needed to make, but he would let her take the book with her before she went out to see her horse. "He was amazing in his last event. The journalist did a great job of describing his skill."

"David really does keep things organized," Sydney noticed, admiring the shelf of leather binders that Jackson was looking through.

"He keeps things running smoothly," he agreed with a smile. "Let's see here," he muttered to himself as he searched though the neatly scripted titles.

"Jackson! It's me, the woman you love most in the world," a voice called out behind them.

Sydney froze, and Jackson turned sharply as Carrie announced her arrival with characteristic flamboyance.

"Sydney and I are back here, Carrie," Jackson announced, sounding to Sydney as if he had deliberately warned Carrie of Sydney's presence.

Carrie's face appeared in the doorway just as Jackson spoke, and she stopped in her tracks, her eyes going from Jackson to Sydney and back again. Sydney could see that Carrie had brought something with her, but as soon as she had stepped into the office, she had quickly hidden it behind her. Though the object was large enough to be seen, Sydney was more focused on Carrie herself. Her rich, dark hair was pulled up into a tousled cluster to give the impression that it had been a last minute effort, yet it looked so perfect in its untidiness that it had to have been done by a professional stylist. If not, life had played a cruel joke on the rest of womankind by making someone as perfect as Carrie.

"Oh, hi, Sydney," Carrie said with a secretive smile as she quickly glanced at Jackson. Some unspoken communication passed between them, and Sydney began to feel a curious sinking feeling in her stomach.

"Hi . . . Carrie." She cleared her throat. "How are you?"

"I'm just perfect," she said, and as if gathering her bearings she breezed into the room and laid an airy kiss on Sydney's cheek before moving on to Jackson. "What are you two up to?" she asked, stepping back to look at them. Before either of them could answer, she swatted at the air as if to dispel any answer they might give. "Anyway, I just stopped by to talk to Jackson. I didn't know that I was interrupting something."

"You're not," Sydney declared quickly. "You're not interrupting anything. I was just leaving." She turned to Jackson. "You can get me that book some other time." She was inching her way toward the door.

"You don't have to leave," Carrie objected, but Sydney got the impression that the words were only a product of her proper upbringing and held no truth at all. Carrie was there for a reason, and it was apparent that Sydney was standing in the way of her getting what she wanted.

"After I'm done talking to Carrie, I'll bring you the book," Jackson said.

"Or I'll stop by this weekend and get it from David. No hurry." Sydney reached the doorway. "It was very nice to see you, Carrie," she added with a brilliant smile. Carrie and Jackson stood near his desk watching her, Jackson with bewilderment and Carrie with amusement. They were beautiful together with their dark good looks. It was no wonder they had dated, and it seemed almost a shame that they weren't still together. Sydney set her thoughts aside before she did or said something to make the situation worse. "See you later," Sydney finally said and, turning on her heel, made her escape.

* * *

A few minutes later Carrie left to talk to Meredith, and Jackson went in search of Sydney. She was not with Romeo, and the grooms said they hadn't seen her. He found her in the parking lot talking to Elizabeth. She was leaning against her Jeep, smiling as his sister went on dramatically about something. Sydney laughed, but when she turned to see him approach, he could have sworn her smile lost a little bit of its sparkle.

"Where have you been?" Elizabeth asked.

"You were going to leave?" Jackson asked Sydney, completely ignoring his sister.

"I didn't want to bother you when you had company."

"It was business." Jackson felt the need to explain.

"Carrie is *not* business," Elizabeth retorted with a bark of laughter. "After meeting Jackson, Carrie's presence at Eagle Crest has never been about business."

"Elizabeth," Jackson warned. He didn't like his sister's tone. Her opinion of Carrie was unfair. Carrie, although a little frivolous, didn't have a mean bone in her body.

"Sorry," Elizabeth said penitently.

His eyes softened as he turned to Sydney. "Here's the book." He handed her a small leather scrapbook.

"Thank you," Sydney said with a tight smile. "I'll get it back to you as soon as possible."

"Take your time," he said, studying her. "You okay?" he asked, ignoring his sister's knowing smile as she watched them both intently.

Sydney's smile was a little too bright. "Of course."

He looked at her carefully for a few seconds and then nodded. Remembering his appointment, he glanced at his watch. "I'm expecting a conference call in a few minutes, but you can feel free to hang around."

Sydney shook her head. "I have to be getting back. I'm sure Adam doesn't appreciate it that I've been skipping out on my share of the work."

Elizabeth sniffed theatrically at the mention of Adam's name.

"Well, I guess I'll see you next week." Jackson could tell Sydney was holding back.

Sydney nodded.

"Give my best to Adrianne and Colin."

"I will. And have fun in Vegas," Sydney said to him and looked at Elizabeth as she straightened from where she'd been resting against the Jeep. "Good luck, Elizabeth. Come back with something shiny."

"If I don't, Meredith will have my hide." Elizabeth smiled and watched as Sydney got into the Jeep.

Jackson and Elizabeth watched as Sydney drove away.

Elizabeth broke the short silence. "She'll make a great sister-in-law."

Jackson rolled his eyes in an imitation of her preferred gesture. "You're incorrigible, and it's way too soon to be talking about marriage."

"Why?" Elizabeth asked as she jogged to catch up with Jackson, who had turned to head back into the stables. "I can tell you're thinking about it."

"And how can you tell?" he asked, distracted. He was thinking about what he had asked Carrie to bring. He had to find a safe place for it, somewhere nobody—especially Elizabeth—might happen upon it.

"Because I've never seen you look at anyone the way you look at her."

Jackson glanced at her sideways but said nothing.

"You see, I don't have this pretty little head for nothing," she said, pursing her lips and tapping at her temple with her forefinger.

Jackson chuckled.

"Aunt Meredith says—"

"Is that all you two do is talk about my love life?" Jackson asked, feeling exhausted.

"Since you happened to finally get one, yes," she said shamelessly. "Anyway, Aunt Mer said that you forgot you were supposed to meet with a buyer last week because you were too busy spending time with Sydney. She said you almost lost a sale."

"David talks too much," Jackson said dryly. That information could have come only from his manager.

Elizabeth shrugged. "So, is it true?"

"Why do you ask if you're so sure already?"

"Because I want to make sure that *you're* sure, too."

"What am I supposed to be sure about, Lizzy?" he asked, being purposely difficult.

"That you're planning to marry her?"

Elizabeth had learned at an early age that if she stated things bluntly it sometimes shocked people into admitting something they would never admit under normal circumstances. However, Jackson knew her antics better than she thought. "I can't make plans without Sydney, and marriage is the furthest thing from her mind."

"So you *are* thinking about it!"

He shook his head in exasperation and quickened his stride, but his sister only hastened her own steps to keep up with him. One of the mares neighed as they passed, and a groom shouted something to another groom somewhere in the background. Everyone was busy doing his or her job, including his sister, who thought her job was to play matchmaker.

"Just admit it, Jackson. Tell me if you're thinking about it. I would love to have Sydney as a sister-in-law. We could ride horses together, and Sydney could come to all of my competitions and actually understand what's going on—unlike Carrie, who thinks that horses are only to be admired from a distance. Heaven forbid she come away smelling like one."

Jackson paused as he stepped over the threshold of his office. He took hold of the doorknob and turned to face her.

Elizabeth stayed just outside the door and watched him expectantly. He knew that if he didn't throw her a bone, she would go in search of one, and he was positive she would start at Sydney's place. "Let's just say that for once I agree with you," he admitted finally.

"I knew it!" she cried out, a massive grin splitting her face as the office door shut inches from her nose.

* * *

"Are you sure it's all right?" Sydney asked.

"Of course it is," David assured her for the third time. "He's your horse, and while he's being boarded here, he needs to be exercised, and you can do it just as easily as one of our grooms. Besides—" he looked at the gelding and then smiled—"you've already saddled him."

Sydney bit her lip and grinned. When she'd called to ask David if she could come over and see Romeo—ride Romeo, actually—he had offered to have the gelding saddled and ready, but she'd insisted she could do it herself.

With her heart in her throat, she had saddled the horse she hadn't seen or ridden in five years. "I've missed you, Romeo," she said, and she smiled when the gelding blew a gentle puff of air and nuzzled her in response. "Are you ready, boy?" she asked softly, looking into his gentle, large brown eyes.

"Why don't you go out to the south paddock?" David suggested. "Ben will show you the way." He nodded toward the young groom who stood next to the stall. "From there, you'll have access to the trails if you get bored of the paddock."

"The paddock will be fine." She smiled.

"If you need anything, let me know. I'll be in the stables."

Sydney nodded. "Thanks for doing this, David. I know how busy you are."

"Don't worry about it. I've been expecting you to call for a while."

"You have?"

"After your first visit, Jackson told me that when you called to ride Romeo, I was to arrange it personally."

"He did?" Sydney didn't know how to respond. It was so characteristic of the man she had gotten to know. He had been perceptive enough to know she would seek out the company of her old horse, yet wise enough to allow her to come to that decision on her own.

She found herself wishing he were there. But she would have to wait for him to return from Las Vegas before she could thank him.

"Let me know if you need anything."

Sydney glanced up. "Thanks again," she said, and she watched him leave. "Where to, Ben?" Sydney asked, turning to the young groom.

Ben led her to a large paddock that was framed by a white, four-board fence and flanked by a spacious grazing pasture and a twisting jumper course that was designed with colorful fences. Sydney felt her pulse pound as she gazed at the setup. "Thanks," she breathed to the groom, and his cheeks flushed as he left.

"Are you ready, boy?" Sydney moved directly in front of the horse so she could look into his face. "What do you say we take a nice, relaxed ride together?"

Romeo blew air from his nostrils, and Sydney smiled. "My thoughts exactly." She lifted her foot into the stirrup. Shifting her weight onto her leg, she hoisted herself up and settled onto his back, biting her lip as a smile broke across her face. "Wow," she whispered, as old, wonderful memories came flooding back.

With the slightest pressure of her legs, Romeo started forward, and Sydney felt his trademark glide as they moved over the ground. She brought him to a trot and enjoyed the smooth, steady pace that he had perfected over the years.

"Look at you. You're practically gliding," she crooned. Riding Romeo was like coming home—the familiar feelings, the familiar smells. He brought with him the love of the sport that she had subsisted on when she was young.

Lost in her thoughts, she took Romeo around the paddock a number of times. When he stopped, she found herself at the fence, staring at the jumper course. Romeo stood tall, his head leaning over the white boards and his eyes trained on the course. He whinnied wistfully.

"Romeo," Sydney chastised, and she nudged him into a canter around the paddock, only to have him stop again at the fence facing the jumping course.

"What's going through that head of yours, boy?" she asked with narrowed eyes.

She pressed with her legs, cueing him to turn around, but instead of turning to the left, he turned toward the entrance of the paddock. Sydney knew what he was doing, and she gently pulled back on the reins. "Romeo," she warned, and he finally stopped.

Sydney bit her lip and looked at the jumper course thoughtfully. She hadn't been through a course in nearly six years, and she'd promised herself she never would again. She had thought she would never want to. Romeo neighed twice, dipping his head as he shifted his weight impatiently.

"I don't think I can," she whispered to Romeo, who nickered loudly. She eyed the course again, nervously learning the layout of the fences.

Releasing her lip from between her teeth and loosening Romeo's reins, Sydney let him take her out of the paddock and toward the jumper course.

"Okay," Sydney yielded, running her hand along his neck as excitement coursed through her. "Now remember," she began as she had before any competition, "this is fun."

Keeping Romeo from taking off into the course, she held the reins in place. She felt his muscles contract in anticipation. "Wait a second," she cautioned softly. "You'll go when I'm ready." His restlessness would have lost them points with the judges, who were looking for perfect obedience in a mount.

With her heart pounding in her chest, Sydney signaled for Romeo to start for the orange-and-white double poles of the hardest jump. She calculated his speed, mentally counting his strides so that they would be perfectly positioned. On the sixth stride, with the fence just before them, Sydney instinctively went into the jumping position by putting her weight on the balls of her feet.

She felt Romeo's muscles bunch beneath her as he lifted his forelegs and pushed off into the air. Sydney lifted slightly off of the saddle, moving forward with the motion of Romeo's body, and flew through the air with him.

For a split second she was in a stadium, surrounded by thousands of people. Colors and sounds disappeared to leave only the rush of adrenaline flowing through her veins and the feel of the powerful horse beneath her as they glided through the air. Her heart expanded in her chest, and the smile that broke on her face was of pure joy.

With a slight jar, Romeo's feet landed back on the ground.

Sydney was laughing loudly. "We did it, Romeo," she shouted, running her hand along his neck and keeping him from heading for another jump just yet. "We did it," she repeated, and her throat was thick with emotion as tears pooled in her eyes.

Swallowing loudly, Sydney looked up at the sky and smiled. "Thank you," she said, closing her eyes. "Thank you."

Chapter 21

White and red flowers filled the large reception tent that had been set up in Adrianne's parents' backyard. The bride and groom had been on the dance floor most of the night, and they were presently dancing to a love song that sounded like it had been written just for them.

"I can't believe she's married," Sydney reflected as she danced with Rob. Adrianne was staring up into Colin's eyes as if looking into the future they were embarking on together.

"Neither can I." Rob spun them slowly until they had a better view of the newlyweds. Adrianne was giggling at something Colin was whispering into her ear.

"I'm going to miss her." Sydney turned back to Rob. "Arizona is so far away." Colin would be attending law school at Arizona State University for the next three years at least, so the couple would be living in the Grand Canyon State.

"That's what we said when you took off to Missouri," Rob said, rocking them to the rhythm of the music.

Sydney smiled. "I know, but I'm back now."

"And in three years, Adrianne will be back too—and most likely with a baby in tow."

Sydney laughed. "If her baby is anything like she was when she was young, she'll have her hands full."

Rob's eyes scanned the room absentmindedly and skidded to a halt when they landed on Carrie. Sydney had noticed that the moment Carrie had arrived at the reception with her parents, Rob's eyes had repeatedly been drawn to her.

He looked away.

"She seems to be enjoying herself."

Rob glanced at Sydney. "Who?"

The corners of her mouth lifted almost imperceptibly. "Carrie."

He shrugged. "I was surprised to see that she came at all."

"Why? Her parents are close friends of Colin's family."

"I know, but people like her only go to red-carpeted, diamond-studded events that are guaranteed to make the front page of the society pages."

Sydney studied him, surprised that he would so harshly judge someone he barely knew. "She doesn't seem so bad. On the yacht she was very hospitable, even."

"And 'yacht' is the key word," he pointed out sourly.

"Just because she doesn't have to work for a living doesn't make her a bad person."

"*You* might not have gotten a chance to talk to her, but I did."

"You did?" Sydney asked, watching the way he avoided making eye contact with her. Suddenly, a thought came to her. "Do you like her?" she asked with suspicion. It would certainly explain a lot. Rob tended to fend for the underdog, and to suddenly find himself attracted to the top dog would be hard for him to swallow.

"No. I don't." He denied it as if she'd accused him of liking a sewer rat. "Don't be ridiculous, Sydney," he said, and he appeared glad when the song finally ended.

"Well, if you don't like her," Sydney began, keeping him from leaving the dance floor by holding her ground, "then why are you so interested in her?"

"Interested in her?" he asked, insulted. "I'm interested in the guy that robbed the bank on Midway Boulevard last week; it doesn't mean I want to date him."

"I didn't say anything about dating," Sydney said pointedly.

Rob went still and scowled. "Why isn't Jackson here?" he asked, suddenly feeling like he was being cornered.

Sydney recognized a change of subject when she heard one, but she went along with it. "His sister is showing a horse in Vegas. He won't be back until tomorrow."

Rob nodded as another slow song started to play.

Sydney caught a glimpse of disapproval in his expression that made her pause. "Do you not like Jackson, Rob?" she asked in confusion.

"Look, Sydney—" He stopped. "I never thought I'd say this, but . . ." He looked down at her, and for a moment Sydney saw the boldness that Josh had displayed the other day when he'd confronted Jackson about his intentions. "Although he's not my first choice for you," he said with a small smile, "Jackson seems like a good man." His expression became serious. "It's plain to see you'll be happy together, and in the end, that's what we all want."

Sydney hugged him, and his arms came around her. She felt overwhelmingly thankful for such a supportive friend. "You have no idea how much your opinion means to me."

Rob pulled back and looked down on her. "I'll remind you of that the next time you take me shopping."

Sydney smiled, because she knew he meant it. "So . . . who's your first choice, then?"

He grinned mischievously. "Me, of course."

"Of course," Sydney repeated dryly.

"Do you want to go get something to drink?" he asked.

"I better sit with my parents." Sydney glanced at their table. "It looks like they're fishing for information."

Rob smiled. "Knowing my mother, she'll be more than happy to give it," he said, and he headed for the buffet table.

Sydney smiled at his retreating back and made her way to where her parents and Rob's parents were seated.

"Rob's mother tells me that he's about to be promoted to detective," Sydney's mother announced delightedly.

"Fingers crossed," Sydney said as she sat down. "Rob deserves the promotion above anyone in his department."

Rob's parents stood up and joined Gabriel and Jane on the dance floor. Sydney smiled when she saw her father dancing with Adrianne. Victor Gabriel Chase had been blessed with looks, superior intelligence, and compassion, but he had been completely overlooked in the rhythm department. "Too bad you have to go back so soon," Sydney said, turning back to her mother.

"Your father has work that needs his attention," she explained. "But you could come visit us. There's nothing stopping you from taking a weekend and flying down to see us."

"I might just do that." She took her mother's hand where it rested on the white tablecloth. "Maybe in a month or two."

"Good. I'll tell your father so he can arrange for some days off."

"Tell me what?" Sydney's father asked as he approached their table and sat down next to his wife.

"Sydney's flying out to visit us next month."

"Maybe," Sydney corrected, although she knew better than to have planted that seed without intending to follow through. Mentioning a visit to her relentless parents was akin to setting the date and buying the ticket.

"So, we'll plan toward the end of the month, then," her father said with a knowing grin.

Sydney chuckled. "For the end of the month," she agreed helplessly.

"So, where is this young man of yours?" her father asked.

"What young man?" Sydney asked, and threads of suspicion began weaving through her mind. "What did Grandpa tell you?"

Her parents were suddenly all wide-eyed innocence. Sydney narrowed her eyes at her grandfather, who was busy dancing with his wife. "I should have known that he couldn't keep from meddling in my social life."

"So there is a social life, then?" her father asked astutely.

Sydney sighed in defeat. "Not really . . . Well, maybe," Sydney stammered, wishing that she had dealt with her feelings before having to explain them to her parents. "I think so," she admitted finally.

Both her father and mother looked delighted at her confession. "My baby is getting married," her mother declared, touching her hand to her heart.

"What!" Sydney nearly shouted, and she immediately glanced around her to see how much attention she had drawn from the guests nearby. "What are you talking about?" she whispered harshly. "No, I am not getting married. I only said that I thought Jackson and I . . . that we're . . . what?" she asked, suddenly confused.

Her parents watched her like vultures waiting for the first signs of a meal. "I'm going to get something to drink," Sydney said in exasperation, and she quickly stood up. She headed for the open tent flaps, where some guests were mingling on what little lawn had been left unoccupied.

There was only a scattering of people standing in the backyard. Wanting to be alone, she was relieved to find that no one had claimed the private gazebo that was concealed in the shadows to the right.

The red, cedar-wood structure had an Asian feel to it that complemented the Japanese-style garden that had taken Adrianne's parents three summers to complete. A trellis, swathed in vines and blossoms, stretched from the two-tiered octagonal roof to the wood railing, and an entrance that faced away from the reception area offered ample privacy. In the far corner of the backyard, there was a veiled opening in the fence, which led into the middle school playground Sydney and Adrianne had often snuck through in their youth.

Sydney made herself comfortable on one of the wicker chairs and relaxed, letting her head rest on the back of the seat. She took a deep breath, smelling the aromatic garden air. Moonlight that was so often concealed by the dense island fog softened everything with a silver glow.

A woman called loudly to someone inside the tent, and the two women made their way onto the lawn. Sydney glanced over and recognized Carrie's mother and a woman she didn't know but had seen with the groom's party.

"Your daughter has really grown up to be a beautiful young woman, Rachel," the blond woman was saying to Carrie's mother as they strolled toward the garden and stopped a couple of feet from the gazebo. "I'm surprised she came alone."

"Well, the young man she would have come with is away on business," Carrie's mother explained.

"So she's seeing someone, then?"

"They've known each other for years," Rachel said with a small smile.

"Is he, you know . . . compatible?" the other woman asked, obviously referring to the size of the man's bank account. *Poor Carrie,* Sydney thought. It was probably really hard for her to find someone who didn't date her for the incredible size of her trust fund.

Rachel smiled uncomfortably. "He does rather well. And what's more, he loves her for who she is and not what she has."

"That's hard to find, whether you have money or not," the other woman said bluntly. "Why hasn't she snatched him up?"

"I believe he was very close to popping the question a couple of years ago, but you know how my husband feels about religion," Rachel said, earning a sympathetic smile from her friend. "This young man doesn't want to make things difficult between Carrie and her father. I think he's just been waiting for the right time." Rachel took a sip of her drink. "They've tried to go their separate ways, but they can't. I think he's still in love with her, and although Carrie doesn't talk about it, it's obvious that she adores him. They've been spending a lot more time together lately. As a matter of fact, he went away on a business trip to Las Vegas yesterday, but before leaving for the airport he stopped by to see her. If that doesn't say something about his priorities, I don't know what else does."

Sydney's eyes narrowed as her suspicion began to mount.

"Do you expect a proposal, then?" the other woman asked.

"I'm crossing my fingers."

"Do I know him?"

"You might. He owns a horse breeding and training facility here on the island."

Sydney felt her heartbeat quicken.

"His name is Jackson Kincaid."

Chapter 22

Sydney froze. Her blood had began to run cold as the suspicion had crept slowly into her mind, but when Rachel had said Jackson's name, it felt like the blood had congealed in her veins. She stopped listening, stopped hearing, as a loud ringing expanded in her ears.

Jackson was in love with Carrie.

Her heart ached. All these years he'd been in love with a woman he couldn't have because her father didn't want a Mormon son-in-law. Hadn't Sydney seen it when they were on the yacht and she had heard Carrie's father tease Jackson about his religion? She had been so blind she hadn't realized that, although he was trying to move on, he was still in love with Carrie.

Sydney shut her eyes tightly. Was that what he'd been doing when he'd taken her out these past few weeks? Trying to get over Carrie? Had she simply been Jackson's attempt to forget the woman he was still in love with?

She felt the agony growing in her stomach.

What a fool she'd been. Everything she had suspected about him and Carrie had just been confirmed. How could she have not seen? *Because he kissed you,* a part of her reasoned. Jackson wasn't the kind of man who would play with someone's feelings if he was still in love with someone else, was he? But he had, hadn't he? Carrie's mother had practically spelled it out. Carrie and Jackson were in love and had been for years. Who would know better than the girl's own mother? *Maybe it was just wishful thinking,* another voice suggested. Sydney shook her head to clear her troubled thoughts.

Sydney got to her feet. She knew she wouldn't be able to go back inside the tent and pretend that her world wasn't collapsing. So, keeping to the shadows and remaining partially concealed by the thick plants and bushes, she made her way to the back of the yard and, unnoticed, slipped through the opening in the fence.

* * *

Rob stood at the opening of the tent and watched Carrie's mother make her way back inside the reception area. He had gone to look for Sydney, and when he hadn't seen her in the backyard, he had been about to return to the tent when he'd heard Carrie's name mentioned. Curious against his will, he stopped and, succumbing to the cop in him, listened for any inside information.

When the conversation had turned to Carrie and Jackson, Rob was suddenly grateful that he hadn't found Sydney. She would be devastated to know that Jackson still harbored feelings for Carrie. Inside him, a profound sense of sadness had quickly been replaced by a fierce sense of protectiveness.

He slipped into the tent in hopes of finding Sydney and keeping her from overhearing something that might hurt her. A small voice within him reasoned that it was most likely a mother's romantic hope that made Rachel Larson believe that Jackson was still in love with Carrie. But the cop in him needed facts. When Jackson returned from Las Vegas, Rob would take a little trip to Eagle Crest and demand an explanation. If his motives weren't good enough . . . well, he'd just have to make sure they were good enough.

* * *

Sydney had intended to leave, but halfway to her car she stopped. She couldn't leave without saying good-bye to Adrianne and Colin, and she couldn't leave without her family. She couldn't run away this time.

She wiped away her tears and put on her best I'm-so-happy-for-you smile. Taking a deep, numbing breath, Sydney headed back to the reception.

Adrianne's younger cousin seized her just as she walked in. "We've been looking everywhere for you. The photographer wants to get some more pictures," the sixteen-year-old informed her with untapped energy.

Sydney followed the young bridesmaid as she left the tent and entered the house, where Adrianne and Colin were posing for the photographer in the formal living room. Two of Adrianne's cousins were waiting to the side in their flowing, lavender chiffon dresses.

The photographers had spent almost two hours on the temple grounds taking pictures of the couple and the wedding party. Sydney hadn't been able to attend the ceremony, but her parents and grandparents told her that it had been absolutely beautiful. From the look on Adrianne's face when she walked out of the temple doors into the idyllic gardens, Sydney could imagine it had been wonderful. *Someday,* she had thought to herself as she had watched her best friend and her best friend's new husband pose for pictures with the white spires of the temple in the background. Someday she, too, might have the privilege of walking through those temple doors and being sealed for time and all eternity to a wonderful man—*to Jackson,* her wistful heart had added.

But now, as she watched Adrianne and Colin, looking no less exultant in the living room of Adrianne's childhood home, she felt that her own dreams of a temple marriage were further away than ever.

"All right, can we have the bridesmaids and the groomsmen line up facing each other?" the photographer requested, motioning with his hand to where he wanted everyone to stand.

"Daydreaming, Syd?" Toby whispered near her ear, making her jump. "Of the day when you'll marry me?" he added with a provocative grin.

Sydney couldn't help but smile then. "Be serious," she reprimanded as she moved into line next to him.

"How do you know I'm not?"

"Because I saw the way you were teasing Carrie earlier . . . and Adrianne's cousins . . . and every other single girl in there."

"I was only trying to make you jealous."

Sydney raised a doubtful brow.

"Well, I did get you to smile, at least," he said with a wink.

"Can I have everyone's attention on the camera, please?" the photographer asked in a businesslike manner, and Toby playfully nudged Sydney's arm.

"Now smile, and remember, your friends just got married," the photographer added for good measure, and the flash went off in time to capture Sydney's elbow connecting with Toby's stomach. The photographer must have noticed, because he glared at them both.

* * *

Sydney waited for Adrianne and Colin to leave for the airport, where they would catch a late flight to their tropical honeymoon. Sydney's parents and grandparents decided to stay and chat a little while longer, so Sydney left them her car keys and caught a ride with Rob.

"Are you sure you don't want to take a drive or get something to eat?" Rob asked.

"I'm really tired." Her ability to keep up the façade was fading fast. "I think I just want to go home." She suspected she would start bawling at any moment, and she didn't want anybody around when she did.

"Do you want me to come inside and we can watch a movie or something?" He seemed worried about her.

"Thanks, but I just want to get to sleep," she explained as he pulled into her driveway. "I appreciate the ride. Maybe you should get back to the reception; it shouldn't be over for a while yet." She glanced at the small time display on Rob's dashboard, which read nine o'clock.

Rob watched her carefully. "Sydney, are you okay?"

She smiled. "Why wouldn't I be okay?" she asked, and then she abruptly turned to get out of the car. "Thanks again, Rob." She walked quickly to her front door. "I'll talk to you tomorrow, okay?" she called and lifted her hand in a wave without turning around.

Her hands shaking, she fumbled with her keys then dropped them on the ground. She bent down to pick them up but couldn't see them past the sheen of tears clouding her eyes. She bit her lip to keep from crying and took a calming breath as she felt around blindly on the ground. Her hand connected with the keys where they'd fallen next to a large potted plant. Just as she was closing her fingers around the keys, a strong, masculine hand snatched them up.

Sydney let her head fall forward, no longer able to stop the tears from falling.

* * *

Rob caught her and held her tight as she sobbed. As her body shook in his arms, he felt like his own heart was being ripped from his chest. He had four sisters and more than two dozen female cousins, so he was used to female tears. He hadn't felt helpless when, a couple of months ago, Adrianne had shown up sobbing at his doorstep after she and Colin had fought and she'd rashly called off the engagement. He had called Sydney, and together they had managed to console Adrianne. Before long, Colin had tracked Adrianne down and was standing outside Rob's house begging her forgiveness. After the newly reconciled couple had left, Rob and Sydney had both expressed their relief that they didn't have relationships of their own to deal with.

He had known what to do then. Now, he was out of his depth. He suspected Sydney's tears had something to do with her feelings toward Jackson, and helping the woman he loved work out her feelings for another man rendered him powerless. Not knowing what to do or say to make her feel better, he said the only thing that came to mind. "Who do you want me to shoot?"

His helplessness must have come through so clearly that Sydney didn't need to look at him to imagine the look of absolute dread on his face. Her laughter started as a chuckle and then grew into loud guffaws that turned into unbecoming snorts, which only served to make her laugh harder.

"Real ladylike, Sydney," Rob teased her affectionately, relieved that she still had a sense of humor. "Why don't we go inside before you wake up the horses?"

They made their way inside the dark house, turning on lights as they went. In the kitchen they found some freshly baked oatmeal cookies that Rob was quick to devour. Sydney made them both some hot chocolate and then sat at the breakfast bar and sipped from a chipped Christmas mug she had picked up at a flea market during her first year at college. Rob, his hunger unsatisfied by the cookies and cocoa, was raiding the cabinets for something else to eat.

"I don't understand. He told me they were just friends." Sydney was staring into her cup, watching the swirls of cream as they settled into soft clouds in her chocolate.

"You don't know for sure that he wasn't telling you the truth." Rob closed one set of cabinets with a soft thump and moved on to another.

"Her mother said that they're practically engaged."

"That doesn't mean anything, Sydney." Why was he defending Jackson? Because he didn't want to see Sydney hurt, that was why. He didn't tell her that he'd overheard the same conversation and that he had every intention of straightening things out with Jackson just as soon as he got back from Las Vegas. "Don't you guys eat?" he complained, finding nothing but raw ingredients and condiments.

"Try the pantry." Sydney absently motioned to the doors on his left.

Rob moved on to the double doors at the end of the kitchen and proceeded to scan the contents. "There's nothing but health food," he complained, picking up a package of rice cakes only to drop it in disgust. "I need to have a talk with Jane about the things she chooses to keep in her pantry."

"Says the guy who just demolished all the cookies," Sydney pointed out dryly. "And what do you mean 'that doesn't mean anything?' It means he lied to me," she insisted.

"Sydney, not everything is what it appears to be. Carrie's mother talking about her daughter might be something like Gabriel talking about you. If I were to believe the things that came out of your grandfather's mouth, I'd have to believe you were perfect."

Sydney glared.

Rob grinned. "You need to go talk to Jackson."

* * *

Sydney's parents had had an early flight back to Texas a few hours before Jackson had returned to Washington. They had expressed their regrets at not getting a chance to meet Jackson, and Sydney had promised that she would visit them within the next month.

Since then, Sydney had done her best to avoid seeing Jackson, but she was running out of excuses. After returning from Las Vegas, he had stopped by to see her, but she'd been out with Adam picking up supplies for the horses. When he had shown up at one of her classes, she had evasively declined his invitation to dinner by claiming exhaustion. Whenever he had called her, she'd been polite but vague.

She knew that she couldn't keep up the cat-and-mouse game much longer. She needed to speak to him, to set things straight. Sydney had spent a lot of time thinking, and she knew what she had to do. First, she needed to know if Jackson was in love with Carrie. If he was, then she would simply walk away, no matter how badly it stung. After all, she couldn't blame him. It wasn't easy to forget someone who had once occupied your heart; she knew that better than anyone. How could she expect Jackson to move on from Carrie so quickly when she herself felt the pain of losing Randy?

There was no need to tell him what she'd heard or to make things more difficult. She would simply tell him that things weren't going to work for her. If what Carrie's mother had said was just wishful thinking, then this would give Jackson the chance to clear it up. But if there was any truth to it, if any part of Jackson was still in love with Carrie, then this would give him an easy way out.

Standing in the stables at Eagle Crest, Sydney gave Romeo one last caress and looked into his huge, almond-colored eyes. "What do you think, old friend?" she asked her cherished horse. "You don't have these kinds of problems, do you?" She rubbed her forehead against his cheek and lost herself in her thoughts. "I'm going to miss him," she whispered sadly.

She straightened and took a last look at her horse. "Wish me luck." Romeo shook his head with a loud grunt.

She wouldn't run this time. She would face her fear and accept the consequences. Sydney took a deep, fortifying breath and headed for Jackson's office.

* * *

The office door was open. Jackson was sitting at his desk with piles of documents and contracts covering the entire surface. He ran a frustrated hand through his already messy hair and leaned back in his chair, exhaling loudly. He raised his eyes and froze when he saw Sydney standing in the doorway.

"Sydney." He felt stunned and relieved to see her standing there. He'd been unable to concentrate on anything, and his work had been suffering. The only thing he had managed to do was think of her.

He knew something was wrong. Sydney had avoided him since he'd returned from Las Vegas, and he didn't have the slightest idea why.

"Hi," she said hesitantly as he watched her.

"Come in." He sprang to his feet and walked around his desk. "Please, come inside. Have a seat." When it appeared that she was planning on just standing in the doorway, he led her to one of the armchairs. When she finally sat, he took a seat across from her. "I've missed you," he confessed, and Sydney smiled uncertainly.

"I . . ." Sydney had been about to tell him that she'd missed him as well and quickly caught herself. "Jackson, I came because I needed to talk to you about something."

Jackson sat back, instantly detecting her reserve. "About what?" he asked, suddenly on guard. She was having a hard time looking him in the eye, and he wondered why.

"I've had a lot of time to think these past few days," she began.

"About what?" he asked again.

She glanced at him and then looked away, her eyes landing on the painting Carrie had done of Patriark, which hung above his desk. "Well . . ." She paused. "What if you had a friend that you were very close to, that you cared for very much? Do you know someone like that?"

"Yes." He wondered what she was getting at.

Sydney nodded.

"And so do you." His eyes narrowed.

"Yes," she agreed. "Well, suppose those feelings didn't go away." When his brow furrowed, she continued. "Suppose that you suddenly didn't just care for them, but that . . . you found that you . . . loved them . . . and that no matter what you did, you couldn't stop loving them." Jackson's eyes sharpened. "But suppose that there were certain . . . people . . . that might be standing in the way of these two people being together." She hoped he understood without her having to go into the details.

"What are you trying to say?" His heart went cold as he watched her. Was she saying that she was in love with Rob?

"I'm asking whether you think that I—" She stopped herself. "If you think the right thing to do would be for the person who's standing in their way to step out of the picture."

Jackson sat silently, his eyes searching hers, but she seemed almost embarrassed to look at him. He had a sinking feeling that although she was too scared to say it, she was in love with Rob and wanted Jackson to step aside so that she didn't have to feel guilty about choosing between them.

"Jackson. Do you understand what I'm asking?" She looked at him beseechingly.

He swallowed, feeling like he had been punched in the stomach. He wanted to shout that there was no way in the world he was going to give her up. He wanted to demand that she tell him in plain words that she didn't want him. But she looked so afraid, and she had been through so much already, that he couldn't bear to add more to the burden she carried on shoulders that seemed so frail. So he nodded.

"You do?" she asked.

"You think that these two people should be together regardless of who else might have feelings for them." He was surprised that he could speak so clearly when it felt like his heart had been twisted in a vise.

Sydney nodded slowly, searching his face. "Do *you*?"

"If that's what you want."

"Is that what *you* want?" she asked.

"I want you to be happy," he said.

"I'll be fine."

"Sydney?" he asked in a last attempt to dissuade her. "Are you sure about this?" He wanted to tell her that he loved her, that he could make her happy, but he said nothing. She had come here for an easy way out, and as badly as it hurt, he would give it to her.

Sydney didn't answer for a while. She glanced at Carrie's painting again and her eyes fell to the floor. Finally, she nodded and looked at him sadly. "I'm sure." She stood up slowly.

Jackson rose to his feet with her, wanting to take her into his arms, wanting to make her see that he was the one for her. Hadn't he always thought there was something between Sydney and Rob? Why hadn't she said anything before? Maybe she hadn't been sure of it until Jackson had come into the picture. "I'll walk you out."

"No!" she blurted. "No," she repeated more calmly. "I'll go alone. You stay. You look busy." She started toward the door, bumping into the armchair on her way out. "I'm sure that you have a lot of work to do." She backed up until she knocked into the open door. "I have a lot of work to do, too." She stammered over her words.

Jackson stuffed his hands in his pockets to keep from reaching for her.

Stopping in the doorway, Sydney looked up with a small smile. "Thank you, Jackson," she said softly. "I think you're . . . wonderful." She swallowed with difficulty. "I hope you will be very happy together."

Finally, she turned and walked out of his office and out of his life. For a long time he stood there, hands in his pockets, staring at the spot where she'd been standing. He didn't want her to think he was wonderful; he wanted her to love him . . . to marry him.

On wooden legs, he walked around his desk and fell into his chair. Her words cruelly ran through his mind. She hadn't had the courage to come out and say it clearly, but she'd had the nerve to wish him happiness? He would have thought she was being deliberately cruel had he not known that she wasn't capable of it.

"I hope you'll be happy . . ." He gave a short, humorless laugh as her callous parting words echoed in his head.

Of course he wouldn't be happy without her. Since the day he'd met her, his life had taken on a different purpose.

He rested his elbows on his desk and let his head fall into his hands. What had happened to change what had been growing between them? He had been sure that she shared his feelings.

He couldn't back down and let her get away. He was in love with her, and he truly felt that she was in love with him, even if she didn't realize it yet. He would give her a little time—a couple of hours—but he wouldn't accept defeat until he had shared his feelings with her, until she knew exactly what he felt for her and how happy he could make her.

"I hope you'll be happy together."

Jackson stiffened. He slowly raised his head out of his hands. What had she said? What had she meant by *together*? Together with whom?

Jackson leaned back in his chair and mentally replayed their conversation. He was almost positive that she had said, "I hope you will be happy *together*." The only person he could even fathom being happy with was Sydney, and if she hadn't been talking about herself, then who had she meant?

Something wasn't adding up, and he intended to find out what.

* * *

Rob was in the process of installing a new engine in his Mustang. He was determined that even if it took him ten years, he would get this car working and have himself a great ride when all was said and done.

He couldn't count the days he'd spent up to his elbows in grease, working in the garage of his two-bedroom house. He had yet to hear the engine turn over, but if there were two things that Rob had in abundance, they were determination and willpower. It wasn't yet nine A.M. on his day off, and he was already covered in grease and grime.

That was how Jackson found him—in an old pair of jeans and an oil-stained T-shirt that had "police" written in big, black letters across the front. Rob had been working on the carburetor and had black grease all over his hands. He wiped them thoughtlessly on his pants and was about to dig back beneath the hood of the car when he saw Jackson walk up his driveway. Rob straightened and reached for the rag he had stuffed into his back pocket.

He wiped his hands. "What are you doing here?"

"Do you have a minute? I need to talk to you about something."

Rob gave a humorless laugh. "That's funny, because I wanted to talk to you, too."

Jackson raised his brow. "Is there a problem?"

"You could say that."

Rob knew that Sydney was in love with Jackson, and he also knew that this wasn't something that happened to her often. She had promised him that she would talk to Jackson and clear things up. Rob had been waiting for her to make good on her promise before he took matters into his own hands. But now Jackson was giving him the perfect opportunity to find out what was going on between him and Princess Carrie.

Gut instinct told him that Jackson wasn't the kind of guy who would do something like that, and his gut had never been wrong. There had to be a good explanation, and he planned on giving Jackson a chance to give it. And if the details and reasons didn't satisfy him, then he would make sure Jackson never went near Sydney again.

"I sense some hostility," Jackson said, his eyes narrowing.

"Curiosity," Rob clarified. "You see, I heard a nasty rumor about you and Carrie." Rob honed in to detect any signs of guilt.

"Carrie Larsen?" Jackson asked with a confused look.

"The only Carrie I know," he answered unblinkingly.

"What kind of rumor?"

Rob watched him carefully. He was either a phenomenal actor, or he really didn't know what was going on. "The one that says you're still in love with her," he said slowly.

There was a long silence as Jackson seemed to digest the information. He didn't squirm or search for a ready excuse as Rob had expected. On the contrary, like a computer, he seemed to analyze and catalog the details. "Who did you hear this from?"

Rob could see him scrutinizing the information like a seasoned investigator. "I overheard Rachel Larsen talking to another woman."

There was a razor-sharp shift in Jackson's expression. "When?"

"At Adrianne's wedding reception."

Jackson stilled. "Did Sydney overhear this conversation?"

"I didn't think so at first. I was the only person out in the garden, besides a few of Adrianne's relatives."

"But?" Jackson prompted.

"Turns out she was sitting in the gazebo and heard every word," Rob said, and he felt the beginnings of tremendous relief as he began to be more sure that what he'd heard hadn't been accurate. Unless his senses were failing him, Jackson was above suspicion.

"She came to see me today," Jackson explained.

"What did she say?" Rob asked with a worried frown. Sydney had promised to go see Jackson to clear the air. If Jackson was here, then something had gone wrong in the process.

"That she hoped we'd be happy together."

"She hoped who'd be happy together?"

"Apparently, Carrie and I."

"Did you tell her she was wrong?"

"I didn't know until now that was what she was implying," Jackson stated simply. "Initially, I got the impression she was there to see me because of her feelings for you."

"Me?" Rob asked in amazement. "Sydney and I are just friends," he defended.

Jackson didn't say anything, but the message conveyed on his face was enough to tell Rob he hadn't fooled him. Rob knew he would have to work on his game face. What kind of a detective wore his feelings like a billboard across his forehead?

"We're just friends," Rob repeated. He was as reluctant to go into the details as Jackson seemed to be to hear them. But there was an unspoken understanding between them. In that moment, Rob knew that Jackson understood the way things were with him and Sydney—understood and sympathized. Nothing else needed to be said.

Jackson nodded once in acknowledgment.

"What are you going to do about it?" Rob asked, tossing his rag beneath the hood and glancing at his watch. "She should be about to start one of her lessons soon."

Jackson shook his head. "I'm not going over there."

Rob's mouth dropped open in surprise. "What do you mean you're not going over there? You need to explain what happened!"

"I will when the time is right."

"When the time is right? Are you telling me you're going to let her continue to believe that you're in love with Prin—with Carrie?"

"I'm telling you nothing at all," Jackson said calmly. "What I intend to do is my business."

Rob raised a brow. In this brief exchange he had learned two things about Jackson: he wasn't easily intimidated, and he didn't take orders well. Rob's opinion of him went up a notch. "She means a lot to me. I don't want to see her hurt," Rob explained, needing to know that Sydney would be all right. By yielding just enough of his feelings, he hoped to encourage a similar capitulation in Jackson. If the man was anything like what Rob suspected, then he would accept the concession and offer one of his own.

Jackson was silent, as if weighing the man standing before him. His eyes gave nothing away, and Rob got the feeling Jackson had missed his true calling. Jackson would have made one heck of a detective.

"I won't hurt her."

Rob nodded. One heck of a detective, indeed.

Chapter 23

"Grandpa," Sydney said with some surprise. She'd been lost in her tumultuous thoughts when a small sound had made Gabriel's presence known. "I didn't see you standing there," she said, straightening, and she released Aladdin's foreleg from where she'd been checking the horseshoe.

"I've missed you lately. A grandfather should never have to make an appointment to see his granddaughter." He leaned up against the barn door. Like always, he was immaculately dressed. He should have looked out of place in the stable in his black slacks and blue knit shirt, but he didn't. Instead, he looked like he had been born and raised among horses.

Sydney smiled up at him and ran an admiring hand over the Arabian's sleek neck. "I'm sorry." She glanced back at the horse. "I've been a little busy lately."

Gabriel nodded pensively. "When's the farrier due?" he asked, looking at Aladdin's hooves, which were in obvious need of a trim and new shoes.

"Scheduled for this afternoon, actually." She glanced up with a smile that was a little too bright. "Good thing, too," she said, and she lifted the horse's leg again. "It's been almost five weeks, and all the horses need new shoes." She dropped the leg and set the pick down.

Gabriel watched the top of her head as she inspected her hands. "Adam's at Eagle Crest?"

Sydney's hesitation was barely discernible. She nodded. "He's gone out a couple of times to see if Duchess is settled yet."

"I would think you'd want to be the first to be there when she's pregnant."

Sydney smiled. "Once she's settled you won't be able to keep me away from Eagle Crest."

"I just got off the phone with Meredith."

"Oh?" she prompted nonchalantly. "What did she have to say?"

"Her birthday is a week from Friday, and she's having a few friends over. She called to extend an invitation. I accepted—for the three of us."

Sydney's smile faltered. "I'm afraid that I won't be able to make it." She took the brush she'd set on top of the stall door and started grooming Aladdin. A couple of the other horses neighed as if they, too, wished to be under the massaging bristles.

"Why not?" he asked. Sydney could hear the suspicion in his voice. She had to think quickly.

"I probably won't be here." She made the decision instantly. "I was thinking of going to visit Mom and Dad."

"How long are you planning on staying?"

"I don't know . . . for a few days," she said, not daring to look at him.

"When do you plan on leaving?"

"Friday morning. I have to teach a riding class on Thursday."

"Well, it sounds like fun," he said slowly. "Anyway, I've got a few things I need to finish before dinner. See you later," he said, and before she knew it he was gone.

Sydney stared at the empty doorway. His exit had been quick— very unlike him. Gabriel didn't do anything—anything—thoughtlessly. She stood there retracing her steps in the conversation she'd had with her grandfather, trying to detect anything that might have caused his odd and sudden retreat. When she was unable to pinpoint anything, she shook her head and dismissed her suspicions.

* * *

Two days later, Sydney hurried to answer the tack-room telephone. Her students had gone home over an hour ago, and she had just finished putting the horses to pasture.

"This is Sydney," she said as she picked up the receiver.

"Sydney, it's Adam."

"Is everything okay?" she asked, instantly alert. Adam had been going to Eagle Crest in her place every day to check on Duchess. Sydney had been too much of a coward to risk running into Jackson. The pain hadn't disappeared, but it had dulled a little, and in its place a fresh sense of anger was growing. Why had she backed away? She should have demanded an explanation. She should have asked her questions more clearly and received a clear answer. She was in love with Jackson and she should have told him.

"Duchess has settled. You might want to come over here," he said, and the excitement in his voice revealed his love for the snooty mare.

"She's pregnant? Are you serious?"

"When have I not been?" he said flatly, and Sydney smiled.

"I'll be right over."

She made the drive in nearly half the time it should have taken and found Adam and David in the breeding stables, where they stood watching the veterinarian examine Duchess.

Adam turned around in time to see her come through the doors. "Dr. Cooper just did the ultrasound. It looks like you'll be the proud owner of a healthy foal in about eleven months."

Sydney laughed and threw her arms around him. "I can't believe it," she exclaimed, controlling her urge to jump up and down. Adam patted her arm paternally and smiled at her enthusiasm.

"It couldn't have gone more perfectly." David grinned.

Sydney released Adam and turned to David. "So what happens now?"

"We'll have Duchess and Patriark stay together for a couple of weeks just to make sure she holds. Then we'll move her into our foaling facility, where we'll have her under twenty-four-hour foal watch. From there, it's just a matter of waiting."

"I can't believe it's really happening." Sydney turned to look at the vet, who was instructing one of her assistants to clean up the ultrasound machine. She stood and joined them.

"Everything looks great." She extended her hand to Sydney. "I assume you own Duchess?"

"Yes. I'm Sydney Chase." She returned the smile and shook her hand. She was a nice-looking woman in her early thirties.

"Dr. Tammy Cooper." She glanced back at her two assistants. "I don't foresee any complications, but we'll keep a close eye on her for the next few weeks."

"Great," Sydney said as a teenage boy proceeded to take Duchess back to her stall. She stopped him and reached up to pat her mare's head. "Hey girl. You did great, didn't you?" She received a few gentle nudges from Duchess as she inhaled her scent. "Yes, you did." She spoke softly and kissed her horse's cheek.

"She's a beauty," Dr. Cooper said appreciatively.

"Yes, she is," Jackson agreed from where he stood leaning back against the wall, his arms folded across his chest. The direction of his gaze made it obvious to everyone that he wasn't speaking about Duchess.

Sydney's head shot up in surprise, her hand inadvertently pulling on Duchess's bridle and causing the mare to recoil slightly. She turned and quieted her horse, scrambling for something to say. She hadn't thought that she would run into Jackson, since Adam had said that he hadn't seen him at all during the past week.

"Well, I have a few more appointments before I can call it a day," Dr. Cooper said, turning to Sydney. "It was nice to meet you, and if you have any questions at all, give me a call," she said to both Sydney and Adam.

"Thank you." Sydney smiled, and the veterinarian turned to her assistants as they prepared another machine. Sydney stepped aside and allowed Duchess to be escorted from the vet lab.

"I've got some paperwork to finish," David announced. "If you want to follow me, I'll get you that information you asked for, Adam."

"Great." Adam started following David out. "I'll see you back at the ranch," he told Sydney, and before she could make a fool of herself and beg him to stay, he was gone.

She tried to stuff her hands into her pockets but realized she was still wearing her pocketless riding breeches. She finally looked up at Jackson and let her hands drop to her sides. Where had all that righteous anger gone, she wondered.

"How have you been, Sydney?" he asked, watching her as if drinking in the sight of her.

"I've been great," she lied. In reality she'd been in absolute agony.

Jackson nodded slowly, all the while watching her intently. "I've missed you."

Sydney frowned, not knowing what to make of his statement. "How's Carrie?"

"Good, I think," he said, not blinking. "I haven't seen her for a while. Come to think of it, I haven't seen much of you, either, except for your short visit last week."

"I've been busy," she explained softly. Couldn't he see that she was in love with him? Didn't he know that seeing him was more than she could bear?

"I know." He came toward her. "And I got to thinking about your parting words," he said, stopping just inches away from her. "It wasn't until after you left that I realized what you had said." He searched her face. "You remember what you said, right?"

She looked away and nodded. How could she forget the words that had shredded her heart into a million pieces—words that she hoped had sounded sincere?

I hope you'll be happy together.

Jackson echoed her thoughts. "'I hope you'll be happy together.' For a while, I didn't know what you meant by that," he said, and she looked up at him with a puzzled frown. "You see, at first I thought you had come to tell me that you were in love with Rob and that you wanted me to back out of the picture."

Sydney's brow was furrowed in confusion and she opened her mouth to speak, but Jackson spoke first. "It wasn't until later that I realized you were talking about me and Carrie, that you thought I was in love with Carrie and hoped to marry her even though I had started something with you. And that you thought I was the kind of man who would do that."

Sydney swallowed as she saw the hurt in his eyes. A small seed of hope began to extend its roots into her chest.

"You were right about one thing. I am in love, Sydney. But not with Carrie, regardless of what her mother wants to believe."

Sydney finally found her voice. "You aren't going to marry Carrie?"

He stared at her so long it seemed that he wasn't going to respond. "I want you to ask yourself what kind of man you think I am. When you can answer that question, you'll have your answer," he said, and then he quietly turned around and walked away.

Sydney watched him go, wanting to shout that she already knew the answer. The way Jackson treated Elizabeth and Meredith was a reflection of his true character, and a man like that would not have betrayed her.

Why hadn't she believed him when he'd said that he and Carrie were just friends? Because she'd been afraid and would have used any excuse to run from what she was feeling for him.

She had willingly been blinded by what she'd heard at the reception. The reason she hadn't been angry at Jackson was because a part of her hadn't believed that he was capable of betrayal. If she could fool herself into believing the worst, then she wouldn't have to admit that she was completely in love with him.

Sydney knew that when you fell off of a horse, you had two choices: get back on or get back on. If you let fear keep you from riding, it would grow so strong it would keep you from what you loved. But if you put your trembling foot back into the stirrup and tried again, only then would you find true freedom. She had taught this to her students, and now it was time for her to learn the lesson herself.

"Are you okay?"

Sydney jumped and turned to look at Dr. Cooper, who stood in the far corner with her assistants, readying the space for another horse. She was standing there watching her with concern. "I'm fine," Sydney answered quickly. "I've got something . . . I have to go," she said, and hurried out.

* * *

Sydney stared out at the water beneath the Deception Pass Bridge. She sat on the same beach where she and Jackson had shared their first kiss. The sun-bleached, skeletal remains of trees were scattered on the beach. She gave in to the temptation to take off her shoes and let the pebbles that lined the coast massage the soles of her feet. The sun had decided to show its elusive face and, as was typical of Washington weather, it would soon be hidden again by a thin cover of clouds.

"I want you to ask yourself what kind of man you think I am. When you can answer that question, you'll have your answer." Sydney felt guilty as she remembered the look on his face.

Two days ago, when she'd seen him at Eagle Crest, she had wanted to run, because seeing him and knowing they couldn't be together made her heart ache. Now, recalling the pain she had inflicted by not trusting him, she knew that there wasn't a place far enough away for her to flee from her regret.

Yesterday she had gone back to Eagle Crest with David to see Duchess, and her legs had actually trembled at the thought of running into Jackson. She wasn't yet sure if it had been born of apprehension or yearning, but she hadn't stuck around to find out.

She'd been running for nearly six years. In the beginning, she hadn't needed an excuse. After Randy had died, her pain had been so raw that she had fled blindly, with no thought for who and what she left behind. As the years went on, she had started excusing her absence from Washington and her reluctance to date by blaming her pursuit of an education thousands of miles away. By the time she had arrived back on Whidbey Island, her excuses had gotten more desperate and feeble. She hadn't even realized that she'd been looking for a reason to end her and Jackson's relationship. But when the opportunity had presented itself in the form of Carrie Larsen's mother, she'd jumped to break off what they had started. She had chosen to believe that there was still something between Carrie and Jackson, because it had meant a chance to break away from the feelings that had burst inside of her since meeting him. Better to hurt a little now than to endure the unbearable hurt that might come later. She was ashamed that she was just now realizing the extent of the damage Randy's accident had caused in her. She had been so caught up in herself that she hadn't been able to see what she'd been doing, how she'd been living.

She was in love with Jackson. She was able to admit that to herself. Now, she needed to admit it to him. She couldn't run anymore. She couldn't pretend that she didn't have feelings simply because declaring them might hurt. If falling in love meant risking her heart, she was going to have to take that chance. It was better than the life she'd been living.

"You're one tough lady to get a hold of these days."

Sydney jumped in surprise and turned to see Rob coming toward her, the smooth pebbles clacking beneath his shoes. "Hey," she said with a wide, welcoming smile. "What are you doing here?"

"I felt like talking to a friend. And since Adrianne is on her honeymoon, that means you."

Sydney smiled. "Am I your second choice, Rob?"

"I love seconds."

Sydney laughed quietly. "How did you know I was here?"

"Adam told me," he said as he took a seat next to her on the massive piece of driftwood. "I must admit that it surprised me a little."

"That I told anyone where I was going?"

He shook his head. "That you came here at all. You usually avoid the water, but lately I've noticed you've been drawing closer to it."

She looked out over Deception Pass. There wasn't a single boat in sight, and there hadn't been for the past hour. "I'm seeing things a little more clearly lately." It was ironic that she had come to the water to confront the ending of one part of her life so she could embrace the beginning of another.

"Is that so?" he said, watching her profile.

She nodded and gave him a quick look.

"Like what things?" he prodded, always the cop looking for details.

Sydney took a deep breath and exhaled slowly as she watched him. "Two things in particular." When Rob patiently waited for her to elaborate, she looked back out at the water. She had realized while sitting on the beach that she had never really been afraid of the water. She had been afraid of how quickly things could change, how suddenly her life could be rearranged without her consent. Now she was beginning to realize that her reactions were a matter of choice—stay down or get back up and fight. She had stayed down for almost six years, but now she was tired of running, tired of being afraid, tired of learning too late that her reactions had hurt people who were very dear to her.

"I saw Jackson the day before last."

"And?"

"He seemed hurt that I had doubted his sincerity."

"Did you apologize?"

"I didn't get a chance."

"What do you mean, you didn't get a chance?" Rob looked at her closely. "If you're alive, then you still have a chance. You're sitting here feeling sorry for yourself and wasting sixty minutes of perfectly good chances."

Sydney watched him, open-mouthed. "By all means, don't hold back," she said dryly.

Rob paid no attention to her remark. "So, are you going to go talk to him?"

She nodded.

"Need a ride?"

Sydney laughed. "No. I don't need a ride, Rob. But I will go. I promise." Her smile lost some of its radiance. "I just hope it's not too late."

"As in, 'two days have gone by and he might not love me anymore'?"

She grinned. "As in, 'I hurt him so badly that he might not forgive me.'"

"If he's in love with you, he'll forgive you."

Sydney watched his eyes, and her smile faded. "That brings me to the second thing I realized while sitting out here."

"What's that?" he asked, sounding relieved to know that she was going to go talk to Jackson. He was scanning the pebbles around his feet and reaching for one the color of pewter and as smooth as glass.

"You."

Rob's pause was almost unnoticeable. She could see why he would make a great detective. His face gave nothing away, and she wouldn't have noticed his hesitation if she hadn't been looking for it. He watched her without saying anything as he rubbed the stone between his fingers.

"You see, after talking to you the other day, I got to thinking about what you'd said about having been in love. I tried for the life of me to figure out who the girl was that had captured and then shattered your heart. I wanted to think up some horrible torture for her." She spoke without humor but looked straight at him with complete candor. She knew he deserved at least that much. "It wasn't until today, sitting here alone with my thoughts, that I realized who that girl was."

Rob's eyes didn't waver, but they softened as he watched her.

"I didn't know, Robby."

Leaning back, Rob took a deep breath and released it. Relaxing his shoulders in defeat, he smiled compassionately. "Don't beat yourself up about it, Syd. I didn't know for a long time either." He chuckled when he saw her expression. "Don't think it's an everyday occurrence that my feelings of friendship grow into something deeper. It blindsided me when I realized it."

"Why didn't you tell me?" she asked miserably.

Rob chuckled. "Why haven't you told Jackson how you feel?"

Sydney nodded in understanding.

"If it makes you feel any better, Syd, I didn't realize what I was feeling until just recently."

"I really had no idea." She swallowed. "Adrianne kept telling me—"

"Adrianne?" Rob frowned.

Sydney nodded. "She kept telling me that you were interest—"

"Wait a second." He stopped her. "Adrianne knew?" When Sydney nodded again, he shook his head in astonishment. "She never told me." He rubbed his hand over his face and murmured something about working on his poker face.

"She probably didn't want to embarrass you."

"We're friends," Rob objected, suddenly insulted. "There shouldn't be any secrets between the three of us." He exhaled with a grin.

Sydney returned his knowing smile. "You should talk."

His smile was heart stopping, and Sydney couldn't help but wonder what the girl he married would be like. He was one of the most handsome men she knew, and he was so good and honest. She couldn't wait to see him fall in love with someone who both deserved and reciprocated his feelings. He deserved nothing but the best; she just hoped he would find it soon. "Let's just agree that if you decide to leave that bum of a horse breeder and fall for me, you'll tell me."

"You'll be the first to know," she answered.

"I would hope *you* would be the first to know, but who's complaining," Rob shrugged.

He reached for her and she went easily into his arms as she had many times over the years. "I love you, Rob," she said as she hugged him.

"That was quick," he said with an arched brow. "Do you want to break the news to Jackson, or should I?"

Sydney's laughter echoed softly off the cliffs.

Rob pulled back to look at her. "I love you, too, Syd," he said, growing solemn. He placed a kiss on her forehead.

Chapter 24

Jackson couldn't think.

He'd been sitting at his desk for the past two hours and had stared at the same contract for half that time. Three days had gone by, and he was in serious danger of losing some clients due to his absentmindedness. David had begun coming in periodically and taking away work to complete in his own office so that they didn't fall so far behind that it caused a problem.

Meredith and Elizabeth had noticed his lack of concentration, but surprisingly, they hadn't broached the subject with him. Word traveled fast in the stables, where everyone was an effective and willing accessory to gossip. He was sure that what had transpired between him and Sydney that day in front of the veterinarian had quickly made its rounds until it had reached Elizabeth and Meredith. He suspected they were just biding their time, like spectators waiting for the curtain to rise on the next scene. Oh, he didn't doubt they would step in and offer their opinions the minute he deviated from what they considered proper behavior in the get-Sydney-back plan. What was worse, he didn't put it past them to go straight to the source and approach Sydney herself.

Although he knew the reason for it, he was hurt that Sydney hadn't trusted him. He had wanted her trust more than he had wanted anything else before. He knew that her reasons for being afraid far outweighed her reasons for trusting, but he had hoped that they were beyond that stage.

He would give her until the weekend before he went after her. He would give her enough time to think about the kind of man she believed him to be. If she didn't come around by then, he would have to convince her. But there was something he wouldn't do no matter what, and that was give up on her. Sydney had opened his eyes and given him a glimpse of what he'd been missing by being alone. If she wasn't ready yet, then he would wait. But he would make sure she knew that he was willing and waiting. He would keep coming around until he became so engrained in her life she wouldn't be able to imagine it without him. He would make himself as important to her as she was to him.

The more she saw of him, the more she would see how much she needed him in her life and how much he needed her in his. And that being the case, he might not wait until the weekend after all. Maybe he would go over there tomorrow. He might as well go over there today. Jackson was halfway out of his chair before he noticed her standing in his doorway.

Neither of them spoke, but Jackson could see the tension in the stiffness of her shoulders and the white-knuckled grip she had on her purse. She had left her hair down, and it framed her face, pronouncing the expressive eyes that reflected her tremendous discomfort.

Sydney had dressed in blue jeans and a simple, white, V-neck T-shirt. Her square-heeled boots were clean and offered her an advantage of another two inches of height, making her look particularly slender. "Hi." Her voice cracked. She cleared her throat and tried again. "Hi," she said more loudly.

"Hi," Jackson replied, not realizing until then that he had remained in a half-raised position. He lowered himself back into his leather chair and waited.

"Can I come in?" she asked hesitantly.

"You're always welcome here, Sydney." He watched her walk into the room, filling it and his life with the light that had been missing since her absence.

Sydney smiled cautiously.

Although she'd been a constant presence in his thoughts, he felt as if he hadn't seen her in years. Watching her standing in his office, it struck him just how breathtaking she was. "Sydney, you're beautiful," he said.

* * *

Sydney reached up to her hair to make sure that it wasn't wind-tossed and sweat-drenched as it usually was after class. But she had prepared. After dismissing her students, she had showered, dressed, and rehearsed everything she was going to say to him. Strange how not a single word of her eloquent speech came to mind just now as she stared into his blue eyes. She felt her control slip slightly and with it some of the bravery that had gotten her to this point. She smiled nervously and forced herself to sit down in one of the armchairs facing his desk. Placing her leather shoulder bag down on the chair next to her, she made a production of every move in an attempt to prolong the inevitable.

You got this far, Sydney. There's no going back now. "I, uh . . . have something to say to you, but you have to promise you won't say anything, or I might not be able to do this," she said, making eye contact with him to see if he agreed. "Please let me get this out and leave and then you can, uh . . . decide what to . . . what you want to do after I leave." She didn't think she could handle baring her soul and hearing his thoughts all at once. She had a terrible feeling he was going to think she was more trouble than she was worth.

Jackson was silent. Finally he slowly dipped his head as if he had carefully her decision and found it satisfactory.

Sydney nodded in gratitude and, straightening her shoulders, took a deep breath. "I'm here to apologize," she said, flinching briefly as she tried to remember what she'd planned to say. Her treacherous memory had taken a hiatus and left her to fend for herself. "I'm sorry, Jackson."

Jackson waited silently, as if knowing what it had cost her to come here.

"I didn't—don't . . . I don't think that you're the kind of person who would do what I thought you did," she blurted out, her eyes pleading with him to believe her. "I know you're not that kind of person, in fact," she admitted. "I came here because . . ." Sydney noticed that she was talking to the collar of his white shirt, and she quickly raised her eyes to his. The quiet intensity with which he watched her made her nerves jump, and she quickly lowered her head again to gather her thoughts. Her mind went blank. Where was the explanation she had composed? Where was that persuasive plea that had taken her hours to perfect? This was not going the way she had imagined.

Regardless of her desire to hightail it out of his presence, she was determined to fulfill her purpose in coming here. She had come to apologize; she'd done that. But she had also come to explain, and she would not leave until she had done so.

With a deep breath, she embarked on the most difficult part of her visit. "I want you to understand that my doubts weren't because you had done anything that was in the least bit untrustworthy or suspicious," she said with a slight tilt of her head. "Although you did act secretive on the phone with Carrie the morning we had breakfast. And a couple of things your sister mentioned made me think that there were still feelings there, at least on Carrie's part." Sydney was rambling, and she was sure that accusing him of acting suspicious didn't constitute the popular definition of apology. "But that still didn't mean you were deceitful," she amended quickly, wringing her hands.

"The reason I didn't trust you was because I was scared," she admitted painfully. "When Randy died, I lost much more than a best friend. I lost my ability to feel and to trust. At least, I thought I did." She was looking down at her hands, glad that he couldn't see they were cold and clammy. "So, when I recognized that I was starting to have feelings for you, I jumped at the chance to mistrust what we have— *had*," she corrected, swallowing past her dry throat. "It wasn't until afterward that I realized how much it hurt . . . to be without you." Her voice was a whisper, and her heart thudded painfully in her chest. She'd never been so frank with anyone in her life and hadn't been prepared for the vulnerability that it caused. She closed her eyes briefly and prepared to significantly increase that vulnerability. "You see," she paused, feeling like she was at the edge of a cliff and about to dive off. "I'm in love with you, Jackson, and it terrifies me." She felt her stomach flip-flop as if she were falling through the air, and she unconsciously wrapped her arms around her middle.

* * *

Jackson felt like the world that had been taken from him had somehow been rearranged, repackaged, and offered to him covered in gold and presented on a silver platter. The words she had said had been more than he could have imagined. More than he had hoped for. The look on her face, the love in her eyes as she met his gaze, pierced him to the core and magnified feelings he had thought couldn't possibly be any stronger. But her words, though wonderful, couldn't have struck him more powerfully than the naked emotion in her eyes.

She stood abruptly, and when Jackson rose out of his chair and opened his mouth to speak, she held out a pleading hand, stopping him. "Please," she pleaded with a breathy gasp as she headed for the door. "Please don't. I've got to go. I just wanted you to know how I feel," she said, avoiding his eyes. Hesitating, she started out the door and then turned back to him. She opened her mouth as if to speak, only to turn quickly and disappear through the doorway.

Jackson stood in stunned silence. He started to go after her but stopped halfway around his desk. He had promised her. He could see how difficult it had been for her to say what she'd said to him. He could at least respect her wishes and give her some time.

He glanced at his watch. There were a few things he needed to take care of before he went in pursuit. He walked back behind his desk and sat down slowly. Leaning back in his chair, he exhaled a big breath as his mind went to work.

It wasn't until much later when Jackson finally stopped rocking in his chair and came to a decision. "If you want something, you don't wait for it to happen," Jackson muttered to himself, repeating what he had said to Sydney when he'd taken her to explore Fort Casey. "You make it happen," he finished softly, and a wide grin slowly grew on his face.

* * *

Sydney was running late. She hurried her pace as she made her way down to the stables. She had just come from visiting Adrianne, who had returned from her honeymoon and was busy starting her life as a married woman. They'd managed to steal a few minutes together while Colin was studying, and Sydney was struck by how completely happy Adrianne and her new husband were. Marriage had perfected their relationship by strengthening their loyalties and increasing their love for each other. Sydney left feeling incredibly happy for her friends.

She hadn't seen Jackson since she'd left his office. She had waited for him. After four days, she had given up hoping that he would ever come see her. After nearly a week, she had regretted having stopped him from speaking his thoughts, knowing that if she had let him talk she would at least know where he stood.

"An important package came for you, Sydney," Adam announced casually, interrupting her thoughts as she walked into the stables. "I left it on the table," he said, taking some stable gear out to the paddock for the riding class.

Sydney thanked him and quickly walked toward the tack room. She didn't have time to see what had been delivered to her, since her students were due any minute for their lessons. She rushed into the office, where she reached for a measuring stick to measure the length of the stirrups. As an afterthought, she picked up a couple of short and long whips in case anyone had forgotten theirs, and she turned to leave. The large package wrapped in brown paper caught her eye from where Adam had laid it on the table. It was square and flat and looked nothing like anything she'd been expecting.

Unable to curb her curiosity, Sydney set her gear down on a chair and reached for the envelope that was attached to the package. Tearing quickly through the envelope, she unfolded the letter and scanned the message. Her stomach sank.

"You told me you didn't want any explanation, but the reasons why I need to give you an explanation far outweigh the reasons you have for not wanting to hear it.

"You said that you thought I acted secretive on the phone with Carrie that day at breakfast. You were right. I didn't want you to know that I was speaking with her. And the morning before I flew to Las Vegas, I drove down to Seattle and met with her. I didn't want you to know about that either.

"I want you to know now why I did it."

Sydney's heart took a painful lurch in her chest as she continued to read.

"I wanted you to have more than just your memories."

Sydney frowned, turning the page over to see if there was more written. Finding nothing, she looked at the package, hesitant to open it. With a fortifying breath she set the letter and envelope aside and reached for the large parcel. Warily, she gently lifted the tape and pulled away the paper, unsure of what she would find. Her brows drew together in confusion when she realized she was looking at the back of a canvas. He had sent her a painting?

Carefully she turned it over and froze.

She gasped and covered her mouth as she gazed at the painting through tear-filled eyes. Romeo was standing proudly against the emerald forests that were so prevalent on Whidbey Island. His noble bloodline was evident in his posture and in his expressive eyes, which peered back at her. Sydney's eyes dropped down to the bottom right corner of the painting, and she smiled in humble appreciation at Carrie's signature.

Carrie Larsen had amazingly captured Romeo's arrogance, which seemed to have become more pronounced in the years since Sydney had ridden him competitively.

It hadn't been what she had thought at all. Jackson hadn't been hiding his feelings for Carrie; he had been hiding his gift to *her*. He had commissioned a painting of her beloved horse—a painting that she was sure she wouldn't have been able to afford in this lifetime.

"Your students are waiting," Adam called, bursting into the tack room without sparing her a glance. "And they're driving me nuts. Nice painting," he commented with a quick glance at the portrait as he went to the far end of the room and hung a saddle blanket. Sydney was glad he hadn't looked directly at her and noticed the look on her face or the fresh sheen of tears in her eyes. "You might want to get out there soon, though, before someone gets impatient and decides to take off at a gallop," he warned with his back still toward her.

Sydney wiped away her tears and, taking a deep breath, set the painting down where it wouldn't be damaged. She was going to have to pay another visit to Eagle Crest Farms today, and this time she was going to let Jackson say whatever he wanted to say.

Mildly distracted, she hurried to the outdoor arena, where her students were chatting with Gabriel and Jane as they saddled their horses. It wasn't unusual for her grandmother to sit in on her class every once in a while, but her grandfather was usually busy elsewhere. Rob had brought Josh and was leaning outside the fence, watching his little brother.

Pulling her thoughts together, she focused on her students. "Hey guys," she called as she ducked under the fence. "Cute shirts," she said to her students, noticing that they all wore white T-shirts with their names embossed in large, black letters on the front. "Mary, I didn't know you spelled your name with two *R*s," she called out, and Mary smiled impishly at her.

"What brings you out here, Gramps?" she asked, and she chuckled at the way he raised a censuring brow at her. "Grandpa," she corrected.

"Just wanted to watch you work."

"Well, make yourself comfortable." She smiled at Rob.

She and Adam proceeded to check each pony to make sure that it was properly saddled. "All right, everyone, mount up," she called. "Trinity . . . the other side." She couldn't help but smile at the large "Me" that the child had printed on her shirt instead of her name.

"You guys, these shirts are so cute," she repeated, glancing around at the various words on each shirt. Instead of his own name, Josh had embossed "Sydney" on his shirt. His crush on her was really cute. "Did you guys want to put on a show for your parents or something?"

"Something like that," Adam said with a smile.

"Jesse, let me help you." Sydney adjusted the reins so that they were held properly in Jesse's hand. "Did you make that shirt all by yourself?" she asked the child, admiring the big "You" that was outlined in sparkling blue paint.

Jesse nodded and Sydney smiled. "It's really pretty," she said, gently pulling on the girl's pigtail. She stepped back from the horses. "All right, everyone. Let's get started." She waited as they all maneuvered their horses into a single-file line. "Give the proper signal to your mount and start moving forward." She moved to the middle of the corral. Everyone but Trinity was off the lead line and able to direct their horses on their own. Adam stayed close to Trinity, lead line in hand, making sure she followed the instructions properly.

"Keep them going around in a circle until I say," Sydney ordered Josh, since he was in front.

"Good, Jesse. And remember to kiss the air if Pepper ignores your leg cues." The little girl kissed the air when her horse began to slow down.

Sydney had them stop and start again a number of times, making sure they were very familiar with guiding their horses. She had them turn around and start in the other direction only to turn again and continue with Josh in the lead once more.

It was nearly twenty minutes before her eyes were drawn to their shirts again. "Don't you think their shirts are cute, Grandma?" she called, surprised to find her grandparents still watching from the fence.

"Very creative," Jane agreed with a little chuckle.

Josh rode by, grinning down at the word "Sydney" on his shirt, and Sydney noted that William, who was right behind him, had embossed his nickname, "Will," on his.

Sydney's smile started to falter, replaced by a bewildered frown as she continued to read the shirts.

Jesse's said "You," and then she saw "Marry," and Trinity was in the back with a big "Me" on hers.

She stopped. Her smile disappeared as she tried to make sense of the words.

"Funny," she muttered to herself, although she wasn't laughing. "Hey, Adam," she called, not taking her eyes off of her students. "Did you notice that their shirts all make a sentence . . ." She froze, the realization hitting her like a freight train. Her eyes shot back to Josh's T-shirt.

"Sydney," she read to herself, "Will You Marry . . . Me?" The last word was nearly inaudible as her throat closed up. She spun around, looking in all directions, trying to find him. She vaguely heard Gabriel mutter something.

Jackson was leaning against the barn door, his arms folded across his chest, obviously waiting for her to understand the message.

A dry sob broke free from her chest when he pushed away from the wall and headed toward her. "What are you . . . doing?" she managed to ask just as he reached her. He was blurry now, as tears clouded her eyes.

"Sydney," he said as he gently pulled her near. "I love you." He brushed a stray lock from her face. "I can't live without you." He was having a hard time speaking past the emotion that had lodged in his throat. "Will you marry me?"

Sydney didn't care that her tears were freely running down her face. She dropped her forehead down onto his chest and wrapped her arms around him. "Yes," she said, and she looked up at him. "I would love to more than anything in the world," she whispered.

"It's about time," Gabriel said impatiently. With a long-suffering sigh, he wiped away the tears in his eyes. "I thought I was going to have to read the proposal to you myself."

Everyone laughed, and Sydney smiled over at her students, who were sitting on top of their horses watching the show. Adam grinned knowingly from where he stood next to Trinity. Rob winked at her and smiled tenderly.

"Everyone knew?" she asked Jackson.

"Everyone but you," he admitted. "Rob and your grandparents helped the kids make the shirts." He glanced at the five children. "And in case you didn't know, Gabriel has a fondness for perfection," he said dryly. "If you don't believe me, you should see the number of T-shirts they had to redo."

She laughed. "I don't think I want to know." Then she shook her head. How could this be happening after she had ruined what had started between them?

"I love you, Sydney. I feel like there was never a moment when I didn't." He searched her eyes.

"I love you so much, Jackson."

An overwhelming joy spread through her whole body. She could see how clearly the road she'd traveled revealed the Lord's hand. When she'd been blinded by sorrow and paralyzed by pain, He had walked with her and had led her here, to this point, and to Jackson. In recognizing His design, she knew that regardless of the trials that were sure to come, the road ahead would be a journey worth taking.

Jackson lowered his head and met her in a tender kiss, marking the beginning of a future that was sure to be better than the past, and even more incredible than the present.

* * *

Jane and Adam smiled fondly, and the children cheered and quickly covered their eyes. Rob grinned, and Gabriel, sighing with satisfaction, silently gave thanks for the answer to a long-standing and heartfelt prayer. With an appreciative glance toward heaven, he winked. "Checkmate."

About the Author

Connie Angeline earned her bachelors degree in Political Science with a minor in French from Metropolitan State College of Denver. She has always had a passion for writing and was lucky to have spent her childhood living in different parts of the world—and growing a fertile imagination in the process. A member of The Church of Jesus Christ of Latter-day Saints, she is currently serving in the Young Women's organization. She lives in the Midwest with her husband and son, where she is working on her next book.

Connie would love to hear from her readers, who can write to her in care of Covenant Communications, at info@covenant-lds.com or P.O. Box 416, American Fork, UT 84003-0416.